I0639637

The Hollow

By
C L Thomas

www.DarkInkBooks.com

First Published by Dark Ink Books, Southwick, MA, 2022

Dark Ink and its logos are trademarked by *AM Ink Publishing*.

www.AMInkPublishing.com

To my Father, without whom, I would have no imagination, and to my Mother, who, through her never ending sacrifices, taught me the meaning of love.

Chapter 1

Peter Briley pulled into an old cracked asphalt lot and parked beneath an oak tree in the far corner. The early morning sun hadn't yet completely risen, so the parking lot was bathed in deep shadows that stretched out across the marked rows like roughly drawn lines on a sheet of blank paper. By late afternoon, when the sun was high overhead, Peter would be glad he had parked beneath the oak tree and its wide branches full of leaves. At this hour, the old, yellow, beat-up VW Beetle was the only car in the parking lot, but it wouldn't be that way for long. Soon, screaming children with parents in tow would flood the lot, prepared for a day of sunshine and swimming.

Peter opened the driver's side door with a loud screech, setting his feet on the asphalt. "A little WD40 will take care of that shit," he mumbled under his breath at the door as he unfolded himself from the Beetle.

Peter worked for the city of Manchester, Connecticut, Parks and Recreation Division. He worked at the town swimming pool known as the Hollow to the locals but named Globe Hollow after the Globe Manufacturing Company, which had owned all the land and the water at one time. Globe Manufacturing used the water from the reservoir above the pool to power their cotton manufacturing company back in the mid-1800s before the start of the Civil War. The pool and all the land were donated to the town of Manchester by the Cheney brothers in 1906. It was the Cheney brothers who first built the pool beneath the reservoir for the locals to use in the summertime.

During the summer months, Peter was always the first person to arrive at the Hollow. His job was to make sure everything was ready before the pool opened at ten a.m. sharp. Standing there in the parking lot beneath the large oak tree, Peter took a last drag off his cigarette while surveying his surroundings. In the soft morning light before the sun rose above the horizon, everything appeared to be in place.

We'll need a sweeper to run through the lot soon, he thought, flicking his cigarette away into the shadows. He watched the butt tumble through the air end over end several times before landing in a shower of orange sparks. A tiny wisp of smoke drifted away from where the cigarette had landed. *I have to quit those fucking things*, he thought, grunting as he walked away from his car.

Peter walked across the parking lot to a chain link fence that surrounded the swimming complex. The fence was meant to keep kids from sneaking onto the grounds at night, but Peter knew it only kept the young and fearful away. Several times a summer, he would arrive for work only to find a couple or two sleeping beneath the trees on the hillside above the pool. A few times, he even found them totally naked wrapped in each other's arms sleeping off the alcohol they had consumed the night before. Peter always chased the kids away, threatening to call the cops every time, but he never did.

At a gate in the fence, Peter took out a ring of keys and selected the key he needed to release the padlock. The gate swung open on hinges that squealed like a cat whose tail had just been stepped on. Peter grunted and coughed as he walked through the gate.

A little WD40 for that too, he thought. Peter locked the gate back up and walked across the wide sidewalk until he stood beneath a blue and white awning that hung above the entrance to the locker rooms.

Peter was an older man in his late forties. He had a bit of a stomach that hung out over his belt and stringy gray hair that fell down over his forehead. He wore a pair of black-framed glasses on his face that magnified his eyeballs. His unruly eyebrows rode atop the glasses like two bushy caterpillars. There was a bald spot at the back of his head shaped like a crooked circle. Tiny brown and black freckles littered the spot, along with a few thin strands of steel gray hair that refused to give up the fight to exist. Peter wasn't a tall man, but he wasn't short, either. He stood just under six feet tall and weighed an even two hundred and thirty pounds. He smoked a pack and a half of Pall Mall Reds every day and drank a six-pack of Budweiser every night in his one-room apartment.

Peter stepped through the door of the men's locker room. A freshly lit cigarette hung from between his lips. The amber glow of the tip lit up his face as he passed through the doorway into the gloomy stale darkness of the locker room. Even through the smell of his cigarette, the odor of wet moldy clothes assaulted his senses. He blew out a cloud of smoke as he reached around the wall for the light switch. He found the switch quickly and bathed the locker room in the glow of pale fluorescent lights that always had a way of making him feel like he was at a hospital.

"Got to make sure to check those damn toilets in the girl's locker room," he grumbled. "Fucking girls always flushing their womanly things and clogging up the works."

Peter coughed and blew out a cloud of smoke that clung to the ceiling between a pair of lights. He watched the smoke swirl above his head before tossing the cigarette into a urinal. "Fucking things are going to kill me one day," he whispered, coughing several times and spitting out a wad of yellow phlegm.

The morning was New England cool for early June, but humid. Typical summer weather for southern New England.

By late July, the thermometer would be hitting the nineties and the pool would be full of screaming brats, but in early June only the most determined or the most desperate swam.

Peter stopped and stood in front of one of the urinals urging himself to pee. It didn't come easy these days. *Need to see a fucking doctor about that shit*, he thought as he zipped up his pants and swiped at the handle. A momentary waterfall raced down the urinal swirling into a pool at the bottom. He watched his cigarette butt tumble and spin around in the yellowish water until it settled back down.

Peter completed his walkthrough of the locker rooms and stepped outside again. He was poolside next to the snack bar between the two locker rooms. He stood on a wide concrete walkway painted a faded green and framed with a thick red stripe along the edge of the water. The walkway traveled to the farthest limit of the pool in one direction and down to a wide concrete beach in the other. Every six feet, bright white letters warned that running wouldn't be tolerated.

The sky was brighter now as Peter looked up and down the walkway for trash left behind from the day before. A thick ground fog wound its way through the trees above the beach. The fog was unnerving the way it clung to the worn grassy hillside, slithering between the trees like a snake on the prowl. Peter swallowed hard and turned away. A thin mist hung over the water riding the tiny waves populating the pool. On the far side of the pool the spillway from the reservoir above was nothing more than a wide dark slice through the skin of grass covering the hillside below the reservoir.

Peter popped another cigarette in his mouth. He cupped his hand over the end and lit it, taking a deep drag. The bright orange glow of the tip lit up his face. He blew out a swirl of gray and black smoke and looked across the water toward the spillway. Through the corner of his eye, he saw something floating in the water out by the diving raft. It was shapeless and dark, really nothing more than a lump of something on the surface of the pool. In the early morning light, he thought it might be a large branch that had dropped down from the reservoir, or maybe the remains of a child's deflated raft.

"Damn it all to hell," Peter cursed, knowing he was going to have to go out into the water to fetch whatever was floating out there before it got caught up in the filters. If that happened, there would be hell to pay, and he would have to spend all day working on them and no one would be happy if that happened.

Peter took another drag on his cigarette and tossed it to the sidewalk, smashing it beneath his foot. He walked into the men's changing room and opened his locker. It was the last locker in a long line of gray steel boxes. On the inside of the door hung a faded picture of a much younger man holding hands with a slightly plump woman with red hair and flashing blue eyes. Peter smiled at the picture. "Good morning, dear," he said to the photo as he removed his swim trunks from the inside shelf. The woman in the photo remained silent, the image forever frozen in a moment of time. Peter reached out and gently brushed the picture with the tips of his fingers.

The woman in the picture was Peter's late wife, Della. She had been the love of his life since his freshmen year of high school, even though she hadn't been aware that Peter existed until they were both juniors. Della had died two years ago in a morphine stupor from breast cancer, leaving Peter all by himself to face the world. They had no children, no relatives close by, and no one to lend support or offer comfort. Peter was totally alone.

It's too damn cold for this shit, Peter thought, stepping out of his pants and into the swim trunks. The morning air bit at his fleshy white legs, raising goosebumps. Peter slipped out of his shirt and tossed it into the locker with his pants. He looked at the picture again and smiled sadly. "Soon," he whispered, turning away from the locker and walking out of the room without bothering to shut the door.

"Fucking colder than a witch's tit out here," Peter mumbled, standing on the walkway again. The concrete felt rough and cold on his bare feet. Peter grunted and spat, walking up to the edge of the pool. He stuck a toe into the water. It felt like a cup of ice against his skin. He shivered and sat down on the edge of the walkway beside a metal ladder that dropped down into the inky darkness beneath the surface.

"Well shit," Peter said, grabbing hold of the ladder and stepping onto it. The water rose to his thighs and took his breath away for a moment. He coughed several times and began to climb down into the pool. By the end of summer, the water would be a nice seventy degrees, but not now—not at the beginning of the season. The water spilling down from the reservoir was still winter cold.

Peter stood shivering with his feet resting on the rough bottom of the pool. He stood on his tiptoes trying to keep as much skin above the water as possible. The water came up just above his chest. It was even deeper farther out away from the edge of the pool. Peter looked across the water from where he stood beside the ladder. The object appeared to have no shape or form. It looked like a strange shadow floating on the surface of the pool. There was an odor in the air, like rancid meat, drifting across the water. Peter wondered if an animal had gotten itself drowned in the reservoir before winding up in the pool below. It's happened before.

"Shit, shit, shit," Peter muttered, beginning to swim out toward the diving raft. He had no desire to touch whatever was out there. He felt bad for whatever creature it might be, but fuck, he didn't want to touch it.

A few feet away from the object, Peter saw that it was a tangle of branches and debris. Something colorful fluttered from the end of one branch and Peter paused, dog paddling in the middle of the pool just a few feet from the raft. It looked like some kind of fabric flapping, like a tiny flag caught in the light breeze blowing down from the reservoir. Peter swam closer, close enough to reach out for one of the branches poking out from the pile of debris. The odor was strong now. Peter was afraid his hand was going to slip into the decaying carcass of a dog or deer that had died somewhere up above the pool. Swallowing hard, he wrapped his fingers around the branch, letting out a slow steady breath. The smell was horrible. Peter wished he had a cigarette going, anything to drive away that overwhelmingly sweet rotting smell of death. He was positive now that something had died. Holding his breath, he tugged on the branch in his hand, trying to move everything toward the raft. He glanced over his shoulder after several strokes expecting to see the gruesome remains of some unfortunate animal, but that wasn't what he saw.

Peter let go of the branch as his arms and legs beat at the water in an effort to escape from the tangled mess in front of him. He slipped beneath the water and screamed a muffled scream at what he had just seen. Unable to hold his breath any longer, Peter surfaced again, still facing the floating pile of branches and the body of a young naked woman caught up in them. Peter screamed again and this time the echo of his scream reverberated throughout the Hollow. The woman's lifeless eyes stared back at him with an emptiness that left him cold in the pit of stomach. He slipped beneath the water again, surfacing a moment later farther way from the body. He spun around, sending up a spray of water and swam for the edge of the pool.

Peter reached the ladder and scrambled up to the cold concrete decking. The rough surface bit into his knees as he dragged himself from the water. Crooked lines of pink blood ran down through the forest of hair that grew on his legs. He pushed himself up and stood, coughing hard, out of breath. He wanted to run out to the parking lot, get back in his car, and drive away, but he didn't. He turned back around slowly and looked out over the water as he shivered in the cool morning air. The pile of branches with its captive prize still floated out there, closer to the diving raft now than when he had first seen it that morning. The girl, really not much older than a child, lay there all stark white, skin peeling away in spots, arms and legs spread wide apart in a grotesque display. Looking at her eyes was the worst part. They looked back at Peter from across the water, a pale cloudy blue color, lifeless and accusing. Peter groaned and threw up. His breakfast splashed across the deck in a hot rancid wave that washed over his bare feet. He wiped at his mouth with the back of his hand, spitting several times into the pool before turning away.

The police; I got to call the police, he thought as he ran into the men's locker room. At his locker, he fumbled for his cigarettes until he had one out in his hand perched between two fingers. He slipped the cigarette between his lips and tried to light it, but the lighter kept shaking, the flame dancing in the shadow-filled room. He felt so alone and scared standing there in front of the photo of his deceased wife. Every shadowed corner in the locker room felt as if it held a ghost. The hum of the fluorescents drilled into his head like sharp knives. He felt himself on the verge of screaming like a madman.

Peter swallowed hard and ran from the locker room, fumbling with his keys as he went. Somehow, he managed to open the door to the snack bar, ducking inside the small office in the back. He sat down at the desk, grabbed his right hand with his left to steady the lighter, and lit his cigarette. He exhaled a gray cloud of smoke and picked up the phone, dialing 9-1-1. An operator answered after the third ring.

"Nine-one-one operator, what is your emergency?" a woman's calm voice asked.

Peter blew out a cloud of smoke and watched it race for the ceiling. "There's a body in the water," he cried into the phone in a hurried rush of words. "Down at Globe Hollow swimming pool."

The operator said something, but Peter didn't hear what she said because he dropped the phone and threw up again into a trashcan beside the desk. He could hear the operator's voice on the phone as he hung his head over the trashcan. It sounded so distant and far away. It sounded like it was lost somewhere inside a tunnel. He wanted to say something into the phone again, but he couldn't, because another wave of vomit was exploding from his body, the chunks sticking to the side of the trashcan.

Chapter 2

Officer Jeffrey Westman pulled into the parking lot at the Globe Hollow swimming pool at 7:00 am. A cup of hot coffee was stuck between his legs while an egg sandwich sat balanced on his thigh. He was dressed in a light blue dress shirt, top button undone, and a tie partially unknotted around his neck. Beside him on the passenger seat was a thin black leather notebook with a pen sticking out of the top. Next to the notebook was a pair of blue surgical gloves, a tape measure, tiny yellow cones stacked together marked with numbers, and a roll of yellow police crime scene tape.

Officer Westman drove a dark green Chevrolet Impala with a small dent in the driver's side door and a cracked windshield. Even from his seated position in the car, a casual observer could tell he was a very tall man. Officer Westman was a thirty-eight-year-old white male with a thin mustache and even thinner light brown hair. He had large brown eyes with heavy dark bags beneath them that always made him appear exhausted. There was a thin white scar shaped like a hook beneath his lower lip. The scar was an old war injury he got fighting a suspect in a bar as a rookie officer. His evening shift trainer told him it gave him character; his wife said it made him look sexy.

The first thing Officer Westman noticed as he pulled into the parking lot was Peter's old beat-up VW and the patrol car parked by the gate. Officer Westman noted the license plate of the VW as he rolled slowly toward the patrol car. An older, slightly overweight officer stood beside the patrol car. Next to him stood a civilian in a bathing suit nervously hopping from foot to foot smoking a cigarette. Westman pulled in front of the patrol vehicle and came to a stop. He took a sip of the now lukewarm coffee and set his practically eaten sandwich on the dashboard. He placed the cup beside the sandwich and picked up his notebook.

"That's the detective," the patrol officer said. Peter nodded and watched as the detective opened his car door and stood.

"He's a tall one," Peter thought as the door slammed shut and the detective approached.

"Good morning, sir," Officer Westman said, watching the gray cigarette smoke curl around Peter's head. "I'm Officer Westman."

"Peter, Peter Briley," Peter said, extending a hand. Westman took the hand and gave it a shake. The skin was cold and clammy. "There's a body in the water, in the pool, floating," Peter said, still holding onto Officer Westman's hand as if he were afraid to let it go.

Westman looked at the patrol officer who nodded, backing up what Mr. Briley had just said. "Alright, Mr. Briley, why don't you take me to where you saw the body and show me what you're talking about." Peter nodded and finally let go of the hand. He started through the gate and paused when he heard the detective speaking behind him. "Patrick, right?" Westman said to the patrol officer. The officer nodded.

"Yes, sir," Officer Patrick answered.

"There's crime scene tape on my seat; go and string it across the gate. When you're finished, stay here and make sure no one gets inside until I say so."

"Yes, sir."

Westman didn't wait around to see if the patrol officer did as he asked. He caught up with Peter at the locker room doors and followed him through the smelly room. Back outside, poolside, Mr. Briley stopped and pointed. "It's out there," he said, indicating the debris floating out near the diving raft.

At first glance, Officer Westman only saw a tangled mess of branches floating in a slow circle on the surface of the water. He glanced over at the spillway. "Must have washed down from the reservoir," he thought as the branches continued its slow lazy spin in the water. Halfway through the spin, Westman saw the pale naked body of a girl. From where he stood, she appeared young; late teens, early twenties maybe. "She hadn't been out there too long," he thought. "Maybe just overnight." He wondered if the pool had been open the day before.

Officer Westman pulled out his cellphone and snapped a few pictures from where he stood on the walkway. He studied the pictures after he finished and took a few more as the body slowly drifted around until he couldn't see it any longer.

Did they leave her like that on purpose? he silently asked himself, swiping through the photos. *It looks like a display.* Westman swallowed hard and lifted the radio mic clipped to his belt. "Unit 23," Westman said into the mic.

"Go 23," a woman's voice answered.

"Twenty-three, we have a body in the water out at the Hollow. Send a crime scene unit and a body car, and notify the M.E. in Hartford."

"Clear 23," the woman responded, as if bodies floating in the water were an everyday occurrence. Peter shivered at the casualness of it all.

Westman opened his notebook and began to sketch the scene. He started with the hill and spillway, adding in the pool below. He sketched the pile of debris and the girl tangled up in it. He added the diving raft and finally the beach and the walkway where he and Mr. Briley stood. Peter watched him drawing and whistled softly when he finished. "That's like a fucking work of art," he said. "Excuse my language."

"No, it's not art; not even close. It's just a rough sketch, Mr. Briley. My photos and the ones to be taken by the crime scene guys will show a lot more detail than I could ever show here." Peter nodded and lit another cigarette. Officer Westman waited for him to take a deep drag and blow the smoke out.

"So, tell me everything from when you first arrived here at work," Officer Westman said. Peter took another drag off his cigarette and began to tell his tale. He finished several minutes later, lighting another cigarette and nervously puffing at it. Officer Westman watched the tip of the cigarette bob up and down several times between drags.

"Would you like to get dressed, Mr. Briley?" Officer Westman asked, realizing that Peter still wore nothing but a bathing suit.

"I would," Peter answered, looking grateful.

"Go on," Officer Westman said. "And make sure you don't touch anything except for your locker. When you're finished, go out front and wait for me." Peter nodded and went into the locker room. Officer Westman watched him go. After the locker room door closed, he began to write his observations in his notebook. Officer Westman finished writing a short time later and stuck his notebook into a pocket. He looked around the walkway until he spotted a canoe latched down to a set of hooks embedded in the wall. He walked over to the canoe and freed it from where it was secured. Carefully, not wanting to get wet, he sat down inside the canoe and paddled his way out into the pool until he was only a few feet from the body.

The girl was young–younger than he had thought when he stood on the walkway, but not by much. She appeared to be in her mid- to late teens, but no older than eighteen. Her wrists were tied to a y-shaped branch, so her arms were positioned above her head. The skin there was red and raw and peeling away. *She might have been alive when he tied her down,* he thought.

The feet were also tied down, one over the other like so many crucifixion statues. All that was missing was a spike hammered through them. *Punishment?* he wondered.

The body was naked. Across the abdomen were several thin cuts. The blood had dried there so she must have been alive for that. Officer Westman took a deep breath and let it out slowly as he continued to view the body. There was bruising around the neck. It was discolored, a deep purple, black along the edges. "Cause of death?" he whispered, snapping several pictures with his phone as the pile of debris continued its slow lazy turn. Officer Westman took several more pictures before paddling back to the walkway.

Peter and Officer Patrick stood by the gate as Officer Westman walked out through the locker room doors. A blue van with flashing overhead lights pulled into the parking lot and stopped beside Officer Westman's car as he approached the two men. A woman exited the driver's side door dressed in gray overalls and a man stepped from the passenger's side door dressed the same. Each of them carried a black and gray toolbox, wore black ballcaps, booties over their shoes, and blue surgical gloves on their hands.

"Patrick, can you show the crime scene unit what we have?" Westman said, stepping through the gate.

"I hope they brought bathing suites," Patrick laughed, waving the new arrivals over.

"We have some suits in the lost and found if they need them," Peter mumbled, fishing a fresh cigarette from his pack.

"That should work, or they could just use the canoe like I did," Westman said. Peter nodded, wondering why he hadn't used the fucking canoe.

Officer Westman waited for Patrick and the crime scene unit officers to disappear through the locker room doors before looking over at Peter. "So, you arrived here at 5:30 this morning?" he asked.

"Yes, sir," Peter answered, smashing the half-finished cigarette out beneath his foot. "I arrive at that time every day. It's my job to get the pool ready for the swimmers."

"And what time did you leave last night?" Westman asked.

"The pool is closed on Sundays and I don't work Saturdays. So, the last time I was here was Friday evening," Peter answered.

"Did you hang around or go straight home on Friday?" Westman asked.

"No, sir, I didn't hang around," Peter answered. "On Saturday it would have been the sisters who closed up."

"The sisters?"

"Yes, Alice and Emily Anderson. Alice has worked here for three years now, but this is Emily's first summer. They're sisters, you see. This should be Alice's last summer before she goes off to college." Officer Westman wrote in his notebook. "I'm sure their numbers are in the office if you need them," Peter offered, watching the pen scratch words out on paper that he couldn't see.

Officer Westman asked a few more questions and told Peter he might call him for more questions later. He handed Peter a card with his work and cell number on it, explaining that if he thought of anything else that he was to call him. Peter thanked the detective and walked across the parking lot to his VW Bug. At the car, he opened the driver's door and sat down on the edge of the seat, lighting another cigarette. He blew out a thick cloud of smoke and watched it drift away up into the branches of the old oak tree that he had parked beneath that morning.

"So, what did ya see?" asked a thin boy straddling a BMX bike in black shorts and blue t-shirt, startling Peter. Peter coughed several times trying to catch his breath as he eyed the boy. He noted the yellow towel over the boy's shoulders and red ballcap on his head. He was a regular at the pool. He'd been here most days throughout the summer. He was only thirteen years old, thin, with blonde hair and blue eyes. He looked and acted older than most kids his age.

"I saw something that will haunt my dreams tonight, of that I'm sure," Peter answered. "Just be glad it wasn't you that found what I found."

"What was it?" the boy asked, looking across the parking lot at the patrol car and van parked near the gate.

Peter followed the boy's eyes across the parking lot before he looked back. He thought of saying nothing at all but decided he was glad to have someone to talk too. "A body," Peter whispered, taking another long drag off his cigarette.

"Cool," the boy said, his mouth open, eyes wide.

"There was nothing cool about it, Matthew Shovinski," Peter said, flicking his cigarette at the boy. A shower of orange sparks fell to the cracked asphalt.

"Hey," Matthew shouted, dodging the cigarette before it hit him. Peter spit and fished another cigarette from his dwindling pack. "Will the pool open today?" Matthew asked.

"I don't know nothing about that," Peter answered. "Do you really want to go swimming where a body was floating?"

Matthew thought about it and smiled. "Sure," he said. Peter shook his head and took a drag off his fresh cigarette, coughing several more times.

"Those things will kill you, you know," Matthew said. "I had an uncle who died of cancer from them."

"Don't I know it," Peter replied, blowing a cloud of smoke at the boy.

Two hours later, Peter watched as the crime scene van, a hearse, the patrol car, and Officer Westman's Chevy Impala rolled out of the parking lot. He walked down to the gate after they disappeared onto Spring Street. Matthew followed on his bike.

"You wait here," Peter said. "Or I'll have you banned from the pool for the whole summer." Matthew nodded. Peter walked through the gate and into the locker room. A bead of perspiration ran down his forehead. *It was going to be a hot day*, he thought. If the pool had opened today, it would have been full by noon.

Peter went to the small office behind the snack bar and called the District Park Manager. The phone rang three times before a voice answered. It was the Park Manager on the other end. Peter relayed what had happened that morning. As he finished, he lit another cigarette. The smoke swirled around a yellowed light fixture clinging to the ceiling.

"I want the pool closed for the next several days," the Park Manger said when Peter finished. "I want it cleaned and then cleaned again and cleaned once more the next day. If the police give us the okay, we'll open up on Wednesday."

"Yes, sir," Peter said, before hanging up the phone. He walked back out front and saw that Matthew was still standing by the gate, trying to see through the building in front of him.

"We're not opening today, or tomorrow, and maybe not for the rest of the week if that's how it goes," Peter said from the doorway.

"Ah, man," Matthew replied. "Can I get a look at where it was?"

"Go home, Matthew."

"Ah, man, that bites," Matthew said, turning away and walking his bike back across the parking lot. Peter watched him go for a moment before locking himself inside the gate.

Chapter 3

Nick's Pizzeria was a small neighborhood shop on Hartford Avenue in Manchester, Connecticut. Inside, there were several tables with red-white-checkered tablecloths draped over the tops. Jars of grated cheese, jars of red pepper flakes, and silver napkin holders stuffed full of napkins stood guard in the center of the tables like soldiers on continuous watch. Three booths with thick red leather cushions and bright silver buttons lined one wall. Above the booths hung several framed photos of famous people who ate at Nick's. A faded yellow counter with an old-fashioned register stood at the back of the shop with a menu board above it. The menu board offered small, medium, large, and extra-large pizzas with a wide variety of toppings. A smaller sign beside the register offered pizza by the slice. Behind the counter were two gray pizza ovens stained and streaked with grease and sauce and flour. Next to the ovens were two leaning towers of pizza boxes unevenly stacked against a cooler stuffed with beer and soda. Nick Jr. stood behind the counter, watching a television mounted to the wall in one corner.

Nick Jr. was a balding, overweight, middle-aged African American. His stomach hung several inches over his belt and bounced if he moved too fast from behind the counter to greet a customer or clean off a table. A thick mustache peppered with gray and black hairs rode above his upper lip and twitched whenever he spoke. Nick Jr. wore faded blue jean overalls and a white apron covered in flour and sauce. A white paper chef's hat sat on his head cocked at an angle.

Officer Jeffrey Westman walked into Nick's and waved a tired hand at the man behind the counter. Nick waved back and went to work on the pizza he knew Officer Westman wanted. A few minutes after shoving the pizza into the oven he came from behind the counter with a bottle of cold beer in his hand. Droplets of condensation dribbled down the side of the bottle as he set it on the table.

"Your brother joining tonight?" Nick asked as Jeffrey took a sip from the beer.

"Yeah, he should be here soon."

"You get that call at the Hollow this morning?" Nick asked, wiping his hands on a white cloth hanging from his waist.

"Yeah, it was a bad one," Jeffrey answered, taking another sip from the bottle and closing his eyes as the amber liquid slid down his throat. A soft, satisfied exhale of air escaped from between his lips.

Nick nodded and went back behind the counter.

Bruce Westman walked into Nick's Pizzeria five minutes later. He saw his brother sitting at the table, his beer three-quarters finished. He knew right away it had been a bad day by the worn look on his older brother's face. He hoped that look meant money in his pocket.

"Hey Nick, two more," Bruce shouted, holding up two fingers as he ambled over to his brother and sat down across from him. "You look like shit," Bruce said, smiling at his brother.

Jeffrey nodded, watching Nick walk across the floor with two more beers pinned between his fingers. Nick set the bottles down on the table and walked away without a word. Jeffrey waited until he was back behind the counter before looking over at his younger brother.

Bruce was nine years younger than his brother. He stood six foot one and weighed an even one hundred and seventy pounds. He had dark brown hair and blue eyes that seemed to cut through all the bullshit the world tossed his way. He wore dark cargo pants with large pockets and a black shirt. An illegal gun was tucked safely in the back of his pants in a holster covered by his shirt. In the cargo pockets he carried a small digital camera, gloves, several Ziploc bags, and a notebook.

Bruce Westman was a private investigator. He worked out of a small office on Burnside Avenue in East Hartford. He had tried to be a police officer once upon a time, but a stint over in Iraq courtesy of the United States Army had put an end to that dream. Now he worked as a private investigator taking mostly cheating spouse cases and the occasional crumbs his brother threw his way. Jeffrey called it consulting and charged the city for his brother's services, but Bruce felt like it was mostly charity. Yet he took the jobs because he had to do whatever he could to survive and pay the bills.

"I heard you got a bad one today," Bruce said, sipping at his beer.

"Yeah, it was bad," Jeffrey said, finishing off his first beer and starting on the second. He set the bottle down after a long sip, wiping at his mouth with the back of his hand. "A girl, a young one. Not sure how she died yet, but whoever did it displayed her like a trophy mounted on a wall. They wanted us to find her." Jeffrey set a folder on the table and shoved it across to his brother.

Bruce took the folder and opened it. The first thing he saw were the photos his brother had taken that morning. They were grisly to look at, yet Bruce forced himself to go through all of them. He looked over Jeffrey's notes after that and everything Peter Briley had said. He pulled a small notebook from his pocket and scribbled *Briley's* name in it. He set the folder down and looked across the table as his brother finished off his second beer.

"I guess you want my help with this?" Bruce asked as Nick Jr. walked up with their pizza. Jeffrey nodded, one eye on Nick Jr. as he set the pizza on the table along with paper plates and silverware.

Bruce snatched the first piece without a word. He shook grated cheese all over it and folded the piece in half along its length, holding it up in front of his mouth. A white string of cheese dripped down from the tip of the folded pizza. Behind the crust, his eyes looked immense as he took his first bite. Nick Jr. smiled and set two more beers on the table.

"Enjoy," Nick Jr. said, walking back behind the counter to finish watching whatever was on the television.

Chapter 4

Bruce walked out of Nick's Pizzeria with his brother an hour later. He said goodbye in the small parking lot at the rear of the building, watching Jeffrey drive off before getting into his small Ford Escort. The car was old and showed its age, but the engine ran and that was all he cared about. The blue paint was fading in several spots, rust had eaten through the body, and black smoke coughed out of the tailpipe, but it was his, free and clear. Bruce turned left onto Hartford Road, his car chugging away, leaving a thin trail of exhaust to mark where he had just been. He was headed to Globe Hollow, wanting to check out the place before it got dark.

He arrived at the Hollow ten minutes later. The parking lot was empty. The sun was setting, but it wasn't down yet. He parked in front of the locked gate, disappointed that he had missed Peter Briley, but it made sense since the place hadn't opened to the public that day. Crime scene tape still clung to several rungs of the chain link fence flapping in the breeze.

Bruce opened the driver's side door and stood. It was muggy outside. The sun was slowly settling to the west. Dark shadows filled the corners of the parking lot creeping in toward the center. The trees along the edges of the lot offered good cover from the street. *Anyone could have hidden back here and the people driving by would never have noticed them*, he thought. *Quiet here*, he thought. *Not a bad spot to hide or commit a crime or sneak over the fence for a late-night skinny dip.*

Bruce slipped his notebook out and wrote his thoughts down on the first clean page he came to. On the next page, he drew a quick sketch of the parking lot, making sure to get the entrance and the exit and how the fence ran along the back of the lot. He slipped the notebook into his back pocket when he finished and walked along the fence until he could see the worn grassy hillside that rose above the green concrete beach. He walked back the other way along the fence until he reached the other end. Peering through the diamond-patterned links, he was able to see the back edge of the pool and the woods beyond. Dark shadows leaked from the trees like spilled ink spreading slowly across a sheet of paper. He tugged at his notebook and wrote down his observations.

Bruce walked back to the gate and shook it. The keyed padlock held. He glanced back at the roadway, realizing that only a handful of cars had driven by since he had been there. *There'd be even less traffic later at night*, he thought, stepping away from the fence to the rear of his car. He opened the hatchback and took out a pair of gray canvas gloves.

"You going to climb that fence?" a voice asked, startling Bruce. He looked up quickly and saw a boy wearing baggy black shorts and a stained blue t-shirt standing beside a red BMX bike. The boy looked to be around thirteen or fourteen. He had blue eyes and dirty blonde hair that covered his forehead and just touched his shoulders in the back. Bruce reached up while eyeing the kid and shut the hatchback.

"I might be," Bruce answered, looking over the roof of the car.

"You work for the police?" the boy asked, his eyes squinting as he studied Bruce.

"Yeah, I do, sort of, so go away," Bruce answered, walking back over to the fence and placing a hand on it.

"I'm Matthew," the kid said. "I was here this morning when they found that woman in the pool," he added, dropping the kickstand on his bike.

Bruce looked at Matthew and considered what the boy had just said. He doubted that he had seen anything worth noting but figured it wouldn't hurt to ask a few questions. The notebook appeared in his hand, opened to a blank page.

"Your name; the full name," Bruce said, his pen hovering just above the paper.

"Matthew. Matthew Shovinski," Matthew answered. Bruce wrote the name down.

"Look, Matthew Shovinski, it's going to be dark soon, so I need to get doing what I came here to do. Can you wait out here for me to finish or tell me where you live so I can find you later if I have any more questions?"

"Why don't I come with you?" Matthew asked. "I mean, it's not like I haven't sneaked inside there before."

Bruce studied Matthew while looking around the empty parking lot. Shadows were creeping across the asphalt.

"I don't think that's such a good idea," Bruce said, turning back to face the fence.

"I go in there all the time," Matthew said. "And I know where everything is that the adults know nothing about."

Bruce looked back at the kid and sighed. He knew it was a bad idea to let him come, but he was curious about the places that the adults didn't know about.

"Fine, but if anything happens to you, I'm not responsible."

"Whatever, I'll be fine," Matthew said, pushing his bike so it sat between the fence and Bruce's car. He ran a chain lock through the back tire, securing the bike so it didn't walk off. "Just in case," he said, looking up at Bruce as he stepped away from the bike.

"Do you need a hand up?" Bruce asked, pointing at the fence.

"Nope, I got this," Matthew said, scrambling over the fence in a matter of seconds. He landed on the other side with a soft whoosh of wind and nothing more. Bruce followed, though he was much slower getting over the fence, and when he landed it was with a loud thump and a slight stumble. Matthew smiled but was smart enough not to laugh.

"Stay with me," Bruce grumbled. "I just want to get a look at the pool and the reservoir above it. Don't make me regret letting you tag along."

"Sure," Matthew said with a slight roll of his eyes. "Do you think you'll find anything up there?" he asked, walking beside Bruce. Matthew was shorter than Bruce, but not by much. Another year or so and he would stand inches above him.

Bruce glanced over at Matthew and shrugged. The hour was late and getting later, and the truth was he didn't really think he would find anything that the police had missed. What he was looking for was a feel for the place, as creepy as it was at night. He was kind of glad to have the kid with him even though he wouldn't admit it. A second pair of eyes on things couldn't hurt and there was always safety in numbers.

"Just stay close to me and keep your eyes open."

Matthew nodded, matching Bruce step for step.

Bruce walked up to the door that led back to the locker rooms and tried it. The door was locked. Even the windows out front were shuttered. A small sign hung between the doors that read, "Closed."

"Come on," Bruce said, leading Matthew through freshly mowed grass that grew between the chain link fence and the building. At the corner, they turned and walked around an A/C condenser and a sign that said *no trespassing*. Bruce hooked a thumb at the sign and smiled. Matthew laughed.

Bruce and Matthew stood on the faded green concrete beach a moment later, staring at the dark water as tiny waves rolled ashore. Dark shadows stretched across the pool as the sun continued to set to the west. Tiny ripples rolled through the water reflecting what little light there was left to the day.

It hasn't changed much since I was a kid, Bruce thought, looking around. On his right was the entrance to the concessions area and the locker rooms. A sidewalk spanned the length of the pool with its yellow warning stripe painted along the edge. The concrete beach was still the same as it had always been. Even when he was young it was painted a faded green that was always chipped and missing patches. Bruce supposed it was all the chlorine in the water eating away at the paint. The beach was poured concrete that was good for skinning knees and scraping the tops of your toes. The beach was twelve feet wide from the water to the hillside and forty feet long, spanning the entire width of the pool to the edge of the manmade waterfall that provided the water for the pool.

The hillside behind the beach was all soft thin grass, fallen leaves, acorns, and tall oak trees. Families who came to Globe Hollow spent many summer days spreading their blankets and towels on the hillside, sunning themselves between the shade of the trees. The grassy hill rose for a hundred yards before reaching another chain link fence that ended at the reservoir on one side and the parking lot on the other. The fence kept animals and trespassers out of the pool most of the time, but wasn't much of a deterrent to those who wanted access to the pool.

The waterfall was a large manmade concrete hill that washed down from the reservoir above. It wasn't painted, just stained from years of water and algae build up. The waterfall was built when Globe Hollow was still a working cotton factory, but it only served the pool now. Water came down from the reservoir above and fed the pool. At its deepest point, the water left the pool from an underground grate that allowed it to flow through a tunnel that ran beneath the street out front. Signs were posted every few feet warning everyone to stay off the falls and out of the reservoir. If someone was caught ignoring this warning they were banned from the pool for the summer. It worked most of the time with the children, but the teenagers were something else altogether.

In the middle of the pool was a large diving platform with a steel slide and a ten-foot diving board. The water was deep out there and very cold once you went down a few feet beneath the surface. Bruce wondered if the platform was the same as the one he had played on as a child. It looked the same, though perhaps a fresh coat of green paint had been applied since his days as a snot-nosed kid.

The platform bobbed up and down in the middle of the pool, rolling with the ripples that ran beneath it. Dark shadows cast by the trees that grew at the furthest edges of the pool crept across the surface of the water looking like the gnarled fingers of an arthritic hand. Bruce swallowed hard and looked away as a shiver crept up his spine.

"Let's get moving," Bruce said. "We don't want to get caught out here after dark." Matthew shrugged, not all that concerned about it getting dark. He followed Bruce toward the waterfall, picking up on his apprehension. Glancing across the water, he thought for the first time in his life that the Hollow felt haunted and creepy, not somewhere full of happier memories. The silence was so loud. It felt like a weight on his shoulders. The trees of the far side of the pool were dark and forbidding. A shiver crept up his spine and he wondered if he had made a mistake agreeing to help this man. He knew his mother would be wondering where he was soon.

At the end of the beach, Bruce removed his sneakers and tied them together, slipping them over one shoulder after shoving his socks inside them. He stepped into the water and then up onto the concrete waterfall. The water was cold as it washed over his bare feet, and the concrete felt slimy beneath his toes. He wrinkled his nose and waited in the middle of the falls for Matthew to join him.

Matthew stepped into the water but kept his sneakers on. Bruce watched the boy and saw that he seemed more stable as he climbed up the algae slick waterfall. At the top, Bruce stopped and looked out over the reservoir. It was dark, full of shadows, and full of the sounds created by the world before day gives way to night. The reservoir appeared very uninviting as Bruce looked out across its expanse. He was wishing that he had waited until morning to check things out.

"Go this way," Matthew said, pointing off to the left. "The water isn't as deep."

Bruce stuck his foot into the reservoir, letting it slowly enter the water. This early in the season the water was very cold. Goosebumps covered his legs and arms as his foot settled on the muddy bottom. It felt even worse than the waterfall. Mud wormed its way between his toes, and he hated how it felt, but he forced himself to set his other foot down. Walking carefully on the tips of his toes, he made his way toward the shore, trying not to imagine what types of slimy creatures were swimming around his feet. Matthew walked beside him on the right. He didn't seem bothered by the water or the mud or what might be lurking just below the surface of the reservoir. *I should have kept my sneakers on*, Bruce thought, finally stepping out of the water.

Bruce leaned against a tall oak tree with a stripe of gray fungus clinging to its bark slipping on his socks and sneakers. It was almost completely dark outside now, so he hurried as quickly as he could.

"I should have just kept them on," Bruce mumbled, stepping away from the tree and glancing at Matthew.

"Yeah, it feels pretty yucky if you don't have something on your feet," Matthew said. Bruce frowned, wondering why the boy hadn't just said something to begin with.

"So where to?" Bruce asked, looking through the trees and brush that were so thick in the dim evening light he couldn't see into the woods beyond.

Matthew looked along the shore. "Follow me," he said, walking close to the water. The ground beneath his feet was so soft and yielding that it squelched with each footfall. Several times Bruce had to yank his foot free from the mud, each time with a loud slurping pop. Not far from the waterfall, Matthew led Bruce into the woods along a thin, uneven path worn from years of sneakered and flip-flopped feet. The path meandered through the trees until they reached a small clearing. Empty beer cans, paper cups, glass bottles, spent cigarette butts, and other discarded debris littered the ground. In the middle of the clearing was an area of leftover burnt coals from where a fire had recently been. It was clear to Bruce that this was a hangout for the older kids.

"I've never been up here at night," Matthew said, looking around nervously in the fading light. "Only the older kids hang out here." Bruce nodded and started looking around the clearing. In the quickly diminishing light he had a difficult time making much out, but he made a few notes in his notebook. There were logs and stumps scattered around the clearing and an old filthy mattress with a towel balled up at one end. Someone had also dragged an old lawn chair up there and a worn coffee table. The top of the coffee table showed the evidence of years of cigarettes being snuffed out on it. Tiny black circles littered its worn wooden surface. Bruce noted all of this and began walking around the clearing. He placed his hand on a tree at the far end of the clearing and felt himself slipping. He fought the urge until his head settled. In his mind, though, he had managed to catch a glimpse of something hidden. He knelt at the base of the tree and brushed away the leaves there. Beneath that top layer of leaves was a pair of pink panties. Bruce took out his cellphone and lit up the flashlight app. The tree suddenly came to life. Years of indignities suffered by the tree were revealed in the yellow glow of the cellphone light. In several spots, initials had been carved into the bark, professing love for so and so or the simple fact that Johnny or Beth had been here. Bruce followed the pool of light down until he clearly saw the panties balled up and forgotten.

In spite of being buried beneath a layer of leaves, the panties looked like a recent addition to the clearing. Time and weather hadn't had a chance to have its way with them. Bruce snapped a photo with his phone, the flash lighting up the clearing like a bolt of lightning. He wrote a few notes in his notebook while spots swam in his eyes. Slipping the pen behind his ear, he withdrew a Ziploc bag from one of his pockets. He used the clear bag like a glove over his hand and grasped the panties between a finger and his thumb, drawing them inside the Ziploc baggie. Matthew stood a few feet behind him watching all of this, waiting for him to finish. Bruce tucked the baggie into one of his pockets and turned.

"Do you think they belonged to her?" Matthew asked, fascinated that they might have found evidence missed by the police.

"I don't know," Bruce answered. "Maybe they do, or maybe they belong to some random girl who came up here with a boy last night to have sex." Matthew nodded, but he didn't think so. In his wild imagination, the panties belonged to the girl they had found earlier that day floating in the pool. The idea sent a chill of fear worming its way up his spine.

"Do you think she was murdered up here?" Matthew asked, stepping back from the tree where the panties had been found. His eyes were wide, and he suddenly looked very scared and very young.

"Why don't we head back?" Bruce said, again thinking it had been a bad idea to allow Matthew to tag along. "I should come back out here in the daylight so I can get a better look around."

Matthew looked relieved. He was ready to go. The last thing he wanted now was to be caught out here in the dark. Turning, he started back down the path that led back to the reservoir. Bruce followed, picking his way carefully through the woods. He used the flashlight on his phone to light the way back to the water's edge. It wasn't totally dark out yet, but the sun was nothing more than a golden glow beneath the horizon.

At the waterfall, Bruce left his sneakers on and carefully made his way down to the pool. He saw the glow of a car passing by on the road. It didn't seem to slow down or notice his car in the parking lot. It was very isolating out here after the pool closed. He could tell that Matthew felt the same way.

"Thanks," Bruce said when they were walking along the concrete beach.

"No problem," Matthew said.

At the parking lot, Bruce removed the panties from his pocket and dumped them inside a paper bag that he took from the backseat of his car. He also dropped the Ziploc baggie into the paper bag, making sure to leave it unzipped so he didn't destroy possible evidence.

"Why'd you do that?" Matthew asked.

"If there's any evidence on the panties I want to preserve it. Things in plastic baggies have a tendency to sweat and that can ruin whatever evidence might be there."

"Cool," Matthew said, unlocking his bike from the chain link fence. "You coming back out here tomorrow?"

"Probably," Bruce answered.

"Can I help again?"

"We'll see," Bruce said and got into his car, starting it up. He rolled the window down as he pulled away from the fence, leaning his head out. "Thanks for the help again, Matthew."

"Yeah, it was cool," Matthew said, waving a hand at Bruce as he pulled out into the parking lot. Matthew watched the brake lights flash bright at the exit before the car turned onto Spring Street and drove away. He stood there straddling his bike until the car disappeared down the street. Glancing over his shoulder, he noted that the shadows had claimed the entire parking lot. A cold shiver ran down his spine and all he wanted to do was be anywhere other than where he was at the moment. Quickly, he turned onto Spring Street and rode away from the Hollow.

Chapter 5

Matthew reached his house thirty minutes later and secured his bike behind the garage. The light from the kitchen window lit up a portion of the backyard so he could see his way to the back door. After the creepiness of the Hollow, he was glad to be safe and sound in his own yard. Just at the edge of the light from the kitchen window sat an old rusted swing set he hadn't used for the last four years and a birdfeeder atop a thin blue pole. Shadows filled the backyard, but none of them appeared threatening.

"Hey, Mom," Matthew said, walking through the back door and into the house.

"Leave those filthy sneakers at the door," his mother said from in front of the stove. Matthew smiled and kicked off his sneakers, heading for the family room after he finished.

"Hey, twerp," an older girl said from a beige couch along the wall. The girl was dressed in torn, faded jeans and a white t-shirt knotted in the front. She had long blonde hair with pink highlights, thick eyelashes, and bright green fingernails. She wore two different colored socks on her feet, the toe missing from one of the socks, and was currently watching television, reading a *People* magazine, and sipping something red and sweet-looking from a cup through a bent straw while glancing at her cellphone.

"Mary, Mary, with legs so hairy," Matthew said, snatching the magazine from her hand and flinging it across the room. The pages fluttered like the wings of a bat before crashing to the carpeted floor.

"Mom! Matthew is being an ass," Mary screamed, jumping up off the couch.

"Matthew, stop being an ass," his mother shouted from the kitchen.

Matthew smiled at his sister and flipped her the middle finger as he shouted back at his mother sweetly, "Yes, Mom."

"Mom, he just flipped me off," Mary shouted as Matthew bounded up the stairs.

"Don't know what she's talking about, Mom, I'm upstairs," Matthew shouted from the top of the landing. Mary glared up at him and threw up her middle finger. Matthew returned the salute and turned away.

Mary waited a second before scooping up her magazine and flopping back down on the couch. She glanced at her cellphone on the floor, but its screen was dark. She huffed and sighed and went back to reading the article she had been reading before her brother had disturbed her.

Matthew walked into his bedroom and closed the door. He stood there for a moment in the dark, enjoying the silence before turning on a light. His bedroom was nothing more than a ten-by-ten square. In one corner was his bed and across from that was a small dresser buried beneath a pile of clothes and forgotten school papers. Movie posters covered one wall, two of them stolen right out of the display cases at the theater, though his mother and father were unaware of that fact. The others were bought at the Buckland Hills Mall. Posters of *Iron Man* and *Thor* faced each other. *Spiderman*, the Tobey Maguire *Spiderman*, hung closest to his bed. There was also an *Avengers* poster from the first movie and one of the Hulk busting through a wall. Matthew loved his posters, especially the two he had slipped out from their cases. He didn't feel any guilt about the theft; instead, he had felt like Indiana Jones slipping out of a cave with a statue or some other lost treasure.

To the right of his bedroom door was a small desk with a Dell laptop on it. His mom and dad had given him the laptop for Christmas last year. It was supposed to be for homework and research, but Matthew used it mostly to watch videos, to play video games, and chat with his friends.

Matthew sat down in front of the laptop and booted it up. The Google search screen came up and he entered the name Globe Hollow into the search engine. Several results came up. Matthew selected one and began to read about the history of Globe Hollow.

Chapter 6

Bruce arrived at Globe Hollow at seven the next morning. Peter Briley was already at work; his yellow VW Beetle was parked beneath the old oak tree in the far corner of the parking lot. Bruce parked beside the VW, leaving his windows cracked so his car didn't get too hot as the morning warmed up. He grabbed his notebook, a pen, several baggies, and a proper camera before exiting his car. He took several pictures of the parking lot, making sure to note the entrance and the fence line before heading down to the gate. He half expected to see Matthew pedaling across the lot to join him. He wasn't sure if he was disappointed or glad that Matthew wasn't there.

"Hello," Bruce shouted through the locked gate. He waited a minute and shouted again. This time, the locker room door cracked open just enough to allow a bit of white light to spill out, along with a lined face.

"We're fucking closed; come back later," a man in his late fifties or early sixties shouted in a thick New England twang that made "we're fucking" sound like one word.

"Hello, I'm Bruce Westman," Bruce shouted through the gate before the door could close again.

Peter stepped through the locker room door and into the early morning light. He squinted his eyes at Bruce as if he were studying him. "You look like that cop who was here yesterday, maybe a little younger, maybe a little shorter," Peter said, wiping his hands on his pants.

"That was my brother," Bruce replied. "I'm helping him out with the investigation."

Peter walked up to the gate and pulled a key from his pocket. He released the padlock and swung the gate open.

Bruce walked inside, and Peter relocked the gate. "So, what can I do ya for, Officer Westman?" Peter asked, spitting into the grass before popping a cigarette in his mouth and lighting it.

"Just Bruce, and I was hoping to get a look around," he explained, lifting his digital camera up so Peter could see it clearly.

"I suppose that'll be alright," he said, lifting one eyebrow. "Ya know, the town would like to keep this shit quiet if that's even possible?"

Bruce looked down at his watch. "I got it."

Peter glanced at his watch and then up at Bruce. "Okay then," he replied, opening the door leading back into the locker rooms. Bruce followed him inside through a thick cloud of cigarette smoke that raced out the door before it could close. He coughed hard once as the door snapped shut. The cold fluorescent lights assaulted his eyes, and the musty odor of wet towels and ancient mold filled his nostrils.

"Fucking things are going to be the end of me," Peter said, coughing thickly several times before spitting into a trashcan in front of a row of lockers.

"Was anything disturbed back here?" Bruce asked, walking down one row over to get away from the cigarette smoke. He noticed that most of the lockers stood with their doors open. In several, towels hung from hooks, and in a few, the odd bathing suit or left behind t-shirt either dangled or sat piled up at the bottom. There didn't appear to be anything of value in any of the lockers.

"Not that I know of," Peter answered, scratching the side of his unshaven face. Bruce followed him back outside. It felt amazing to breathe in the fresh air and feel the light of the rising sun on his face. "I saw her over there, yesterday. She was all hooked up in that pile of floating crap," Peter explained, pointing a crooked finger toward the diving raft in the middle of the pool. Bruce took a photo of the raft even though he knew his brother's people had already done so. "You can do what you need to here, and I'll be around," Peter said, flicking his cigarette onto the ground and stumping it out. He bent and picked up the spent butt, tossing it into an empty trashcan.

"If I may, I'd like to ask you some questions later," Bruce asked.

"I suppose that will be alright, as long as it doesn't get in the way of things," Peter replied, before ducking back inside the locker room. Bruce watched the door close before turning back around to face the pool. It looked much as it had the day before, minus the creepy shadows lurking across the water. He noted that the caretaker had turned on the sprinkler in the shallow end of the pool where the younger kids played. Colorful rainbows danced in its mist.

It's all the same today as it had been when I was a child, Bruce thought, walking along the sidewalk toward the concrete beach. He stopped at the end of the sidewalk, noticing a pile of branches at the top of the hillside behind the beach. In the failing light yesterday, he hadn't noticed the pile, or it hadn't been there, but he saw it up there today. "I bet that's what she was tied to," he whispered, walking across the beach and up the hill.

At the top of the hill, he stopped and examined the pile. Even the next day it was obvious that the piled wood had been in the water recently. Damp mold clung to the bark and the ends of the thicker pieces were still soft and spongy. Bruce poked through the pile, removing one piece of wood at a time until he had everything spread out in the grass, side by side. He took pictures from several angles with his camera and then one with his cellphone. He took out his cache of baggies and set them at his feet before slipping on a pair of gloves. He saw a piece of white string clinging to a bent branch and carefully tugged at it until he had it free of the bark. He laid the string across the grass to get an idea of its length. It was three feet long. After taking a picture, he placed the string in a plastic bag and made a note in his notebook.

Might be something left behind from whatever they used to hold her down to the pile, he thought, looking for more evidence that the crime scene unit may have missed yesterday. He found a bit of tattered denim clinging to the end of a limb that had been buried at the bottom of the pile. White thin strings of cloth dangled from the ends of the material. It was still damp from the water. He took a picture of the denim, tweezed it away from the wood, tucking it inside another plastic bag.

"Yep, that's what she was tied to, poor little thing," Peter Briley said around a cigarette poking out of his mouth as he climbed up the hillside.

Bruce straightened up and nodded. "Did you pile all this up here?"

"Sure as fuck did. Someone from the town is supposed to haul it away today," Peter said, coughing several times and spitting into the grass. It was a thick wad of yellow phlegm that landed just in front of his feet. "Fucking things," he mumbled, shaking the hand that held the cigarette. Smoke twirled into the air like dark gray snakes curling up in the morning sunshine.

"Did you remove this from the water?" Bruce asked, waving a hand at all the branches set out in the grass.

"One of those cops with the cameras and the jumpsuits did," Peter answered. "He waded out there and guided it over to the shallow end." Peter snubbed out his cigarette in the grass. He picked up the butt after it was out and stuffed it into the back pocket of his jeans.

Bruce looked out over the water. "Does anything filter the water before it runs off?" Bruce asked.

"Sure, sure," Peter answered, stuffing another cigarette into his mouth.

"Did the police check the filter out?"

"I don't believe so, at least not while I was here, and I was here until I shut this bitch down." Bruce smiled. "You know, it's not much of a filter down there. It's more like a steel screen that keeps the large shit from getting into the Hockanum River," Peter explained, eying the debris scattered across the grass. "You going to stack that shit back up?" Bruce nodded, mopping his brow with the back of one gloved hand. Peter laughed and walked away, lighting another cigarette as he went. The smoke trailed off above his head.

Fucking things are going to kill you, old man, Bruce thought, watching Peter Briley walk away. He waited until the caretaker ducked back inside the locker to turn back to the wood. He didn't want any witnesses to see what might happen next. He knelt in the grass and took hold of one of the branches. The bark was soft and wet in his hand. He tossed it aside and did the same with another and another, closing his eyes each time and simply feeling the wood in his hand waiting for something to happen.

"Not even a twinge," he said after everything was piled back up. Standing, he turned away and walked toward the waterfall. He left his sneakers on this time and began climbing up the slick concrete. At the top, he admired the reservoir for a moment in the light of day before stepping into it and making his way to the strip of mud and cattails that ran along the water's edge. He made sure to snap a few photos of the reservoir and the waterfall before walking away.

Bruce found the path quickly that Matthew had shown him the night before. It cut right into the woods through the trees and overgrowth like a healed over scar carved into the land. After walking only a few feet, the reservoir was nowhere to be seen behind him. Bruce took a photo of this before following the path further into the trees, thankful that, in the full light of day, the path didn't appear as spooky as it had the night before, though shadows certainly ruled beneath the overhanging branches.

Through the fractured sunlight that managed to penetrate the thick canopy above, the clearing looked filthy and abused. Thin shadows covered the ground in the twisted shapes of dying spirits. Trash was scattered everywhere on the ground along with other paraphernalia left behind by the older kids who came out there to smoke pot, drink, or fuck. Bruce shook his head, feeling sad and angry. Everything from the night before was just as it was, but in the light of day it appeared so much worse, so much sadder.

Bruce took several photos of the clearing from several different locations. He took a photo of the tree toward the back of the clearing where he had found the panties hidden beneath the fallen leaves. In the light of day, he saw something else there that he hadn't seen the night before. The ground at the base of the tree was darker than the rest of the ground around the clearing. It was stained.

Bruce turned on the flashlight application on his cellphone and studied the patch of earth where he had found the panties. In the light of the cellphone, it looked like several leaves were stained with dried blood. Bruce took a picture and then used his tweezers to loosen the leaves from the dirt. He dropped the leaves into a baggie. In a separate bag, he scooped up a handful of dirt and dropped that in as well. He set the baggies on top of a stump and continued looking around the clearing.

Bruce found another piece of frayed denim a few minutes later. It was snagged in a Japanese Barberry bush just outside the perimeter of the clearing. The bright red berries clustered at the ends of the branches rocked back and forth in the stiff morning breeze. Bruce took a picture of the denim before freeing it from the bush and placing it inside another plastic bag for safekeeping.

Bruce walked around the clearing again, searching for more evidence. After a third trip, he widened his search, picking his way through the trees and underbrush, avoiding the thorn bushes as best he could. He saw that the ground cover beyond where he found the denim appeared as if it had been tamped down by someone recently. *Maybe it was the crime scene techs,* he thought, *or maybe it was the killer.* Branches close to the ground were broken here and there and the weeds and grass that grew over the forest floor looked smashed and beaten down. Bruce took pictures, following a razor-thin path deeper into the trees.

At the end of the path was a smaller clearing a couple hundred yards or so from the first. This clearing appeared more recent than the first. There were no signs of teenage rebellion or things left behind and forgotten. In the middle of the clearing were rocks and sticks piled on top of each other, forming what appeared to be, to Bruce at least, a very uncomfortable platform or altar. Bruce took several pictures of the stones as he approached. A few of the rocks were darkly stained. Bruce glanced over his shoulder half expecting to see someone watching. He was still alone, so he turned back to the stones and reached out a finger, setting it right in the middle of a dark stain. It felt tacky to the touch. Bruce felt his world begin to slip sideways and he yanked his hand away, but not before he caught a glimpse of a child struggling for her life. He held his hand against his chest, swallowing hard.

"I don't need to see that shit," he whispered, stepping away from the stones and fumbling his cellphone from his pocket. He called his brother.

Chapter 7

The killer stood upon the Case Pond Bridge. He admired the careful stonework that had gone into the building of the bridge. It spanned Case Pond, which was part of the Case Mountain Recreation area in Manchester. The bridge was built by the Case Brothers and the killer knew all of this. He knew the history of Case Mountain and how it came to be the property of the Town of Manchester. He knew that the Case family hadn't been the pillars of the community that they had pretended to be, but who really was after all?

"You know, this whole area was a papermill at one time," the killer whispered to a bound and gagged girl at his feet. There was no one around that could have heard him speak, but years of careful existence had taught him not to take any chances. The girl's eyes went wide, and tears rolled down along her cheeks. She tried to speak but couldn't form the words around the gag in her mouth. "No, no, no, of course you don't," the killer replied, as if she had spoken. "Alfred and Albert Case were twin brothers and they formed Case Brothers, Inc., in 1861. They supplied washed cotton to the Union Army," the killer explained. "Most of this land, that you can't see at the moment, because you're lying here at my feet, was given to the town in the 1960s by the family."

The girl mumbled around her gag. The killer smiled. "Yes, yes, you are very welcome for that bit of knowledge," the killer said, leaning out over the wall, looking down at the waterfall that fell away just beneath him into the darkness. The forest beyond the falls were nothing but dark shadows, but the killer knew the water ran for quite a way down into Birch Brook. He took a deep breath and exhaled sharply, reaching into a black leather case as he did so. The leather bag looked like an old doctor's medical bag. It had a clasp at the top and a strap for carrying.

"Let me see, let me see," the killer whispered gleefully. The girl at his feet began to buck and twist. Even in the meager light from a partially hidden moon, the killer could see the terror in her eyes. He watched her fight against the carefully tied ropes. Scrapes and cuts opened along her naked skin. The back of her head bled, but she continued to fight.

"Look at what you've done to yourself, child," the killer said, withdrawing a long silver-bladed knife from the bag. The blade sparkled in the moonlight as he held it up. The girl screamed a muffled scream around the gag, her struggles becoming more violent and desperate. The killer smiled, kneeling alongside her body. Her frenzied movements stopped.

"Child," the killer said, drawing the tip of his finger over one breast. The girl whimpered. Tears left streaks on either side of her face. The killer smiled, placing the blade of the knife beneath her chin. The steel was cold like a chip of ice. "You are such a sweet little thing. So young and full of life," the killer whispered, trailing his other hand across her stomach. Goosebumps covered her slightly sweaty skin. "I'm saving you, child, don't you know that? If it wasn't for me, you would become a whore just like the rest of them," the killer said, moving the blade further down below her chin. She could feel it there, against the soft skin of her throat. Just the tiniest bit of pressure. She didn't move.

"My mother was a whore, and so was her mother, and I bet your mother is a whore, too, but not you. Not yet. I can save you. You want to be saved, don't you?"

The girl screamed her muffled screams. The killer's smile widened, and he drew the tip of the knife across her throat. Bright red arterial blood spurted out across the stone bridge washing over the killer's shoes. He took hold of the girl's throat with both of his hands, allowing the blood to pour through his fingers. Its warmth felt comfortable, enjoyable. He sighed deeply, looking into her eyes, watching and waiting for that moment when salvation took her. He saw the light go out. He saw the very moment when her soul slipped free of its prison.

I have saved her, the killer thought, lifting the girl up into his arms, cradling her against his chest before hefting her up over his head. The girl only weighed a hundred and twenty pounds. He lifted her easily enough, stepping up against the stone wall that overlooked the waterfall.

"You are welcome," the killer said, before tossing the girl out over the waterfall. He heard the body splash somewhere below. He heard it slam into rocks and debris, but he couldn't see it now. She was gone. He hoped the water carried her away, but he didn't care. He had done his job and fulfilled his mission. She was safely saved now.

The killer placed his knife back in the bag and zipped the bag closed. He walked back along the bridge until he stepped off into the shadowed forest. The path here was wide and led back to the Spring Street parking area down below. The killer only followed the path a short way before stepping off and walking over to the pond. He dropped to his knees along the shore and washed his hands in the cool water. Standing back up, he made his way back to the path, looking back at the bridge. A smile spread across his face and he reached down between his legs. He was hard and it felt good to be hard. It felt magical.

The killer left the path again, walking into the trees, setting his bag down in the dirt and leaves at the base of a tree. He unzipped his pants and removed his hard-on from inside his white underwear, masturbating among the nighttime shadows. It felt incredible as the world shrank.

The killer stood in the shadows beneath the forest trees catching his breath as he softened inside his hand. He enjoyed the feeling of his dick all slick with cum shrinking inside his hand. He didn't mind the sticky wetness between his fingers. Eventually, he zipped up his pants, wiping his hands off on the legs of his jeans. From a pocket, he withdrew a pair of white panties and placed them against his face. There was a musky smell there that he inhaled deeply. The panties were soft and silky, and he enjoyed the feeling of them as he smashed them against his face. It was intoxicating. It was the finest kind of drug that he knew.

The killer twisted the panties into a ball and bent over. He shoved them beneath the fallen leaves slowly rotting away at the base of the tree. The killer smiled and walked away, leaving the panties behind. Standing on the path again, he followed it back to the parking area, pausing before stepping out of the shadows. Sure that it was safe, he walked quickly across the small parking area and out onto Spring Street. He kept to the curb, clinging to the shadows before reaching his car. The killer drove off down the Spring Street Extension toward Wyllys Street and safety. There were no other cars on the street. Everything and everyone was sleeping safely behind locked windows. It was his world now as he drove away from Case Mountain.

Chapter 8

Bruce arrived at the Case Mountain Recreation Area at ten the next morning. His brother had called him several hours earlier, waking him up at the crack of dawn. As Bruce was pulling into the recreation area, the crime scene officers were getting into their van, preparing to leave. Jeffrey's city-issued car was parked beside the crime scene van in the Spring Street parking lot.

"Hey, little Westman," one the techs said through a rolled down window as Bruce got out of his car. He hated the name but forced a smile.

"Hey," Bruce said from behind the dark sunglasses concealing his bloodshot eyes. At the rear of his car, he popped open the hatchback and rummaged around, gathering the items he needed. The crime scene techs chuckled at this before leaving the parking area in their white van with Manchester Police Department emblazoned across the rear and sides. A blue, white, and amber lightbar sat on top of the van. A blue bumper sticker with white letters was affixed to the rear bumper declaring, "In God We Trust." Bruce watched the van roll away until it disappeared down the long driveway leading back out to Spring Street.

"What took you so long?" Jeffrey asked from a path at the end of the lot, close to where Bruce had parked. He wore a white dress shirt, no tie, top button undone, dark blue slacks, and brown loafers. A pair of dark Ray-Bans rested on the bridge of his nose. He looked fresh, clean, and rested--nothing like how Bruce felt that morning.

"Long night," Bruce explained, rubbing the bridge of his nose between his thumb and index finger. "After I left the

Hollow last night, I went into Hartford for something to eat and a few drinks. A few drinks turned into several and before I knew it the bartender was shouting last call. Not really sure how I made it home."

"I bet it was a long night," Jeffrey said, pointing a finger at Bruce's sunglasses. "Sun too much for you today?"

"Maybe, or maybe I just happen to think I look cool with these on," Bruce said, licking his lips, wishing he had stopped at a gas station for something to drink.

"Whatever, your life," Jeffrey replied, shaking his head. "Anyway, we have a body near the pond, below the bridge. It looks like she was killed on the bridge sometime last night and tossed over the side. It's just you and I out here right now so we'll be all alone."

Bruce nodded, following his brother down the path. "Same guy from the Hollow, you think?"

"I think so, but we're not totally sure. I want you to look things over with fresh eyes and see what you think about it. Maybe you can get into this guy's head that way that you do." Bruce nodded.

"Who found the body?" Bruce asked.

"A groundskeeper. He's around here somewhere. Found her this morning at seven while he was walking the grounds and called the police." Bruce continued following his brother along the path. "We have a body car headed out here, so you might want to pick up the pace, so you can do your thing in private."

"What's the groundskeeper's name?" Bruce asked, taking out a pen and his notebook.

Jeffrey glanced down at his own notebook, which he slipped from a pants pocket. "His name is Frank DeMasso. Old guy in his late sixties. Been working out here over twenty years."

"Anyone see anything last night?" Bruce asked, enjoying the shade overhead as he walked. It felt good to be out of the direct sunlight. Even at ten in the morning he could tell it was going to be a hot and humid Southern New England day.

"Don't know. We got uniforms canvassing the area, but I'm not too hopeful," Jeffrey answered. "Nearest house is around the corner."

They reached the bridge a few minutes later. Bruce was sweating. Jeffrey looked as fresh as he had when he had shouted for Bruce in the parking lot. Holding his cellphone, Bruce took a picture of the bridge as he walked up to it. It hadn't changed all that much since he was a kid, maybe just a little older looking.

The Case family built the bridge by hand from stones taken from the surrounding property. The stones, now covered in a thin film of green moss and long tangling vines, were carefully stacked one on top of the other. There were five stone arches in the bridge that allowed the water from the pond behind it to flow through to the brook below. The water fell in a twelve-foot waterfall, forming three small pools before washing out into the brook. Stones littered the pools and the brook beneath the waterfall allowing the water to flow over them or around them. It was upon these stones that the girl's body had come to rest. Bruce sighed and took a picture from the middle of the bridge. His head hurt a bit more as he leaned out over the falls.

The girl was naked, her skin swollen from being in the water overnight. Her lips were parted around a gag that dug into the flesh of her face. Twigs clung to her long brown hair. She was young. If Bruce had to guess, no more than seventeen or eighteen. Her head was bent at an odd angle where it had struck a stone during her fall from the bridge. The eyes were open and vacant, staring up at the sky. A jagged cut parted the skin a few inches beneath her chin. It looked ugly and cruel and completely out of place on someone so young. The edges were white and puffy from spending the night exposed to the water. Looking at it from above, the cut almost looked like a second pair of lips.

"She was killed here, I think," Jeffrey said, pointing at all the dried blood on the surface of the bridge. Bruce walked to within a foot of the blood that covered the stones and ran into the cracks and crevices. He took a picture with his phone, wrote a note in his notebook, and stepped away.

"He tossed her from here," Bruce said, looking down at the body again. "I don't see any lights around here, so the killer had plenty of privacy. Any idea who she is? Is she local? Was she reported missing?"

"Nothing yet," Jeffrey answered.

"She's a kid; someone's missing her," Bruce said. "Check East Hartford and Glastonbury and Vernon."

"It's already being done, little brother."

"Can I go down there?"

"Sure," Jeffrey said. "Whatever evidence there was, and there wasn't much, has been gathered up."

Bruce walked to the end of the bridge and picked his way over and through the mess of brush that cluttered beneath it. He stopped beside the girl's body and took several pictures, noting that her hands were tied behind her back, and her feet were bound together. The killer used twine instead of rope or zip ties. It was wrapped over and over around her wrists. Her feet had been tied together in a similar fashion at the ankles. Strips of skin were torn away beneath the twine. Dark blood had soaked through the thin frazzled string, turning it crimson where the water hadn't gotten to it.

"She doesn't look as if she was sexually assaulted," Bruce shouted up to his brother. "I don't see any bruising or blood around her thighs, but you never know."

"No, we didn't see anything, but she's been in the water for a while. The girl found at the Hollow didn't look like she had been assaulted either. We'll know something for sure in a day or so when we get the autopsy report from Hartford," Jeffrey said.

"That's so strange," Bruce said. "This feels like it's sexual in nature. Did anyone find any panties anywhere?"

"Nope," Jeffrey said, glancing into his notebook. "There really isn't much evidence here. I'm sure the brook had its way with anything left on the body. This guy is smart."

Bruce climbed back up the slope and stood at the end of the bridge. He faced the pond and closed his eyes, standing absolutely still. Jeffrey watched until his brother's eyes opened back up. Bruce didn't acknowledge him. It was as if he no longer saw his brother.

Bruce turned back to the bridge and kneeled beside the bloodstained stones. He set a hand on the stain, closing his eyes and taking a deep breath. A moment later he stood and walked back to the end of the bridge and looked down the path. His eyes narrowed as he took in the pond.

Jeffrey watched his brother step off the bridge and follow the path. He walked slowly as if in another world. Jeffrey kept silent and waited. Bruce paused on the path before stepping off and walking to the edge of the pond. He fell slowly to his knees and leaned out over the water. His hands slipped into the water, and he began rubbing them together as if he were washing them in a sink.

"He had to wash up here after he finished his deed," Bruce mumbled. "Cutting the girl's throat can be so messy." Jeffrey, standing on the path now, wrote in his notebook.

Bruce stood and faced the path again. He didn't seem to see his brother standing. His eyes were focused on the trees beyond the wide trail. Slowly, he began walking again, stepping around Jeffrey, crossing over the path, and heading into the woods. Jeffrey watched. He knew not to speak. He knew that Bruce wasn't Bruce at the moment, but the killer. Bruce called what he was doing "drifting." Jeffrey didn't know what to call it, but he knew it worked.

Bruce stopped several feet inside the trees. Deep shadows filled the forest as thin beams of sunlight fought to break through from above. The woods were dark and full of things hidden and ancient. Birds chirped up in the trees along the branches, and squirrels scurried about the ground searching for acorns and nuts. Bruce felt all of this as he settled in front of a tree. There were trees everywhere, oaks and pines mostly, but the tree he stood in front of was a tall maple. The trunk filled his vision. He felt excited, turned on, stimulated. Every nerve ending was firing. He wanted to touch himself but somehow resisted. Looking around he saw that the ground at the base of the tree appeared disturbed. The leaves seemed to lie unnaturally. He reached down and brushed the leaves aside until they revealed a pair of white panties.

Bruce looked up and saw the killer standing at the base of the tree jerking himself off. He heard the man cum with a groan as he leaned into the tree. Bruce felt himself release and shame swept over him. He watched the killer inhale the panties before hiding them.

The drift ended. Bruce was back in the forest. The sun was out. The shadows not so threatening. He wanted to throw up but swallowed it back. He could feel the mess inside his pants and hated himself for it. He took a few breaths to steady himself before stepping away from the tree. He looked down at the panties. His heart ached for the owner of the panties and the pain and horror she must have felt before dying. Another deep breath to calm himself before joining his brother back on the path.

"It's the same guy," Bruce said. "He left another pair of panties at the base of that tree buried beneath the leaves." Jeffrey walked carefully into the woods and snapped several pictures before recovering the panties and stepping back out on the path.

Bruce and Jeffrey stood in the Spring Street parking area watching the body car pull away. They waited in silence until it was gone, and they were alone again, Jeffrey turned to Bruce.

"Nice catch with those panties," Jeffrey said.

"Just lucky," Bruce muttered, feeling a sense of guilt at how aroused he had become.

"No, you're not lucky. What you have is a gift," Jeffrey said, shaking his head.

"It doesn't feel like a gift," Bruce said, rubbing his forehead. "It feels like an invasion of my soul that leaves me damaged and broken inside," he said, remembering again what had happened out there.

"Well, whatever it is, it tied these two killings together, and that's something."

Bruce forced a smile and opened his hatchback. He put his things away. He needed a drink in the worst way and wanted to leave.

"Why don't you come over tonight for dinner?" Jeffrey asked.

"Maybe," Bruce said, knowing he wouldn't…knowing he would probably spend the night in the city again at some bar drowning his pain in a flood of alcohol.

Jeffrey watched his younger brother get into his old Ford and chase three Ibuprofen with something hidden inside a brown paper bag. He knew what was inside the paper bag but kept silent. Bruce started the engine after setting the bag on the passenger seat. He didn't care that Jeffrey had seen him take a swallow. He rolled the window down and set his arm on the sill.

"I'm serious, a good meal and family might be just what the doctor ordered," Jeffrey said.

"We'll see," Bruce said, glancing over his shoulder. "I might come back here tonight and check things out in the dark."

"I can come with you after dinner," Jeffrey said, stepping away from the car. Bruce forced a smile and rolled his window up. He didn't want to continue the conversation. Jeffrey waved as he pulled away from the parking area.

Jeffrey waited until the car disappeared before walking over to his own vehicle. The door opened with a squeal and he sat down, turning on the engine. The cold blast of air through the vents felt good. *It's going to be a long hot summer*, he thought, pulling away.

On Spring Street, Jeffrey turned right, heading away from the recreation area. He wondered as he went if he would ever be able to go out there again to hike or enjoy a picnic alongside the pond. It was such a nice place for something like that to have happened. Families and couples always came out here when the weather was good to enjoy a picnic or just be together.

If we catch this asshole, I'll make sure to tell him fuck you for ruining a good park, he thought, picking up his cellphone. He selected Baby from his list of contacts. The number rang several times before going to voicemail. He waited for the beep.

"Hey, Baby," he said into his cellphone. "Bruce might join us tonight for dinner. And I just wanted to say, I love you and miss you." Jeffrey hung up and dropped the cellphone into his pocket as he took the entrance ramp to Highway 384.

Chapter 9

A man in a Red Sox ballcap walked down the sidewalk holding tightly to a blue leash. At the end of the leash was a small dog weighing no more than twenty pounds. It was a Boston terrier mix of some kind, short haired and brindle. The dog pulled aggressively against his leash as his owner fought to control him. The man was of average height, maybe one hundred and eighty pounds. He wasn't fat, but he wasn't built either. There was really nothing that stood out about him. His arms were lightly tanned with a thin covering of hair; his face was clean shaven. He wore dark sunglasses with large lenses that revealed nothing of the watchful eyes behind them. The shadow from the bill of his ballcap and the sunglasses he wore in fact hid most of his face without looking as if that was what he was trying to do. No one walking casually by would have been able to describe the man with much accuracy beyond the gray cargo pants and solid blue t-shirt he wore, and of course the ballcap. In Manchester, you were either a Red Sox fan or a Yankees fan, so the cap didn't stand out unless you rooted for the Mets or the dreaded Dodgers.

The dog paused to pee on a for sale sign planted in the grass between the sidewalk and the street. The man studied his surroundings from behind the sunglasses while the dog took care of his business. The street was like any other street across Suburbia, USA. The houses on either side were older, built in the forties and fifties after World War Two. Tall oak trees and thick pines grew in the front and backyards, casting long shadows on hot summer days. The man didn't live on this street or any of the nearby streets. In fact, he didn't even live in Manchester, but he looked as if he did. The man was careful, very careful, not to hunt in his own backyard. He may not have lived in Manchester, but he was very comfortable there, as he was with most towns in Connecticut.

While the dog continued sniffing at a message left behind in the grass by a German Shepherd, two kids walked down the sidewalk on the opposite side of the street. The man watched their approach with great interest. He felt his pulse increase and his heartbeat speed up. One of the children was a girl in her mid- to late teens, sixteen or seventeen…not much older than that. The other was a boy. The boy was younger than the girl by a couple of years.

Brother and sister, the man thought as the dog finished his sniffing and began pulling on the leash again.

"Easy, Max," the man growled, his eyes never leaving the two children walking down the sidewalk. As they drew closer, the man saw that the boy had a green towel over his shoulder, swim trunks on instead of shorts or pants, and a white t-shirt with Sponge Bob displayed across the front. The girl wore tattered shorts revealing her long well-tanned legs, a white t-shirt balled up in the front, so it showed off her naval and the piercing dangling beneath it, and sunglasses with lenses that were much too large for her long slim face. The t-shirt was knotted so tight that the strap of a swimsuit top was exposed over one shoulder. The man smiled. His thin pink tongue parted his lips before darting back inside his mouth. He adjusted his ballcap with his free hand, pulling it down lower, bathing his face in shadows.

"Matthew, look at the dog," the girl said, just loud enough so that the man heard her voice. The boy glanced up and across the street, smiling at the man and his dog. The man pretended to pay no attention to the children until he saw the girl was holding her cellphone out, snapping a picture of him and the dog. Startled by what she had just done, the man yanked roughly on the dog's leash. "Come on, Max," he snapped, dragging the dog back onto the sidewalk.

Matthew watched the man and his dog walk off quickly down the street. "I guess he doesn't like his picture being taken," he said as the man disappeared around a corner.

"I guess not," Mary said. "He's even weirder than you are," she added, stuffing her phone into a pocket.

"At least the mirrors don't crack when I look into them," Matthew teased.

"Asshat," Mary said, taking a playful swipe at her brother as they walked away.

Around the corner, the man paused and crept slowly back so he could watch the children walking away. *Going to Globe Hollow?* he wondered. *Too bad they removed my gift from the pool already.*

The man watched the children turn onto Spring Street and disappear. He noted that the girl had long blonde hair with pink highlights that danced in the sunlight. He felt himself growing hard, but knew better than to touch himself in public. *No more than seventeen*, the man thought, licking his lips. "So young and pretty and innocent. She could be in need of saving, Max," he whispered. Max glanced up, wagging his tail. His human looked pleased and Max wagged his tail even harder, tugging at the leash, sniffing at another message left behind by another dog. It was a good day to be a dog on a walk.

A half-hour later, the man sat in the front seat of a beige colored Chevrolet Impala. The car, like the man, didn't stand out. It drew no attention to itself. Max sat beside the man with his nose pressed tight to the passenger side window as an air conditioner vent blew cold air on him. The man drove away from the curb in a manner that drew no attention. He thought of the girl and the picture she had taken earlier.

He wondered if he should be worried but decided he had nothing to worry about. *They were just kids, after all, doing kid things,* he thought. "No, no, no," the man whispered, pressing his free hand against his groin, feeling the hardness there beneath his cargo pants. From across the seat, Max glanced at his human. The man smiled at the dog as he placed his hand back on the steering wheel. "Ten and two will always do, anything less could cause a mess," the man whispered, heading down the well-shaded street. Max wagged his tail and went back to looking out the passenger side window again. It really was a wonderful day to be a dog.

Chapter 10

Bruce didn't go to his brother's for dinner or back out to Case Mountain as he had thought he would that night. Instead, he went into the city and drank hard late into the night. The bartender, a man dressed in a black t-shirt one size too small with a white towel tossed over his shoulder, announced last call at two. Bruce lifted his glass and downed what was left before stumbling out of the downtown Hartford bar. He found his car where he had left it, parked against the curb beneath a streetlamp. The pool of light was not kind to his car. It revealed patches of rust, scratches, and a few dings and dents, some left there by him, some by a previous owner. Bruce noticed none of this though as he dropped into the driver's seat and started the engine. He listened to the engine chug and cough before smoothing out to a steady idle.

Bruce had no memory of driving away from the bar or how he had gotten home that night, but there he was sitting on the floor of his one room School Street apartment in his stained boxers. The clothes he had worn that night were scattered around the room. He lived on the second floor of an old three-story, three-family, faded-red brick building that needed a new a roof in the worst way. The building, built back in the late twenties, stood next to a vacant lot which stood next to a business. Discarded cars and trash littered the vacant lot. Tall weeds grew up between everything.

Bruce sat in the middle of his floor on top of an old threadbare carpet that had lost most of its original color. There was very little padding left beneath the carpet so he could feel the uneven wood floor beneath the rug through his boxers. He sat with his legs crossed, hands resting on top of them, and his eyes closed. He wasn't sleeping, he wasn't meditating…he was drifting. This is what Bruce called it, what he did to get inside a killer's head. His control over it was tenuous at best. Jeffrey called it a gift, but Bruce didn't think so. He thought of what he could do as drifting because that is how it felt when he went away. He simply drifted on waves following unseen currents until they took him somewhere.

Sometimes the drift felt like he was floating upon the ocean, riding calm seas, and other times, it felt like being caught in the middle of a storm, the tempest raging around him. On those occasions, his body was whipped around like a yo-yo at the end of a string, slammed this way and that, but no matter how it felt though, it all came down to the same thing. He was drifting along to some unknown destination that, if he was honest with himself, he'd tell himself to get the fuck out of there. Whatever you called what he did, it wasn't a gift or a superpower or anything like that. It was a curse. It was a horrible fucked up curse that he would do anything to give away.

Bruce sat there on the floor of his apartment with his eyes closed even though he wasn't really there. The apartment and its four walls no longer existed. Well within the drift, Bruce had traveled back to Case Mountain, and the night before last. The scene before him was dark. Everything felt strange and foreign. He stood at the end of the Case Brothers' stone bridge in the half-hidden light of a half-moon, and he wasn't alone. The bridge was covered in shadows that crept over the uneven stone surface like starving ghosts in a haunted graveyard. The killer, a faceless man of average build and average height, stood further down the bridge, and he wasn't alone either.

He works hard to remain so average, Bruce thought, making a mental note upon a mental notepad.

The killer stood over a body that lay at his feet. Bruce approached and quickly saw that it was the girl, but unlike the killer, she wasn't faceless. Bruce could see all of her and the naked terror in her eyes. He wanted to help her, to spirit her away from all of this, but he was helpless, because these were events that had already happened, and all he could do now was watch as they played out again like a scene from a horror movie.

The killer reached into some kind of bag that sat on the ground beside his leg. The bag looked familiar somehow, like something out of an old movie, but Bruce wasn't sure because it was just too dark to see clearly. The shadows were like greedy children hungry for a sweet treat swallowing everything.

A knife appeared in the killer's hand, reflecting what little light there was from the moon overhead. It bounced off its steel blade causing it to sparkle like glass. The knife wasn't anything special or noteworthy. It looked like something found in any kitchen across America, or like something from one of those *Halloween* movies starring Jamie Lee Curtis. The killer pressed the blade just below the girl's chin. It stood out against her pale skin. The killer ran his other hand slowly, deliberately, over her naked flesh and Bruce felt goosebumps covering his body as tingling energy raced beneath his skin. The killer smiled as he drew the blade across the girl's throat. Blood sprayed out like a fountain and the killer allowed it to wash over his hands and run through his fingers. He mumbled something as he did this, but Bruce couldn't make out what he said. The killer stood, picking up the girl as if she weighed nothing and threw her over the side of the bridge.

Bruce heard the smack and thwack and splash of her body as it tumbled down the falls. He felt himself cringe against the sound until there was no more noise to be heard and the silence of the night took back control. The killer walked away while Bruce stood there transfixed, looking beyond the bridge. When he turned away, he saw the man standing up from washing his hands in the pond water. Bruce knew what came next and wished he didn't have to observe it again, but whatever controlled the drift forced him to watch.

The killer finished and stepped back out onto the path and walked away. He was still a faceless man, but Bruce thought if he ever saw him he would know who he was just the same because they were joined together somehow. They were connected by what had happened there in the park.

Bruce's eyes opened. He was back inside his apartment again sitting there in his boxers in the middle of his floor. His body was covered in sweat, and much to his disgust, he was aroused. He felt sick seeing his erection poking at the underside of his boxers, but he was also helpless to leave it alone. He reached inside the boxers and began to slowly stroke himself. Tears fell from eyes as he completed the act. He felt shame and anger at himself, and horror. He sobbed softly for several minutes sitting there in the middle of the floor in his unlit apartment, one hand still inside his boxers covered in semen.

Bruce stood after a few minutes and made his way to the kitchen sink. He washed his hands in tepid water and dried them off with a flowered patterned paper towel. He shot the paper towel across the kitchen toward a trashcan but missed. Sighing, he walked over to the refrigerator. Its cold light instantly flooded the small apartment. He stood there for second in the glow of the light, as the cold air blew against his naked legs. It felt like being inside a cold drawer at the city morgue. He shook that image away and snatched a cold bottle of vodka from the middle shelf of the icebox.

Darkness returned to the apartment as the refrigerator door closed, chasing away the shadows that had been crawling over the walls. Bruce guzzled the vodka until he felt nothing. He made his way over to his bed. A pair of jeans and a t-shirt lay there where he had discarded them earlier. The bed was unmade, the sheet and blanket crumpled up in a pile at the end. A flat pillow hung over the side, teetering on the edge as if deciding if it wanted to fall or not.

Bruce dressed quickly and made his way down to his car parked out in front of the apartment building. The car was parked in the street, one of its tires sitting cocked at an angle on top of the curb. He had no memory of how that had happened or how he had even gotten home from the bar earlier. Looking around the street, he didn't see anyone or anything threatening. It was still dark outside. Something chirped in the grass. Opening the driver's side door, he fell into the car and slipped the key into the ignition. The old clock on the dash said it was four in the morning. The engine started with a rough growl.

Bruce looked out the windshield and saw a small dog, maybe twenty pounds, walking down the sidewalk. He sat there watching the dog sniffing at whatever attracted him, hiking his leg up and peeing. At the corner, the dog turned to the left and disappeared. Bruce let out a breath he hadn't been aware he had been holding. A name came to him out of the blue. "Max?" he mumbled at the windshield, wondering if that was the killer's name or something else. It didn't feel right, but it meant something, so he jotted it down on a pad of paper stuck to his center dash beside the endlessly running clock. The handwriting looked childish.

Bruce drove away from the curb with a rough thud as the tire dropped to the street. He managed to make it only a few feet down the street before slamming on the brakes and throwing the driver's side door open. He hung his head out and vomited onto the black asphalt. Wiping his mouth with the back of his hand he spat several times before closing the door again.

Manchester was quiet after four in the morning. In fact, on most nights, Manchester was quiet not long after midnight. The streets were lit by overhead lamps that cast wide pools of light on the dark asphalt below. The houses and businesses along the streets were dark and closed to prying eyes. Bruce loved the world at this hour when there was no one out there but him and those he hunted. He felt as if he owned the city at this hour.

He drove with his window down and arm hanging out over the side. The cool night air felt good against his skin and helped to keep the nausea at bay and his eyes open. He craved a cigarette when he drove like this. One of the few memories he had of his father was how he always had a cigarette planted between his index and middle finger while he drove. It was a good memory for Bruce, and one he had come to copy until he quit three years ago.

Bruce stopped at the gate to the Spring Street parking area. The parking lot was closed and blocked by the red and white striped gate, so he left his car there and entered the Case Mountain Recreation Area on foot. It was only a short walk to the actual parking area and the path that led away from it. Bruce carried a flashlight, a baggie, and a small garden shovel with him as he picked his way through the darkness. His stomach was still doing flip flops, but he didn't think he would vomit again.

There was very little light at this hour. Nothing from above managed to pierce the canopy of branches over the path. Even though it was a warm muggy night, he felt a chill creep over his body as he walked. It left his skin feeling clammy. He was disgusted by the idea that he had driven back out to the park at this hour, but he was determined to follow through with it. He wasn't sure if what he had planned would work out or not, but he had to try.

Bruce followed the path that wound its way back to the pond and the falls. At the end of the path, he came upon the stone bridge. It was bathed in deep shadows that hid most of its shape. He paused before walking out to the middle of the bridge. It wasn't something he wanted to do in the dead of night after what he had seen, but he forced himself to take a step, and then another and another, until he stopped where the killer had done his work.

Bruce gazed down into the darkness below and for a moment thought he heard the thwack and splash of the girl against hidden rocks and debris. He shivered and hugged himself thinking that he might throw up after all. Goosebumps covered his exposed flesh, leaving him wishing he were tucked safely in his bed.

"Why?" he asked aloud. His voice sounded far away. "Why do you have to kill?"

A frog croaked from somewhere below. Bruce sighed and sat on the wall, his legs dangling over the waterfall. He listened to the water splash and roll away. He watched the darkness for the ghosts of murdered children. He waited for some kind of answer to his question, but none came.

"What did you whisper to her before you killed her?" he wondered aloud as the back of one foot bounced against the bridge. Somewhere in the distance something scrambled through the underbrush. Another frog or toad croaked. Mosquitoes buzzed around his head. Something chattered up in one of the trees.

Bruce hopped off the wall and kneeled where the blood had been the night before. He ran his fingers over the spot, the rough stone biting into his skin. The stone was warm. He wondered if the heat was left over from the day or if it was the child's life spilling out that had heated its surface. He closed his eyes and pressed down on the stone until the palm of his hand was pressed flat. The bridge felt alive beneath his hand. He thought he felt a distant heartbeat thumping along at a quick pace from within the bridge. He took a deep breath and held it. A word formed in his head. It formed one letter at a time until it was complete. The letters were tall and crimson. They ran like blood over a white lined sheet of paper. He studied the letters as they swelled and pulsed with life.

"Salvation," he whispered, tasting the word, feeling it upon his lips. His mouth was dry, and the word sounded like sandpaper. He stood slowly. *Does he think he's saving these girls?* he wondered, looking back out into the darkness again.

Bruce returned to the parking area an hour later. In his hand he clutched a baggie of dirt that had dug up from beneath the tree where the panties had been found. He couldn't bring himself to look at the baggie. He wasn't sure if he had wasted his time or not. He didn't know if Jeffrey's people would be able to get any DNA from it, but they might.

Bruce returned to his car and tossed the baggie onto the passenger seat. He leaned his head back and closed his eyes. "Salvation," he whispered, starting the car. He rolled the window down, looking out into the darkness. "Salvation is mine, saith the Lord," he cried out the window. He wasn't sure what book of the Bible that came out of, but he knew it had just the same. "I am, the truth, the way, and the light," he whispered, driving away, pleased with his recall.

Bruce reached across his seat as he drove away from the Case Mountain Recreation Area. He opened his glovebox without taking his eyes off the road and removed a bottle. It was the same paper-bag-clad bottle his brother had seen earlier. He unscrewed the cap from the bottle and took a long swallow. The hot liquid felt good going down.

It was almost six in the morning now. He was tired and hungry. He made his way through the streets of Manchester and down Silver Lane to Main Street East Hartford. He turned right onto Main Street and drove to the Triple A Diner. It was open. It was almost always open. There were even a handful of cars parked out front. The real breakfast crowd was still an hour away. He parked among the few vehicles that were there and went inside. The bright fluorescent lights hurt his bloodshot eyes. He groaned softly and dropped down into a booth, not bothering to look at a menu.

"Food," he thought. "Then sleep."

Chapter 11

The afternoon sun filtered through the blinds and the thin blackout curtain over the one window to his apartment, waking Bruce up. The light stabbed painfully at his brain making him wish he could gouge out his eyeballs. He wasn't hungover exactly–that didn't happen very often anymore–but he didn't feel all that good either. He wore only boxers and a single sock on his left foot. His pants, shirt, shoes, and the other sock were left in pile on the floor at the foot of his bed where they had fallen. He added the sock he wore to the pile and stumbled into the bathroom to begin his day.

Thirty minutes later, Bruce walked out of his apartment building with a piece of toast in one hand and his car keys dangling from the other. It was already well into the eighties and the humidity was thick. He was sweating as he stumbled to his car. He had a massive headache that threatened to blow his head apart. Glancing up at the clear skies he thought it was going to be a busy Saturday down at the shore, but thankfully he wasn't going anywhere near a beach today. He hated crowds of people; they always made him uncomfortable. He only enjoyed the beach after the kids went back to school.

Bruce stuck his toast in his mouth and fumbled around with the keys, trying to get the correct one in the door. He managed to do this on his third try and yanked the door open. A blast of heated air rolled out of the car like a wave from a furnace. It smelled stale and trapped as it hit him like a fist, forcing him to take a step back from the door.

"God, I hate summer," he thought, making himself sit down inside the car. The seat felt like the electric coils on a stovetop as his butt and back made contact with the sizzling vinyl. The steering wheel was a circle of hell as he wrapped his fingers around it. *Summer sucks so bad*, he thought, rolling his window down and starting the engine. Hot air coughed through the closest vent, adding to his misery.

Bruce drove away from his apartment building, tossing the last bit of toast from the window. He saw it land in the street in his side view mirror. At Park Avenue, he turned right and followed it out to Main Street. From there, he made his way to the Dunkin' Donuts and bought two cups of coffee and four donuts. Pulling out of the parking lot, he turned back onto Main Street, heading toward Saint Christopher's Catholic Church on Brewer Street.

Saint Christopher's Catholic Church had been the church he attended ever since he was child. He went to catechism there every Saturday morning, made his first Holy Communion there, and had his uncle stood up for him at his Confirmation. He and his brother Jeffrey had also been baptized there as babies, and his brother had been married there ten years ago. Bruce still attended mass when he could, which wasn't very often, but Father Murphy always made sure to let him know that he appreciated him being there.

Bruce parked his car at the back of the parking lot beneath the shade of a large elm tree. The branches were full of leaves and birds and squirrels. It was his favorite spot to park. He took his keys from the ignition, left his window down, and made his way to the front of the church. He climbed the three steps to the four towering wooden doors stained a fleshy beige color. Walking inside to the vestibule, he paused and dipped his fingers into the holy water before entering the sanctuary. The water was cold and sent a shiver through his hand as he crossed himself.

The church was silent, cool, and deeply shadowed on the inside as he stepped through the second set of wooden doors. Tall stained-glass windows set high in the walls only allowed a muted fractured light to pierce the subdued atmosphere of the sanctuary. Row after row of pews rolled up either side of the church leaving only a six-foot-wide aisle down the middle. The aisle ended at three steps that led up to the altar. Behind the altar hung a large wooden cross with a crucified Christ nailed to it. As a child, Bruce had always expected that one day that figure on that cross would simply step down and walk out of the church, perhaps disgusted by what he saw sitting there in the pews. He had nightmares about it as a child where the crucified Christ, like a giant in a fairytale, stepped on all the parishioners, smashing them beneath his pierced wooden feet as he made his way out the doors. Even now as an adult he looked cautiously up at the cross behind the altar making sure the figure nailed to it was still there safe and sound. Bruce smiled when he saw that it was and made his way to the confessional to the right of the altar.

At the front of the sanctuary, just to the right of the altar, were two wooden booths stained the same fleshy beige as the doors. Thick red curtains hung down over the entrances to the booths, so no one could see inside, and no one inside could see outside. Bruce stepped into one of the confessionals and sat down on a small wooden bench. He placed the coffee and donuts on the floor at his feet. The curtain swished back over the entrance, bathing him in darkness. He sat facing a small window cut into the wall in front of him. On the other side of the window, a priest sat waiting to hear his confession. There was a dark screen inside the window that allowed whoever sat there to speak to the priest on the other side without him being able to see who they were talking to. Even now as an adult, the confessional left Bruce feeling creeped out. It felt so alien to be inside that tiny room spilling out your transgressions to a priest. It made no sense to him that, if you could pray to God, why did you need to confess your sins to a priest?

Bruce sat there inside the confessional thinking about what he was going say to the priest. His head pounded and the bench he sat on, though cushioned, was not all that comfortable. It was also incredibly musty inside the confessional and smelled of sweat and an old lady's perfume. A thin shaft of light from high above pierced the screened ceiling. Motes of dust floated within the shaft drifting around the enclosed space like tiny planets. Bruce watched them, wondering what might be happening on so many worlds.

Bruce's thoughts were interrupted by the scrape of wood against wood. A small square of faint light appeared in the window as the shadowed shape of a head filled the screen. Bruce looked into the window and took a deep breath.

"Forgive me, Father, for I have sinned," Bruce said as he made the sign of the cross.

"Make your confession, my son," the priest said. It was Father Murphy on the other side. Bruce could tell by the sound of his voice, a little raspy from years of smoking and drinking.

"Father, it feels like it has been a lifetime since my last confession. In that time, I have committed many sins. I have lusted after others and engaged in sex with strangers. I have drunk alcohol in excess to the point where I have blacked out several times," Bruce confessed, pausing and swallowing hard.

"Is there anything else, my son?"

"I suppose I have coveted and taken the Lord's name. I'm sure there is other stuff that I have done that I need forgiveness for but just can't think of it right now."

"My son, say the Lord's Prayer, three Hail Marys, and an Act of Contrition, and go and sin no more," Father Murphy said. "After that, your sins are forgiven." Bruce watched the shadowed figure of the priest make the sign of the cross.

"Thank you, Father," Bruce said, before exiting the confessional. The curtain swished behind him. A little old lady passed him on his way to do as the priest had instructed him.

Bruce sat among pews toward the front of the church and did as Father Murphy had instructed. When he finished praying, he heard someone sit down beside him. He looked over and saw that it was Father Murphy. He smiled thinly, feeling embarrassed after his confession.

"Good afternoon, Bruce," Father Murphy said, setting a hand on Bruce's shoulder.

"Hello, Father. How are you?" Bruce replied.

"I am fine, son. How is everything with you?"

"I'm okay. My brother is doing well, and still married. My mom is driving everyone nuts, threatening to move to Florida and live with her sister."

"Good, good. But how are you doing?"

"I have good days and bad days, Father. Maybe more bad than good, but they're still days, I suppose," Bruce answered, handing the priest a cup of coffee and pointing at the small bag of donuts. Father Murphy smiled, sipping at the coffee.

"I worry about you, Bruce," Father Murphy said. "Your abilities to see into the minds of others comes with such a heavy price. I can see the toll it takes on your face, and in your eyes, and I can hear it in your voice."

Bruce looked closely at the priest. He knew that he was coming from a place of concern for him, but he still felt uncomfortable talking about the things he could do even though Father Murphy knew all about his abilities. "It's okay, Father, I can deal."

"It's alright, Bruce, you don't have to talk to me now if you don't want to. I'm here anytime as you well know." Bruce forced a smile as he watched the priest take a donut from the bag. "Just make sure you bring more coffee and donuts." Bruce chuckled.

"Father, can I ask you something?" Father Murphy nodded, setting the cup down on the pew. "What does salvation mean to you?"

Father Murphy took a moment to think. "According to our faith, Christ died on the cross for our sins. His death was our salvation. He saved us from being separated from the Father and spending eternity in Hell."

"So, what if a child dies? Are they sinners when they die or does God make an exception for them?"

"According to the Church, as long as a child has been baptized, they are free of the punishment of sin until they become old enough to understand what sin is."

Bruce rolled the words over in his mind. "So, the baptism in water is like the priest washing away our original sin."

"Yes," Father Murphy answered. "It is a sacrament like your First Holy Communion or the Last Rites."

"Thank you, Father," Bruce said, stepping out of the pew, his coffee cup in hand. "I have to go now, but you've been very helpful."

"I'm not sure what I did to help, but you're welcome." Bruce smiled and headed to the doors. Father Murphy watched him walked away.

Outside, Bruce took out his cellphone and called his brother. Jeffrey answered on the third ring.

"Hey, what's up?" Jeffrey said into his phone.

"Hey shithead," Bruce said.

"You're the only shithead I know, now what do you want?"

"I think the killer is trying to save his victims like in a churchy way," Bruce said.

"Well, he's doing a shitty job of it," Jeffrey said.

"No, he's not trying to save them from dying. He's trying to save them from sinning and going to Hell," Bruce explained.

"Okay, so he's saving them from whatever. How does this help us catch him?"

"Check out priests and pastors who have been excommunicated from their congregations for inappropriate behavior. Look for anyone named Max or something like that." There was silence on the other end of the phone for several minutes as Jeffrey wrote everything Bruce had said down.

"Anything else?" Jeffrey asked when he finished.

"Yeah, water is very important to this guy. It's always going to be a part of what he's doing, like his signature," Bruce said. "I think he believes he's somehow washing away their sins or something, like a priest baptizing a baby."

"Real sick fuck our guy," Jeffrey mumbled into the phone.

"Yeah, he's a sick fuck alright," Bruce said.

Chapter 12

Amy Patterson was seventeen years old and a junior at East Hartford High School. She was a pretty girl but still a bit tomboyish, tall and thin, always dressed in jeans and t-shirts. She had long straw-colored hair tied back in a ponytail that twisted halfway down her back. Black and red ribbons held her hair in place, so it flared out at the ends. She wore cat-eye-shaped prescription glasses with tiny fake diamonds curling down each arm. A vintage Alice Cooper t-shirt hung from her shoulders and baggy blue jean shorts. The shorts ended just above her lightly tanned knees. On her feet, she wore dirty white Converse sneakers with intricate designs drawn on them in blue and black ink. She had done this while sitting in fourth period study hall when school was still in session. Her mom hadn't been pleased, but what did she know about how a seventeen-year-old expressed herself?

It was later in the evening–more evening than afternoon–as Amy walked down Hill Street after leaving a friend's house. She was walking slowly without a care in the world toward the entrance to Governor Jefferson Gates Elementary School. The worn rubber bottoms of her sneakers slapped against the uneven concrete sidewalk. At the school entrance, she turned onto the deeply shaded driveway and made her way down the long hill. Her eyes were focused on her cellphone, checking out her Instagram for likes and comments on the pictures she had posted earlier that day. The sun was quickly setting behind her but there was still just enough light to see by.

On Hill Street, there were only a few cars passing by, their headlights not yet on. None of the drivers noticed the skinny little girl turning into the school and heading down the driveway. Most were concerned with other things—adult things—that prevented them from noticing a seventeen-year-old girl. Even with the two murdered girls in the news, no one saw Amy...and truth was she preferred it that way.

On the sidewalk, several houses down from the entrance of the school, a man walked with his dog. Unlike the drivers passing by on the street, he noticed the girl turning into the school, and like her, he preferred to go unnoticed as well. None of the people safely tucked away inside their cars really saw him or his dog as they drove down Hill Street. If they had been asked to, none could have described the man because nothing about him stood out or screamed threat. He just looked normal. He wore ordinary clothes and a Red Sox ballcap. Nothing about him screamed out see me, notice me. Even his dog was small—nothing special to make him stand out.

The man knew he was safe as he watched the girl turn from the sidewalk into the school driveway. He knew no one ever paid him much attention because for most of his life no one had ever paid him much attention. His mother ignored him, his father was nonexistent, and the only time other children paid him any attention was to tease and make fun of him. The only one who had ever paid him any kind of attention at all was Mr. DeAllan, and that had been the wrong kind of attention.

The dog paused along the sidewalk and lifted his leg to pee on a clump of grass. The man frowned and yanked on the leash. "Come on, Max, we have very important work to do. Very, very important work to do," the man whispered as the girl disappeared down the driveway.

At the top of the driveway, the man paused. Max peed again. The man watched the girl turn at the bottom of the hill and walk across the parking lot to the right of the driveway. She disappeared again, and the man smiled. The last thing he saw was the bounce of her ponytail as she looked up from her phone.

The man waited at the top of the driveway before proceeding. A few more cars drove by. He thought of Mr. DeAllan and his thick mustache shot through with black and gray hairs, and the glasses he wore that made his eyeballs look three sizes bigger than they really were. He thought of the mint green house Mr. DeAllan lived in all by himself across the street from his own house, and the dark cold basement beneath the main floor. A chill ran down his back. The man swallowed hard and tugged at the leash. "Come on, Max," he grunted, starting down the driveway, forcing all thoughts of Mr. DeAllan from his mind.

At the bottom of the driveway, the man didn't see the girl anywhere. He wasn't worried. If she was meant for him, God would provide, for salvation is his to bring to the lost. The man walked across the parking lot/pick-up area to the corner of the school building. He peeked quickly around the corner and was just in time to see the girl duck through an opening in a chain link fence on the far side of the playground. On the other side of the fence the woods hid everything from view. The trees were tall and thick; pines, oaks, and maples. Long shadows trailed back toward the school building. The sun was almost down now, but there was still enough light to see by.

"Come, Max," the man whispered. Max followed his owner across the field of grass to the chain link fence. He paused to pee on the fence before following his owner through the opening. Max knew not to linger because the man had very little patience for lingering. On some level, Max was very aware that the man was hunting prey now, and this was very important to his human.

Inside the trees, the man found a thin path worn down to dust by the thousands of tiny feet that must have come before him. The path wound its way into the thick shadows of the forest. It was dark and private—the perfect place for what he had to do. The man quickened his pace now that he was beneath the trees, hidden by the shadows. He felt safe here in the woods, as if he were wrapped inside of God's very protective hand.

The man came upon the girl after a few minutes of ducking and darting through the forest, avoiding low hanging branches and bushes full of thorns. She was walking with her eyes focused on her phone, the bright screen lighting up her face. She paid no attention to anything around her. The path was familiar to her because she had walked it many times before and because she was seventeen and the world revolved around her. *She is not long for this world*, the man thought as he slowed, paying attention to each step he took as he closed the gap. In front of him, the girl slowed.

Amy stopped walking. Something was off. She looked up from her phone and out into the shadows that surrounded her. Goosebumps rose on her flesh and the tiny hairs on the back of her neck came to attention. She spun around quickly, expecting to find another kid out there in the woods with her, sneaking up on her to scare her. She froze at the dark shape she saw though. It wasn't another child. It was an adult with a small dog. Even in the deep gloom of the forest she could see the dog pulling on its leash, lunging at her aggressively, but the adult, a man, held it back.

Amy took a backward step feeling the danger all around her. The isolation of the woods pressed in on her. A voice shouted in her head for her to run, but she hesitated. The man smiled. His teeth glowed bright white behind plump red lips. Amy swallowed hard. *Fang*s, she thought, frightened beyond belief. She turned to run but it was already too late, the man was on her before she even managed to lift her foot from the path.

An incredible weight suddenly forced her to the ground. All the air in her lungs exploded from her body in a useless blast that left her gasping for oxygen. A filthy hand that tasted of sweat and dirt covered her mouth while another hand drove her face down into the well-worn path. Fingers wrapped around her hair, lifting her head back up before slamming it back down again. Bright flashes of light exploded like stars before her eyes. The hand lifted her head up again, and again slammed her face into the dirt. The stars in her eyes went dark. She stopped struggling. Somewhere far away, she heard a dog barking. The sound of the barks seemed to come from miles and miles away.

"Shut up, Max," a man's voice growled. The voice sounded distant, like a whispered thought from somewhere inside her head.

Amy's eyes opened a few minutes later. She tasted blood in her mouth. It made her want to gag. She tried to speak, but something sticky covered her mouth. She tried to probe at it with her tongue, but it was sticky and yucky tasting. She tried to move but her arms and legs were held together. A man squatted in front of her. He was smiling. His lips were so incredibly red, and his teeth were so large and white. An image of fangs flashed through her mind again. Something wet and warm lapped at her face. It was the dog licking the tears from her eyes. His breath stank. The smell made her feel nauseous. She wished the dog would stop.

"Now, I want you to stay here until I return," the man whispered in a voice full of gravel. He smelled sour and dirty, much worse than the dog. More tears fell from her eyes. The dog licked even harder. "Enough, Max," the man snapped, standing up. He paused, looking down at her. He smiled again, revealing those hideously white teeth.

He's a vampire, she thought, watching him straighten and walk away. He went back toward the school. All she could do was watch him go until he disappeared into the shadows with his dog. Amy kept still, waiting for several minutes, watching the shadows spread across the world. Waiting to see if the man was going to return to drain the blood from her body. She let out a slow breath through her nose chased by a stream of snot after several minutes passed.

Stop crying, she thought, looking down at herself for the first time. She hadn't realized until then that she was naked. At some point the man had undressed her. She wore no clothes, no under clothes, nothing on at all. She had no memory of how it had happened. She took another shuddering breath, determined to figure something out.

Her body hurt everywhere. Her head and her face throbbed like a drum. She was scared and frightened and so alone out there beneath the trees. She could feel dirt and rocks biting into her skin. Insects that she couldn't see, crawled over her exposed body. She tried to struggle against the ropes that held her, but it did no good. She drew in a deep breath through her nose and screamed from behind the tape that covered her mouth. The scream was barely audible. More tears fell from her eyes again, soaking into the ground.

I should have allowed Patricia's mother to take me home like she wanted to, Amy thought, and then she remembered the two girls found in Manchester and wondered if this was the same guy. "Fuck, fuck, fuck me," she mumbled beneath the tape covering her mouth.

Chapter 13

Amy couldn't remember when she stopped crying. All she knew was that the tears did her no good. They didn't free her or make everything go away. Whether she cried or not did nothing to change the fact that she was tied up and left in the woods all alone. It was completely dark now outside. The woods were alive with sounds that she had difficulty figuring out what they belonged to. It was all so overwhelming. She wanted to scream, but the tape over her mouth prevented that. All she could do was lay there in dirt listening to the forest and praying someone came along to rescue her.

As she lay there, a new sound invaded the forest. This new sound didn't fit in with the other sounds. There was an odd rhythm to this new sound as it slowly grew louder and louder, closer and closer. Thump, thump, thump, thump it went like a beating heart. She swallowed and blew out a slow breath through her nostrils. Twigs snapped somewhere down the path. Leaves crinkled on the forest floor. Thump, thump, thump.

"Footsteps?" Amy wondered. She heard another sound now, just under the thump, thump, thumping. This sound was lighter. It paused and stopped, scratching at the earth before starting up again. *An animal*, she thought, trying to twist her body around so she could see, but the effort was useless; she couldn't move herself enough and the forest was simply too dark to see anything.

As the two competing sounds drew closer, Amy became aware of a threatening presence in the woods. Other creatures seemed to sense this presence too because everything else quieted down. Even the mosquitos had paused in their endless search for a meal. She felt the goosebumps rise on her exposed skin. *The man and his dog,* she thought. *He's finally come back for me.*

Amy felt something hot pass between her legs and realized she had just peed herself. Fear quickly overwhelmed her as images of what he might do to her flashed through her mind. So many horrible things crept through her thoughts. Her breath whistled through her nose as fresh tears washed down her cheeks. Panic filled her and she began to struggle against the ropes again.

"It's time, my dear," a man's voice said cheerfully from the shadows. He sounded so relaxed. Amy twisted her head enough to look up and saw a shadowed giant standing above her. A dog stood beside the giant and even he looked like a mountain lion standing there, sniffing at her with its cold wet nose. Shivers convulsed through her body. She swallowed hard and tried to speak, but only soft mumbles came from behind the tape. She wanted to beg for her life, but she couldn't get the words out.

"Always lift with your knees, not with your arms," the man whispered, squatting down beside her. His hands dug beneath her body, the nails scratching deeply into her skin. His fingers felt like iron claws gouging at her back as they inched further underneath her. All at once, she was off the ground like a helicopter lifting from a pad. The man tossed her over his shoulder as if she weighed nothing. She bounced twice painfully against his back before settling back down.

The man smelled of sour sweat and stale clothing as he stumped along the path through the woods. He smelled as if he hadn't bathed for several days. The odor made her want to vomit but she fought against the urge, knowing it all would have to explode through her nose. Branches lashed at her exposed back and face from either side of the path. She tried to focus on where they were going but it was impossible. She had no idea what direction they were headed. Nothing looked familiar hanging upside down as they lumbered through the woods.

After a million years that in reality couldn't have been more than ten minutes, they emerged behind the school. Tears blurred her eyes, but Amy was able to make out the building that had been so familiar to her for so many years. The man paused at the side of the building. He was breathing hard. His shirt was soaked with tears and sweat and pee. Amy looked down and saw that the dog was pooping in the grass.

Some kid is going to step in that, she thought absently. The man waited for the dog to finish. Amy kept looking around the schoolyard for anything or anyone that might help her, but she saw nothing. She wondered how late it was. The outside lights along the building were on casting pools of pale-yellow light. It felt late but she wasn't sure. When the man attacked her, it hadn't been quite nighttime yet, but for how long had she lain there in the darkness beneath the trees? She wondered if anyone even knew she was missing yet.

Why didn't I take the ride home? she thought sadly.

The sky overhead was full of stars and thin dark clouds. She didn't see the moon but that didn't mean anything. Shadows, like hungry zombies, stretched out from the woods across the schoolyard searching for a meal. She saw a car waiting at the curb. It looked tan or beige in the little bit of light that reached it, but she wasn't positive. She couldn't tell what kind of car it was because she didn't know much about cars. If she had to try and describe it to someone, all she could say was that it wasn't small, but it wasn't big either. It was just a car with four doors.

"Come on, Max," the man growled at the dog as it kicked dirt on the present he left in the grass.

At the car, the man stopped and reached into a pocket, withdrawing a ring of keys. He slipped one of the keys into the lock and opened the trunk. A tiny bulb of white light flashed on from beneath the lid. In the circle of light, Amy saw that the trunk was empty. A sheet of plastic covered the interior.

"You keep still in there; I'd hate for you to bang yourself up," the man said before whipping Amy off his shoulder and dropping her into the trunk. She landed with a painful thump that echoed in the empty parking area in front of the school. Amy looked up at the man as he reached for the trunk lid with one hand. He needed a shave. A thick scruff covered his chin. She thought of her father on Saturday mornings waking up and forgetting to shave. His face always felt like sandpaper. More tears fell now as she remembered rubbing her hand against his cheek and telling him he needed to shave. He always went into the bathroom and shaved for her, always returning and asking, "How's that?" She always told him, "Much better, Daddy." She missed those days more than she would ever admit to her father.

Amy prayed silently that the man would just leave, but he only smiled at her and slammed the lid down. The tiny light bulb winked out like a flash of heat lightning across a summer sky. She was in total darkness with gray after-images floating in her eyes. It smelled of gas and mold and plastic inside the trunk. She wanted to throw up again but fought it off once more.

The car started a few minutes later. Her whole body vibrated as the car began to move. She felt every bump and rock on the driveway as the car climbed the steep hill to the street. She rolled back against the front of the trunk and things she couldn't see poked and stabbed at her skin like angry knives. She hurt everywhere.

He must be on the street now, she thought as she felt the car turn and then level out. The street was just as bumpy as the driveway. The car came to sudden stops and starts, and every time she rolled across the trunk. She heard muffled barks from inside the car and at times she heard the man mumbling something that she couldn't understand. She didn't know if he was talking to the dog, to himself, or to something outside the car.

The trip to wherever they were going lasted a lifetime. How long that lifetime was, Amy didn't know, but it felt like forever. Her body screamed with pain. Everything seemed to hurt. She felt bruised and bloody from rolling back and forth across the trunk. The plastic beneath her body was slick in spots and tacky in others. She felt her skin sticking to it every time she rolled one way or the other now, and at some point, she vomited through her nose and pissed herself again. The smell of her own vomit and pee choked her and caused her to gag even more, and still the car kept moving.

The car finally came to a stop and the engine turned off. She heard a door open and close. She heard footsteps outside and claws scraping against concrete. She heard a key slip into the lock, turn with a click, and the trunk creak open. Light from inside and outside the trunk flooded into the compartment. It stung her eyes. She tried to turn her head away, but she couldn't. It hurt too much to move.

"I'll have to clean that mess up," the man said, his face scrunched up in disgust. Something touched her, and she opened her eyes. It was the man's finger. He was dragging it over one tiny breast. She wanted to scream. She wanted to melt into the trunk and disappear. The man withdrew his hand and shook his head back and forth. "That will not do, no, not at all," he said, forcing a tight smile.

The man licked the tips of his fingers and reached down to her face. She twisted painfully away from his touch, but he grabbed her by the chin and wrenched her head back so she was forced to look up at him.

"I am your salvation, child. Do not look lightly upon this gift." He released her head after wiping away a bit of vomit from one cheek and scooped her up from the trunk.

They were inside a garage. It was dark in the corners. Shadows climbed the walls. Only a single uncovered bulb hung down from the ceiling, but it was bright enough to see by. The garage smelled of gas and dirt and oil. The door was closed, and there were no windows to see out of. Max, the dog, stood at the man's feet looking up into her upside-down face. Fresh tears fell from her forehead, splashing on the gray concrete floor, leaving dark spots wherever they fell. The dog sniffed at her tears but left them alone.

The man took several steps and paused. Amy heard a door open. The hinges screeched. The man walked through the doorway into a dark room, and then through another doorway and into a kitchen lit by a nightlight that was plugged into the wall by the door. The tiles on the floor were black and white. The white tiles were dull, absorbing most of the light, and the black tiles were shiny, reflecting the light. From where Amy lay across the man's back, she saw bits of food and other droppings littering the floor. It was so gross and filthy. The man walked right on through the kitchen without pausing.

The next room was dark and full of shadows. The man stopped near the center. Amy saw a coffee table close to her head and a threadbare couch. The man tossed her off his shoulder and onto the couch. She bounced on the cushions several times before winding up with her face pressed against the back of the couch. The whole thing smelled of piss and sweat. The man grabbed her shoulder and forced her onto her back, pinning her down so she couldn't move. She felt so naked and exposed beneath his rough hand.

"We will begin in the morning," the man said, scratching at his chin. He yawned deeply and eased the pressure on her. The only thing Amy could do was watch as he picked up a length of rope from the floor. A bit of black tape was wrapped around the end of the rope.

"Be still now," the man whispered, moving his hand so it was placed squarely on her chest, squashing her small breasts, pinning her to the couch. Sinking deep into the cushions, she felt all sorts of things biting into her skin. The man ran the rope through a hole in the back of the couch, pulled it out from underneath, and brought it back up. He did this several times through several holes in the back of the couch until she was tied down securely. The rough rope scratched her skin, peeling it away in spots.

"Now, you try and get some sleep," the man said, kneeling beside her, leaning over her body, his eyes tracing a path from her head to her feet. He ran the tip of a finger slowly across her stomach. Goosebumps rose on her flesh. She heard herself moan. She was scared out of her mind, her body shaking. "It's okay, little girl. I'm not going to hurt you. I'm going to save you." The finger dropped between her legs and her mind screamed. He pulled the finger back and smiled. "For I am the truth and the way and the light," the man said, squeezing the inside of her thigh until it hurt.

Amy looked up at the man through tear-filled eyes and saw that his eyes were closed, his lips pressed tightly together. A deep moan passed through his body that she heard. His hold on her thigh tightened until she thought the tips of his fingers were going to meet on the other side. She cried out from behind the tape and his eyes opened. She saw him look down at his hand as if surprised that it was even there. He let go of her leg and stood. The pain lingered. There was a sad smile on his lined face. "Come on, Max," he whispered.

Through a flood of tears, Amy watched the man walk away with his dog. She watched him climb a flight of stairs and disappear somewhere inside the house. She cried even harder after he was gone. Snot ran from her nose. Her lips hurt from the tape that covered her mouth. She struggled against the ropes, but they held. There was no give in them, no relief from their constricting pain.

Amy forced herself to look around the room as best she could. She didn't see any windows, but it was dark inside the house. She saw the coffee table clear enough and the glow of the nightlight inside the kitchen. She smelled tobacco and coffee, and the dog. She smelled the filthy couch she lay upon and the sweat covering her own body. It all smelled so bad and then she added to the smells pissing herself again. She felt so embarrassed. She thought of her mom and dad and felt guilty for how worried they must be about her. She closed her eyes and pictured her mother sitting beside her bed and reading a story to her like when she was small. She would give anything now to hear her voice and feel her touch.

Chapter 14

Bruce's cellphone rang, interrupting what was a pleasant dream for him. It had something to do with the Incredible Hulk and unicorns. The ringtone on his phone was the theme from the first *Avengers* movie, so the Hulk showing up in one of his dreams wasn't all that surprising. The ring tone was for his brother, who liked to smash things when he was younger. Bruce opened one eye from beneath his pillow and glanced over at his nightstand where his cellphone sat charging. *Stupid fucking phone*, he thought, wishing much disaster upon his brother for waking him up.

"What?" Bruce grumbled into the phone, thinking his voice sounded a bit too loud.

"They have a missing girl in East Hartford. The chief asked me to lend a hand since we're working our two cases," Jeffrey explained, his voice definitely sounding much too loud on the other end of the cellphone. Bruce held the phone away from his ear while rubbing at his temple with his free hand.

"Age?" Bruce asked, sitting up slowly, leaning back against the headboard, both of his eyes closed against the little bit of light that managed to pierce his blackout curtains. His head hurt, his eyes burned, and his stomach felt like a churning ocean. Beside him was a half-empty glass of what he suspected might be vodka, but he wasn't sure. He reached over for it and sniffed as his brother went on, oblivious to his pain. *Definitely vodka*, he thought, setting the glass back down inside the ring of moisture that had dried on his nightstand.

"Seventeen," Jeffrey answered while Bruce considered purchasing a set of coasters. "Just finished up her junior year in high school."

"Pick me up in thirty minutes," Bruce said before hanging up the phone. He rubbed at his forehead with his thumb and two fingers. It relieved the pressure there somewhat and he was able to get off the bed and stumble into the kitchen. Cold water ran in the sink while he searched for the aspirin.

Thirty minutes later, Jeffrey sat in his department-issued car at the curb in front of Bruce's apartment. He glared up at the dark windows where his brother lived, watching and waiting for him to appear. *Stupid shit is probably hungover*, he thought, honking his horn for the third time.

Just as his brother had earlier, Jeffrey Westman rubbed at his forehead with his thumb and two fingers, sighing deeply as he did so. Jeffrey was dressed in black jeans, a clean dress shirt, cleanshaven, and wearing dark sunglasses. His dark brown hair was combed neatly and straight back with a side part. Beside him in the cupholder sat a cup of coffee from Dunkin' Donuts and a white paper bag with a glazed donut inside for his brother. On the radio, classic rock played softly.

Jeffrey glanced out the window and saw an older African-American man walking a small dog on the sidewalk across the street. He raised a hand and waved at the man, but the man didn't wave back. The dog shit in the grass and Jeffrey watched the old man pick it up in an orange poop bag. The dog pissed against a telephone pole and then followed his owner further down the sidewalk. Jeffrey sighed again and turned back to the front door of the apartment building, wishing his brother would appear.

Bruce stumbled out the door a few minutes later. He ran a hand through his damp hair, combing it back with his fingers. He wore wrinkled faded jeans, sneakers, and a black t-shirt that looked like it had been picked up off the floor and tossed on. Jeffrey honked the horn and gave his brother the middle finger. Bruce grimaced. "Stop with that shit," he shouted at his brother, crossing the sidewalk to the passenger side door. Jeffrey rolled down the window and leaned across the seat without unlocking the door.

"Be ready when you say you're going to be ready and I won't have to do that shit," Jeffrey said. "Now go back upstairs and dress a little better. We're going to the friend's house where she was last seen." Bruce rolled his eyes and sighed at his brother before turning around and going back inside. He came back out several minutes later wearing clean Dickies, a light blue polo shirt, and his sunglasses. His hair still looked like he combed it with his fingers.

"Better?" Bruce asked, standing outside the passenger side door.

"Better. Now get the fuck in the car." Bruce opened the door and sat down on the passenger side. "And don't slam my door," Jeffrey said as the passenger door slammed shut. "Asshole," Jeffrey whispered, pulling away from the curb. As he drove, Jeffrey began explaining what he knew so far about the missing girl. Bruce munched on his donut and sipped at his coffee while listening to his brother.

"Our guy is evolving," Bruce said, as Jeffrey finished up. "He's learning, growing, getting better at what he does. He likes what he's doing, but I'm not sure why he's doing it yet."

"You still fixed on that religious thing?" Jeffrey asked.

"Yeah, I guess," Bruce answered. "What I have so far isn't concrete, but it feels right. What I saw was a guy who thinks he's saving these girls from something. Maybe from themselves, maybe from something else. Who the fuck knows? He hungers for them, too, but he doesn't touch them, even though he wants to. It hurts him to think about touching them, like it might spoil everything he's doing. I don't know."

"Well, it fits. He hasn't had sex with any of the victims, dead or alive. The medical examiner says that both girls were still virgins when they died, hymens still intact." Bruce nodded, setting his coffee in the cup holder.

"How would he even know if they were virgins?" Bruce asked, wondering why that made a difference.

"Maybe he checks," Jeffrey suggested. "Maybe that's why they're always naked. He could be a doctor or a nurse or something in the medical field. He could work at or at one time have worked at one of those private religious hospitals, like Saint France in Hartford."

"So, what does he do if he finds out they're not virgins?" Bruce asked as Jeffrey pulled away from a light.

"I don't know, but you can be sure these aren't his first kills. He has to have started somewhere; we just haven't figured it out yet." Bruce looked out the window. "You know, if this shit keeps up, the FBI is going to want to take it over," Jeffrey added, turning left. Bruce nodded and leaned his head back against the seat. He closed his eyes and simply felt the ride beneath him. It was hypnotic. His head felt better as he leaned into the motion of the car. It had been a long time since he had woken up feeling so trashed. His body was trying to tell him to slow down, to stay away from the alcohol, but he was always so thirsty, and the alcohol helped so much. Bruce opened his eyes and saw that they were parked in front of a small yellow single-story house. He looked over at his brother.

"This is the friend's house," Jeffrey explained. Bruce looked at his brother.

"What are the odds that he found two seventeen-year-old virgins?"

"Probably better than you think," Jeffrey answered. "I mean, the movies and television make it sound like teenagers are nothing but horny animals, but I bet they're not all that much different than when we were kids."

"Maybe," Bruce said, turning back to the house.

A marked police car was parked in the driveway behind a green Ford Explorer. In the yard was a girl's purple bike leaning against a tree and a small plastic chair tipped over to the left of the front door. The grass needed to be mowed and the curb edged. White curtains hung behind the windows. Alongside the garage were two garbage barrels, one green and the other blue. The driveway was black asphalt and recently tarred. The house was old and in need of fresh paint.

"She was here most of the day yesterday and left around seven-fifteen according to the mother. The mom wanted to give her a ride home because of the missing girls in the news, but she refused. Her social media shows she checked her Instagram around seven-thirty. After that, nothing. We're trying to ping her phone, but having no luck. Either the battery is dead or the phone is turned off."

"Where does she live from here?" Bruce asked, looking down the sidewalk in either direction. The neighborhood was quiet. Only a few cars were on the roadway. It was an older neighborhood. Most of the houses were built back in the fifties and sixties. It should have been a nice safe place to grow up.

Jeffrey glanced at his notes. "Milton Drive."

"Off Oak Street, right?" Bruce asked.

"Yeah, that's it."

Bruce and Jeffrey walked up to the front door. It was painted a light blue with a brass knocker below a peephole. Jeffrey knocked. An older woman in her late forties answered the door. She was short and slightly overweight with long curly blonde hair and wide-rimmed glasses. There was a brown speckled mole on her left cheek that made Bruce think of Cindy Crawford, even though this woman would never be confused with a supermodel. She had that tired mother look about her. A look that said she worried about everything. Thin crooked lines ran from the corners of each eye and her forehead was deeply carved. She eyed Bruce and Jeffrey, forcing a tight smile that didn't touch her eyes.

"I'm Officer Westman with the Manchester Police Department and this is one of our consultants."

"Bruce. You can call me Bruce, ma'am," Bruce said, holding out a hand that she didn't reach for. The woman nodded at them instead and stepped aside so they could enter her home. She held a red-and-white-checkered cloth in one hand, nervously picking at it with the other hand.

"Could I speak with your daughter?" Bruce asked as the door closed behind him.

"Patricia?" the woman asked, glancing down the hallway.

"Yes, I would like to speak to Patricia if that is alright," Bruce explained.

"She's already talked to the other officers," the woman explained. "Does she have to do it again? I don't understand why you're even here. This isn't Manchester."

"No, it's not, ma'am, but I am the lead investigator on another case that is possibly similar to this one," Jeffrey explained.

"There's been others? I read about those two missing girls. Wasn't one of them found in that pool?" she asked, pulling on the cloth.

"Yes, that's correct," Jeffrey answered.

"I promise to keep it short, ma'am. Just a few questions for your daughter," Bruce said, looking down the hallway at three closed doors. He wondered which door Patricia was behind.

"I suppose," she said, twisting the cloth into a ball as she spoke.

"While he speaks with your daughter, could I speak with you?" Jeffrey asked, glancing at the kitchen.

"Oh, I don't know," she said in a quiet voice. "This is all very unusual."

Just then, a light appeared in the hallway as one of the doors opened. Soft music rolled out of the room followed by a young girl. She was just as short as her mother and a bit on the chunky side. She had fair skin, full of freckles, and red hair that tumbled down over her shoulders. She held a cellphone in her hand and a frown on her face as she glanced at the three people standing at the end of the hallway.

"Patricia?" Bruce asked, stepping away from Jeffrey and the girl's mother.

The girl looked at Bruce and then glanced at her mother. Her mom nodded, letting her know it was okay to speak.

"Yes," Patricia answered.

"My name is Bruce, and I am working with Officer Westman here. I'd like to ask you some questions if that is alright with you. We can do it in the living room or in the kitchen if you like. Wherever you feel most comfortable."

"Living room is fine," Patricia said, walking toward them before stepping into the living room. She sat on a recliner next to the couch. Bruce sat on the couch and set his notebook down on the coffee table. Jeffrey and Patricia's mother went into the kitchen.

"What were you looking at on your phone when you walked out of your room?" Bruce asked.

Patricia looked at Bruce. For a moment he thought she was going to tell him to go to hell, but then her expression softened. She took her phone from her pocket and glanced at the screen.

"I was texting Amy again, but she hasn't answered," she explained. "I know it's dumb, but I just thought she might answer me. I've called her like a million times this morning."

"Was Amy upset with anyone? Was anyone upset with her? Would she have run away?" Bruce asked.

"No, she wasn't, and no, she wouldn't," Patricia answered. "Amy was like anyone else, you know. She had things, but nothing was so bad that she would run away because of it." She brushed at her hair with one hand, forcing it back away from her forehead. Bruce saw that her nails were painted pink.

"Okay," Bruce said, jotting something down in his notebook. "So, she left here yesterday evening after spending the day with you. Was she going home or somewhere else?"

"I'm sure she was headed home. I mean, like, it was late, and she didn't like to worry her mother, so yeah, she was headed home, I'm sure."

"How would she have gone home? Would she have followed the sidewalk down to Oak Street or would she have taken a shortcut somewhere?"

Patricia thought about the question. None of the other officers had asked her that so far. She thought about lying to keep Amy out of more trouble just in case she turned up, but decided not to. "She would have taken the shortcut behind the school through the woods. It dumps out onto Davis Street."

Bruce wrote in his notebook before looking up at the girl. "What school?" he asked.

"Gates," she said. "Behind the school along the fence is a path through the woods that dumps you out onto Davis Street. From there, you just walk over to Oak Street and bam, she's home," Patricia said before turning sad. Tears welled up in her eyes. She was about to cry. "Or she would have been."

"We're going to try and find her, Patricia, I promise," Bruce said, setting a hand on Patricia's shoulder.

Bruce and Jeffrey sat in the car twenty minutes later. Bruce filled Jeffrey in on everything Patricia had said.

"That's good," Jeffrey said. "The mother told me that Amy was troubled like most teens her age, but nothing out of the ordinary. She didn't think she had a boyfriend or anyone she was seeing. She feels guilty about not forcing her to take the ride home."

"Why had the mother described Amy as troubled?" Bruce asked as they pulled away from the curb.

"Her parents were separated, and the father is living with a younger woman. According to her mom, it was recent, and Amy had been spending a lot of time with Patricia."

"Patricia hadn't said anything about that. I wonder why?"

"Maybe to her it didn't matter. I mean, they were friends, and Amy was spending time with her, and I didn't get the impression that either one of them had a lot of friends from the mother."

"Maybe," Bruce said. "Let's go to the school and check out this path in the woods."

"Already headed that way, brother," Jeffrey said, driving through the quiet neighborhood.

Bruce watched the houses stream by as Jeffrey drove down Hill Street. Most of the homes were set back from the roadway in well treed lots. Here and there, a few older people puttered in their yards, but for the most part it was a deserted neighborhood.

Where are the kids? he wondered. *They were inside playing games or on social media. Who even played outside anymore?* Bruce thought, shaking his head.

Chapter 15

Jeffrey turned down the school driveway a few minutes later. He drove down a steep hill with tall trees growing along the sides, making it impossible for anyone not standing directly at the top of the driveway to see anything. At the bottom of the hill, he turned into a parking area that also served as a pick-up and drop-off area. He parked in front of the school just outside the turnaround and turned the car off.

It was close to noon, and the sun was high overhead and hot. Only a few wispy clouds populated the sky. Rolling waves of heat baked off the asphalt. It was going to be a hot Southern New England day. A day better spent at the shore than searching for a killer.

"Global warming, got to love it," Bruce said, walking to the side of the school building and glancing at the field behind it. To his right was a fenced-in baseball diamond and in the distance soccer goals stood across from each other. A short chain link fence ran around the entire schoolyard separating it from the trees beyond.

"Remember when we were kids?" Jeffrey asked, walking beside his brother. "We would have been all over this place, all summer long, playing ball or just hanging out, making shit up about how we were going to be something one day. It's sad to see it forgotten like this."

"Kids today would rather have their faces buried in their phones or tablets," Bruce said, noting the empty soccer fields. It was deathly quiet here, a perfect spot to attack someone.

"It's just sad; that's all I'm saying," Jeffrey said.

To the right of the ballfield there was an opening in the fence, and beyond that, a twisting path through the trees. Bruce stopped at the fence and squinted at the path. "I guess this is the shortcut she took," he said, turning sideways so he could fit through the opening. Jeffrey followed.

"Do you think the killer knew about this path?" Jeffrey asked as they walked into the woods.

"It's possible, or maybe he just followed her here."

"You know the shit is about to hit the fan about this. The press is already blowing the story up." Bruce nodded, continuing down the path.

Bruce and Jeffrey followed the path until it ended at a cul-de-sac. The street it came out onto was Davis Road. The houses were newer here, built in the '70s. The neighborhood was quiet and well shaded. Tall oaks stood in most of the yards, their branches twisting and bending high overhead full of dark green leaves. Like Hill Street, there were no kids playing outside. No one rode bikes or played ball in the street. A lonely dog barked somewhere in one of the backyards. A car backed out of a driveway, paying no attention to Bruce and Jeffrey as it drove away.

"Typical street in a typical neighborhood," Jeffrey said, looking down the sidewalk. "Perfect place for a killer to hunt." Bruce nodded again, looking back at the path.

"Let's walk back," Bruce said. "But this time you walk in front of me. Just keep going even if I fall behind."

"Okay, you do your thing and I'll be waiting for you at the fence," Jeffrey said, taking off down the path. Bruce smiled and watched his older brother walk away. He continued to stand there at the end of the cul-de-sac for several minutes studying the houses at the end of the street. Most appeared dark, as if whoever lived within them were gone for the day. Like the schoolyard, it felt strange and wrong. *Where are the children?* he wondered.

Just as he was ready to walk away, an older man walking a small dog appeared on the sidewalk. The dog looked like one of those Pomeranians. Its fur was puffy and tan colored to the point where it looked almost orange. The fur stuck out at all weird angles. The dog walked on thin legs, prancing along like a princess. Bruce smiled as the man walked buy. The man glanced at Bruce suspiciously but kept walking. The dog snarled softly but kept on sniffing at the grass at the edge of the sidewalk. Bruce nodded at the two of them, continuing to watch as they walked away.

"Max," Bruce thought as the man with the dog disappeared down another street. "Is Max a dog?" he wondered. "Could that be how he goes unnoticed? Just another person walking his dog in the neighborhood?" Bruce wrote in his notebook, placing a question mark after the name, *Max*. He shoved the notebook back in his pocket and looked at the street where the man and his dog had disappeared. *He needs to blend in and go unnoticed*, Bruce thought, wondering if the killer had just been there for no other reason than to see what would happen while he walked his dog. *Could that be how he finds his next victim?* The answer to that question didn't reveal itself to him. Bruce waited a few more minutes before finally turning away and starting back along the path through the woods. Jeffrey was nowhere to be seen.

Halfway back down along the path, Bruce paused. The hairs on his arms stood and goosebumps covered his skin. It suddenly felt cold where he stood, and so dark. The shadows haunting the forest seemed to collapse around him like a thick blanket falling over his head. *Here*, he thought, closing his eyes and quieting his mind.

Bruce sat down in the center of the path, setting the palms of his hands down on the cool soft dirt. All sounds disappeared and the woods became silent like a grave. He heard nothing. Felt nothing. Everything had simply disappeared, and slowly, the drift came upon him. It was a slow and easy trip that swept him away. The world became all darkness as he floated through an ocean of space. Gently, he settled down until he was once more on the path.

It was nighttime now. He heard footsteps thudding through the forest, growing closer with each step. The shadows that surrounded him drew back until he could see into the trees just the tiniest bit. There was Amy walking along the path, her head down, looking at her cellphone. The light from the screen was bright upon her face. It sparkled off her eyes. He could see her eyes darting over the screen studying whatever was there for her to see like it was the most important thing in the world.

"Amy," he thought, wishing he could call out to her, to warn her.

Behind Amy was another presence. It was large and tall. It loomed over her like a dragon ready to strike. He knew it was the killer, but from where he sat, the killer appeared otherworldly. He was monstrous, gliding over the path like a specter. He made no sounds as he drew closer to that poor girl. She had no idea that danger was just a step away and then she looked up much too late.

Bruce watched the monster in the woods attack Amy, knocking her to the ground. He watched as the killer fell on her like a hungry animal wishing to devour its meal. He witnessed how the killer drove her face down into the dirt over and over. He saw her cellphone fly from her hand, spinning off into the underbrush, disappearing somewhere into the night.

The killer stood. Amy was unconscious at his feet. Bruce watched as the monster dragged her off into the trees. He couldn't tell what was happening there. All he saw was the killer's back as he set about doing whatever he was doing. After a few minutes the killer was back on the path, and he wasn't alone. There was a small dog with him on a leash. Bruce wondered where the dog had been during the attack but couldn't puzzle it together. *Fucking Max*, Bruce thought, watching the man and his dog walk off down the path, disappearing into the darkness.

Bruce opened his eyes and looked around. He was still sitting there in the middle of the path. His head hurt. A thin line of blood ran from his nose. His face felt like someone had smashed it into the dirt. He reached up and rubbed his forehead. He tasted dirt in his mouth and spit.

Her phone, he thought, crawling on his hands and knees into the trees and brush that grew alongside the path. He made his way over into a mass of branches and thorns, digging his way inside, feeling every scratch and cut as the thorns attacked and defended their territory. The tip of one finger touched something smooth hidden deep inside among the thorns and branches. It was cool to the touch. It felt clean and out of place. It didn't belong out there in the woods. He slid the object toward him just enough so he could grasp at it and yank it free of the underbrush. It was Amy's cellphone. He pushed a button but the battery was dead. He smiled anyway and stood.

Chapter 16

Amy woke up bound and gagged in a shadow-filled room. The space she occupied smelled stale and dusty with just the tiniest touch of urine and shit to mingle in with the other odors. She was still in the living room inside a house. It was dark and dusty wherever she was, and it was almost totally devoid of light. She lay strapped down to a couch facing up at the ceiling, but she could turn her head just enough to see out into the room, but there wasn't much to see except for a coffee table in front of her. Everything else was drowned in shadows.

She had no memory of how she had gotten to where she found herself. She tried to think, but all she could remember was being out in the woods behind the school. Her head hurt, and her ears rang. The rough fabric of the couch cushions rubbed against her naked skin, leaving it feeling raw and abused. She was scared and frightened and hungry, and every joint and muscle seemed to beg for movement. She tried to shout, but the tape covering her mouth made everything sound like a muffled mumble. She tried to move to ease her discomfort, but the straps holding her down were just too tight. She closed her eyes and began to cry.

I was attacked, she thought suddenly, opening her eyes again. *There was a man in the woods. Yesterday it was, or at least I think it was yesterday. It happened after dark while I was walking home. He smashed my face into the ground and brought me here.*

A sound from within the house drifted down to her. She froze, all thoughts of yesterday fleeing in the panicked realization that she wasn't alone. She strained her eyes to look through an archway into the next room, but it was nothing more than a shadowy abyss. The sound kept coming, drawing closer and closer without ever revealing itself, and then something began to emerge from the shadows. It was small. It padded toward her, its nails clicking on the hardwood floor beneath its paws. It was a small dog. The same small dog that had licked the salty tears from her face.

Max or Mike or Mick, she thought, but wasn't sure. The dog stopped at the couch and sniffed at her face. A thin pink tongue like a slice of bubble gum from a pack of Garbage Pail Kids trading cards shot out of its mouth and licked her right eyeball. Its tail wagged back and forth vigorously like a windmill. Amy moaned and blew a sharp breath through her nose. Her head screamed with pain and her slathered eyeball only added to the pain. She wished she could ask the dog to help her somehow.

"Max, leave our guest alone," a man's voice said from the dark hallway. Amy looked away from the dog and across the room. A man stood there on the other side of the living room just beneath the archway. He wore a stained white t-shirt and gray boxers. She realized immediately that he was aroused. His boxers tented out as he stood there looking at her. She looked away, embarrassed that she had noticed and praying that he hadn't noticed that she had noticed.

The man stepped into the living room and drew closer to the couch. She saw that he needed a good shave. His face was covered in rough stubble. The hair on his head sprung in all directions. In one hand, he held a piece of toast, and in the other he held a book. He jammed the toast into his mouth and walked up to the couch. Crumbs tumbled over his chin and down to the floor. Amy heard her stomach grumble with hunger as she watched the man chew and swallow.

"I am the truth," the man said, after swallowing. "I am the only truth you shall ever need to hear," he added, holding out the book so she could see it better. It looked like a Bible and the words he spoke sounded like they could have come from a Bible. There was gold lettering on the cover, but she couldn't make out the words written there.

"I have been sent to save you from yourself, child," the man said, sitting down in a wooden rocking chair beside the couch. The chair creaked every time he rocked back. The sound twisted sharply inside Amy's head. She began to cry, her tears soaking into the couch cushions on either side of her head. Max sat below her, his tail swishing back and forth on the floor, kicking up clouds of dust.

The man watched Amy from his chair, his fingers tented beneath his chin. She felt his eyes crawling over her body. She wanted to bury herself into the stinking couch cushions and hide herself from those creepy eyes, but she couldn't move. Her body was racked with sobs. Snot ran down over her upper lip. She felt so exposed and broken.

The man stood and approached the couch, his hard-on obvious behind the thin fabric of his boxers. She tried to look away, but he stood over her now, leaning down. His hard-on swayed just above her head like a twig dangling down from a tree. His body pressed down upon her like weight. She saw the outline of his penis against his boxers, the yellowed stains that clung to the faded material. His odor was overwhelming. She wanted to vomit.

"Oh God, oh God," Amy thought. "Please don't let him rape me, please don't, please, please, please, Daddy, help me. " She cried behind the tape, breathing so hard that snot and tears ran down the side of her face. The man bent further until his face was only a few inches above her own. His breath was rancid, cutting through everything. He set a hand on her bare shoulder, touching her with just the tips of his fingers. The skin was rough and callused. She screamed a muffled scream from beneath the tape. His fingers dug hard into her flesh, crushing the muscle.

"Everything is going to be fine, child," the man whispered in a voice laced with sand. His breath felt hot against her skin as he spoke. It felt like thousands of ants crawling across her body. "I am not here to harm you, but to help you," he explained, releasing his grip on her shoulder. He loosened the straps that held her down to the couch and picked her up easily enough. He laid her over his shoulder, and she fell down across his back. Max looked up into her upside-down face, his whiplashing tail almost hypnotic.

Amy struggled to free herself, but it was useless. The man had her legs in a death grip that she couldn't break. She felt the rough unwashed cotton of his t-shirt against her face. It felt like sandpaper and smelled of filthy back sweat. She gagged and thought that the vomit was going to come now. The world spun as the man stomped through the house and into the kitchen. He carried her over to a door beside the stove. She saw streaks of yellow grease running down the chipped and faded white enamel. She felt the shift of the man's shoulder beneath her stomach as he grasped the doorknob and opened the door. It made a dry creaking sound as it swung open.

Amy looked across the kitchen as the man stepped through the doorway. She saw dishes poking out above the sink. Streaks of water ran down the cabinets beneath the sink. A box of cereal stood on the counter. *Lucky Charms*? she wondered or maybe a knockoff brand. Above the sink was a small curtained window. Only the barest amount of light managed to make its way into the kitchen through the window. She saw none of the outside world through the curtain.

Halfway down the basement stairs, a bright light came. She heard the click of the switch just a millisecond before the light appeared. At the bottom of the stairs, the man stepped onto a gray concrete floor littered with mouse-size mounds of dust and dirt that blew away with each footfall. Amy felt sick. She knew that if it hadn't been for the tape covering her mouth, she would have blown chunks all over the floor. Even now she could taste the vomit in the back of her mouth.

The man came to a stop somewhere deep in the basement. His shoulder shifted and another light came on. Amy glanced up and saw a naked bulb hanging from the unfinished rafters. The glare stung her eyes and more tears fell. The man laid her gently on top of a padded table. The fake leather felt cold against her skin. A rough belt cinched quickly across her stomach. It was so tight she could barely breathe. She glared up at the man, wishing he would just drop dead.

"Now, I am going to free your legs, child," the man said. "But I want you to feel something before I do."

Amy felt sharp cold steel beneath her left breast. It sent shivers through her body. The steel bit into the skin under her breast and goosebumps rose all over her body as white fire flamed beneath her breast.

"This is a very sharp blade that I hold, and if you should get it in your head to kick me, I will simply slice off your left breast," he said. "It is better to enter paradise missing a breast then to go to hell with both of them, after all." He sounded excited and out of breath as he spoke. "Do you understand me?" he asked. Amy nodded her head quickly. The blade disappeared and a moment later her legs were free.

The man forced her legs apart, holding tightly to each one. He took the left leg in his hand and set her left foot into a stirrup. A strap was quickly cinched over her shin, squishing her calf muscle against a cold metal rod. The pain was sharp. Amy lifted her head to watch as the man placed her right foot into another stirrup. It was like she was in a doctor's office laying on top of an exam table. She began to shake violently as he strapped the right leg into the stirrup.

The man stood back when he finished and looked down at her exposed body. She felt his eyes on her again. She felt them traveling over her body as he sucked on his lower lip, running the tip of his tongue over it like a snake scenting the air. Burning spikes of fire crawled over her naked skin as she watched him studying her, drinking her in. Screams erupted from behind the tape and the man simply smiled down at her from the foot of the exam table. The smile widened the more she screamed.

"There was an old man from Nantucket, and he had a prick so long he could suck it, so he said with grin as he wiped off his chin, if my ear were a cunt I would fuck it." The man laughed and laughed at his limerick as a hand slid down her leg until it was so close to touching her that her eyes went wide. *Daddy please, Daddy please, Daddy please*, she cried over and over inside her head, wishing the hand would go away.

The man looked up into her wide eyes while his hand remained on her thigh just short of touching her, just short of violating her. The smile was gone now, and he looked very serious. His nostrils flared. His cheeks were pink. He looked as if he had just finished a workout in the gym.

"Shall we begin?" the man asked, walking the fingers of his hand to the edge of her vagina. Amy's mind exploded in one long scream that threatened to shatter her world, and then she just drifted away.

The man was nowhere to be seen when Amy opened her eyes again. She was still secured to the exam table, her feet still in the stirrups. The light above her was off, and the room was only shadows and the soft clicks and clacks of an old house. She let out a slow trembling breath as the damp chill of the basement settled over her. She hurt down there where the man had been looking, but she didn't think he had forced himself on her while she was blacked out. She wasn't positive about that, but she thought if he had she would have hurt so much more than she did. She let out another trembling breath and peed herself. The warm liquid ran between her legs, puddling on the exam table before splattering down on the floor. A sigh escaped her lips as she finished. It felt good. It felt naughty. It felt like fighting back somehow.

Fuck him if he doesn't like it, she thought to herself, enjoying the tiny victory.

She wasn't sure if it was night or day. There were only shadows surrounding her. The only window she saw was boarded over. She had no idea how long she had been down there in the basement. Goosebumps crawled across her skin as the warmth from the pee went away. She closed her eyes and tried to think warm thoughts.

I love you so much, Mama, she thought, her teeth chattering. *I wish I had been a better daughter.* No tears fell as she prayed to her mom. She didn't have any more tears left to cry.

Above her head, the floorboards creaked. The clickity clack of tiny nails against the wood floor drifted down into the basement followed by heavier steps. A door closed somewhere inside the house and a few minutes later the muffled sound of a car starting filled the gaps of silence. The engine sound disappeared quickly, and she heard nothing else but the moans and groans of the house. She was totally alone now. Not even the dog was home.

Chapter 17

In his hot empty apartment, Bruce sat up in his bed. His head felt heavy and fuzzy. He wasn't sure just how long he had been asleep, but something had disturbed him. He looked around his small one-room apartment trying to repair the frayed edges of whatever nightmare had awakened him, but most of it was gone now, lost to whatever universes existed within the many worlds of our dreams. The apartment felt wrong, out of joint, as if the world had expanded somehow while he slept.

On the nightstand beside the bed sat his cellphone. He reached down and touched the screen, causing it to light up. The tiny clock at the top of the screen said it was just ten-thirty at night. Frightened and confused from the nightmare, and needing to pee badly, he swung his feet from the bed and onto the floor. The threadbare carpet felt solid beneath his feet when everything else around him didn't. He wiggled his toes, enjoying the feel of the rough threads as they scratched at the bottoms of his feet. The nightmare drifted further away, and the world began to shrink back to normal. He stood and walked to the bathroom, his knees popping and cracking with each step.

Bruce stood in front of the toilet peeing and thinking about Amy. He knew, or maybe just felt, that she was still alive. It was like a tickle at the back of his brain, but it was there.

Finishing, he flushed the toilet, washed his hands, and returned to the bed. He didn't remember falling asleep so early. It was so unusual for him. Looking at the nightstand, he saw a half-empty glass. On the floor beside the nightstand was an empty pint bottle of cheap vodka. He picked up the glass and sipped at the liquid inside, grimacing at the taste.

"Warm, watered-down vodka," he snarled, setting the glass back down inside the wet ring on top of the nightstand. "Fuck it," he mumbled and stood back up. Dressing quickly in clean clothes, he headed out the door, calling his brother as he walked away from the apartment.

"Hey," Jeffrey answered on the third ring.

"She's still alive," Bruce said, walking outside into the warm humid night air. Thick clouds raced from the west to the east across the sky. It felt like a storm was coming.

"You pick that up somehow?" Jeffrey asked.

"Yeah, I did," Bruce said, walking up to his car parked at the curb.

Bruce sat down inside his car and started the engine. It coughed several times but sprang to life. He pulled away from the curb slowly.

"I'm going to drive around for a bit and see if I get anything else," Bruce explained, turning onto Park Avenue. He rolled down his window and rested his elbow on the sill. The air was still hot and humid, but it felt better at forty miles an hour than it had standing outside his apartment building.

"You're going to call me if you get anything?" Jeffrey asked. "I'm serious, Bruce. You can't go acting all super soldier and shit. We don't know how much time we have before he kills her."

"I got it," Bruce said, disconnecting from the call.

For the next hour, Bruce drove around Manchester and East Hartford. He drove up and down random streets waiting to feel something, anything, but he felt nothing. Eventually, he found his way back to the Globe Hollow parking lot and parked beneath the tall oaks in the back. It was so dark back there in the corner of the lot that it felt like a dirty secret shared between friends. The security lights around the entrance to the pool didn't reach into the far corners of the parking lot. In fact, they didn't even reach into the parking lot. He was completely hidden from any cars passing by on the street. It was a perfect spot for dirty deeds.

Bruce turned off his engine and sat back in his seat, listening to the night, enjoying the cool breeze drifting into the car through the open windows. There was the scent of decaying leaves, chlorine, and something else in the air. It took a moment to place the something else and then he had it. It was something alive, something hungry, and deadly. It crept along the shadows at the edges of the parking lot hunting for prey. A shiver crawled up Bruce's spine and the hairs on the back of his neck stood.

"Stop freaking yourself out," he whispered, reaching across the seat and opening the glovebox. His hand fumbled around expired insurance cards, a faded owner's manual, and other forgotten discarded items and tools until he found what he wanted. It was a paper bag with a bottle hidden inside. He withdrew the bottle, a pint of Smirnoff's Vodka, and twisted off the cap. The wonderful odor of the alcohol filled his nose. He smiled and tipped the glass to his lips, enjoying the liquid fire as it ran down his throat. He took a second sip, this one burning less. The third sip didn't burn at all as he set the bottle between his legs.

He gazed out the windshield at the empty parking lot. "Where oh where are you tonight?" he sang in a whispered voice out the driver's side window. The sound of his song sounded lonely as it carried out into the night. He searched the shadows that fell over the chain link fence. Nothing jumped out at him; nothing answered his whispered question. He opened the driver's side door of his car and placed his feet on the cracked and broken asphalt. He stood, shoving the bottle into his back pocket, and walked down to the fence. No cars passed by on the street. He peered through the chain link fence for several minutes, searching for answers.

"Fuck it," Bruce said, pressing his lips through one of the diamonds in the fence. He stepped back and began to climb until he lifted his leg over the top and dropped down on the other side. He landed with a thump, stumbling on the walkway but remaining upright. Walking quickly, he made his way around the building to the concrete beach.

On the back side, the building the security lights cast a soft yellow glow over everything. The pool looked cold and dark and dangerous. Tiny waves rolled ashore, lapping at the concrete. There was nobody but him inside the Hollow. The grounds were empty; no kids had snuck into the pool to skinny dip that night or make out on the hillside above the beach.

Bruce walked along the edge of the pool to the waterfall and climbed up the slippery embankment. At the top, he paused to turn on the flashlight application on his cellphone. Its dull glow only penetrated so far over the water. The shadows that crawled over the reservoir swallowed up the light, keeping its secrets hidden. Bruce stepped into the water, its icy bite soaking through his sneakers and pants. It was so cold that it made his bones ache as he hurried to the shoreline.

The reservoir was a creepy lonely place at night. He wondered why teens would come out here to fool around and get drunk when there were so many other places much less creepy than this. He followed the shoreline, using his cellphone to illuminate the ground. Frogs and toads croaked, and mosquitos swarmed. Unseen creatures roamed just beyond the shadows. The water buzzed with unseen life.

In the feeble light, the water appeared black and impossibly deep. Bruce knew it wasn't, but knowing that didn't change anything. A chill crawled up and down his back and he resisted the urge to hug himself. Tiny ripples rolled across the surface looking like disjointed fingers reaching for something to hold onto. On his left there was only the darkness of the forest and whatever monsters it might be hiding. Branches and bushes and shadows marked where the woods began, making it impossible to see anything beyond, even with the aid of the cellphone.

Bruce walked quickly, searching for the opening in the trees where the path lay. He hated that he was alone. He missed Matthew, even though he knew it wasn't safe having the kid around. He felt so exposed out there walking along the edge of the water. In the dim light, anything could be lurking just beneath the surface, waiting to attack. He told himself those thoughts were silly, that only little children believed in monsters, but wasn't he hunting a monster? Goosebumps crawled up his arms like insects on the march and he blew out a long stale breath. His mouth felt dry. He took a swig from the bottle in his back pocket before walking any further.

The glow of the cellphone finally fell on a patch of emptiness among all the thick growth along the edges of the reservoir. At night, the path appeared much smaller than it did in the light of day. It really was no more than a foot wide and totally encased in a canopy of overhanging branches and limbs. Demented shadows crept across the soft yellow glow of the cellphone. It looked nothing like a place where kids would come to hang out and get drunk or fumble around with each other in the dark. It looked like a scene straight out of a horror movie. Camp Crystal Lake from the *Friday the 13th* series.

Bruce looked over his shoulder, expecting to see a swamp monster crawling ashore, or a hockey mask wearing killer stepping out of the water, but he only saw the slow ripples from the reservoir washing ashore. Everything around him felt old and ancient. The water seemed to call out to him like the lost souls of so many missing and dead children. The cries of suffering that only he could hear. They were the moans the ghosts of the long dead waiting for that perfect moment when the layers separating the living from the dead became so thin that crossing over was possible.

Bruce swallowed hard against his irrational fears and forced his eyes away from the reservoir. Licking his dry lips, he fumbled for the bottle again. The cool glass felt comforting in his hand. It was so steady, so real. Just holding it chased away the demons that his imagination drew up. He took a long quick sip from the bottle, swallowing slowly so he felt every bit of the alcohol draining into his body before shoving the bottle back into his pants pocket and looking down into the darkness along the path.

"Fuck it," he whispered hoarsely and started down the path.

He emerged without much difficulty into the first clearing at the end of the path. In the glow of his cellphone, the clearing appeared even more depressing than it had in the light of day. The shadows stretching across its expanse appeared like trapped prisoners struggling to escape. Bruce couldn't imagine anyone ever wanting to come down there to have sex on a filthy mattress beneath the drooping branches of a weeping willow tree. The idea felt so desperate and filthy. It felt like the raping of one's soul.

He walked across the clearing to the stump and sat down. He set the cellphone on the ground, the light flowing back toward the path, and slipped the bottle of vodka from his pocket. He drank deeply, enjoying how good the vodka felt rolling down his throat. The experience of that clear liquid drove away the ghosts and the unease that he had been feeling.

He emptied the bottle and tossed it at the filthy mattress. He heard it bounce and tumble away into the darkness.

"Where are you tonight?" he asked aloud, looking through the darkness of the forest beyond the clearing. His eyes closed slowly and his head tipped back. For a second he felt himself begin to lose his balance and then it all went away. He was no longer tethered to this world. He was floating along, drifting on an ocean free from fear and pain. The sensation enveloped his whole body until this new world slowed and stopped.

Everything inside his mind lightened up until another world came into focus. In this world, a girl appeared beneath him. She was young and pretty. She was the girl found in the pool by the caretaker. She was alive but looking scared. Her eyes were wide round blue orbs of fear that glowed like chips of glacial ice. She lay on her back in the second smaller clearing that he had found the other day. She fought against the ropes that held her. Her hands and her feet were tied together. There was duct tape over her mouth. The faceless man stood on the other side of her like a tall giant looming above the landscape of a tiny village. He was Godzilla, ready to crush Tokyo, and she was one of the helpless citizens screaming in fear.

The faceless man was all shadows, nothing more than a formless shape without features that might distinguish him from someone you passed by on the street. It was impossible to tell if he was even black or white or some other race that fell somewhere in between. He wore dark pants and a black or dark blue long-sleeved shirt. Nothing was written on the shirt he wore. It was just a solid color of darkness like his soul. A ballcap sat on the man's head with a red capital B in the center. *My killer is a Red Sox fan*, Bruce thought.

The killer bent low over the girl, cupping her chin in his hand. He tilted her head back slowly so she was forced to look into his eyes. Teeth appeared on the faceless face and Bruce saw the killer smile with a mouth full of shark's teeth. The teeth were large and white and bright and hungry looking. Bruce saw a knife appear in the killer's hand. It came from a bag at the killer's feet. The blade flashed bright and sharp in the light and the killer placed it against the girl's throat. Deathly stillness filled the clearing. The world was silent. Everything, every creature, every insect, held its breath, waiting for the killer to act.

"I am the way and the truth," the killer whispered in a hushed voice that sounded like gravel on a back country road. "I am the instrument of your salvation from sin," he said, drawing the blade of the knife across the girl's throat. Blood sprayed out in a terrifying fountain across the killer's hands. He flexed his fingers in the flow until the girl's heart stopped pumping and the spray settled down to a slow trickle. He stood, rubbing his hands together, drawing them up beneath his face, taking a deep trembling breath. Dark eyes appeared on the faceless face, joining the mouth full of teeth. The eyes were large, oval-shaped, and the deepest darkest brown that Bruce had ever seen. The eyes rolled back into their sockets until nothing but the whites appeared. The faceless face began to melt like putty in the hands of a sculptor. It lengthened and shrank. It expanded and drew inward, stretching and pulling slowly as a face began to slowly take shape. A nose appeared beneath the bill of the ballcap. For the first time, the killer had a face.

Got you, motherfucker, Bruce thought as he began to take mental notes. *Mid-thirties, early forties. Cleanshaven, brown hair sticking out from beneath the ballcap. Brown eyes, slightly crooked nose, as if it might have been broken once upon a time,* Bruce thought as the face began to swim away, melting like ice cream spilt on a sidewalk on a hot summer's day. The face disappeared, hidden in the shadows again, but Bruce didn't mind. He had what he needed.

The killer leaned over the body, caressing one tiny breast, tweaking one bloodstained nipple. His hand trembled and he pulled it back to his chest. He stood, walking over to the trees at the edge of the first clearing. A pair of panties were wrapped tightly around one hand. He held onto the panties while he masturbated. When he finished, he buried them where Bruce had found them.

Bruce tumbled from the stump and fell to the ground, his face landing atop damp leaves that smelled of decay and rot. He saw leaves and trash just inches away from his face. A soft groan rolled up his throat and he pushed himself back up, brushing the dirt and leaves from his clothing. He felt sick and disgusted by what he had seen and somehow aroused at the same time. Like the killer, he wanted to touch himself and release the pressure down there, but he didn't. He had what he needed. He knew what the killer looked like.

"Fuck him," he whispered into the darkness, standing and walking back down the path in the glow of his cellphone flashlight.

Bruce sat in his car ten minutes later in the dark parking lot beneath the tall oaks. His body felt like it was on fire. He was antsy, full of electricity. He wanted a drink in the worst way, but had nothing in the car left to drink. He leaned his head back against the seat, closing his eyes, trying to expel the energy flowing through him. Wired as he was, he was ready to explode. He started the car and drove out of the parking lot. It was almost midnight now as he drove away, but he knew where he was headed.

Chapter 18

Light filtered into the apartment through a window set across the room from the bed. It wasn't all that bright, but that didn't matter; it still hurt his eyes enough to draw out a groan. Bruce sat up, covering his eyes with the palm of his hand as he fought against the stabbing pain slicing through his brain. He looked around the bedroom from beneath his hand, unsure just where he was or how he had gotten there. He knew it wasn't his place because he woke up in a real bedroom and not in a one-room apartment where the bedroom, the kitchen, and the living room were all the same. He looked slowly around the shadowed bedroom, trying to remember what had happened the night before, but found he couldn't piece anything together. A digital clock on the nightstand read eight-thirty in dull red numbers.

"So fucking early," he mumbled, rubbing his forehead. Across the room, a bathroom door stood open. The soft glow of a nightlight lit the bathroom. He could just make out the sink. The urge to pee struck him and he got out of the bed, stumbling across the room wearing only his boxers. Inside the bathroom, he did what he had to, noting that whoever lived in the apartment kept the bathroom very clean.

Definitely not my place, he thought, flushing the toilet.

Finished in the bathroom, and proud of himself for fighting the urge to snoop in the medicine cabinet, he walked back into the bedroom. His clothes were on the floor at the foot of the bed. They looked out of place in the otherwise clean bedroom. The odor of bacon frying elsewhere in the apartment made his mouth water. He was suddenly very hungry. He dressed as fast as he could and stepped out into a short hallway. The sharp sizzle of frying pig flesh filled his ears as he stood there just outside the bedroom door. His stomach grumbled as he tried once more to remember the night before, but just couldn't recall anything. *Fucking blackouts*, he thought, walking quietly down the carpeted hallway in the direction of the frying bacon.

Bright light flooded the entrance to the kitchen as a dark shadow moved across the wall. Bruce stopped at the entrance and watched as a tall man in white boxers and a white wife beater t-shirt flipped an egg in a pan. He was well muscled and attractive with short blonde hair and a tattoo of a star inside a circle on his left bicep. The man looked slightly older than Bruce, but not by much. His legs had no hair and Bruce wondered if that was natural or if he shaved them.

"Good morning," the man said, catching Bruce by surprise as he turned around, still holding the spatula.

"Morning," Bruce said, the sound of his voice thudding through his head. His throat felt raw. He needed coffee. *How drunk did I get last night?* he wondered.

"I figured you might be hungry," the man said, pointing the spatula in his direction. Bruce glanced at the stove and saw three frying pans sizzling and smoking and an old-fashioned coffee pot perking away.

"Coffee, dark," Bruce mumbled, taking a few steps into the kitchen. He spied a small table against the wall between the kitchen and the living room and sat down. The man placed a cup of coffee in a blue mug on the table in front of Bruce. Curls of hot steam lifted from inside the cup. Bruce took a deep breath and picked up the mug. He drank slowly, savoring the taste of the coffee.

Breakfast was two eggs over hard, toast, and crispy bacon. Bruce ate everything without speaking and drank a second cup of strong coffee, no sugar, no cream. The man sat across from him sipping at his own cup of coffee while Bruce ate.

"I guess you liked that," the man said as Bruce finished off his plate by mopping up the remains of his eggs with his last bite of toast. "I'm Julian, by the way—in case you forgot or don't remember. You were pretty drunk last night when we left the bar. Both of us were, I guess."

"Bruce," Bruce said, standing up from the table and taking his dish and cup to the sink. "Thanks," he added, turning back to face Julian. He smiled.

"Not a problem," Julian said, setting his cup down.

"So, I have to work," Bruce said, looking everywhere but at the man sitting across from him. "Do you know where my car is?" he asked, his eyes finally settling on him.

"Yeah," Julian said. "I can take you to it. Let me get dressed."

Bruce watched him walk down the hallway and into the bedroom. The door closed, and a light came on from the other side.

That wasn't totally uncomfortable, Bruce thought, feeling overwhelmed by shame and guilt mixed with a touch of desire. He found himself wanting to walk down the hallway and into the bedroom, but knew he wouldn't. In spite of what might have happened last night, Bruce knew nothing else was going to happen. It had all been a moment of weakness, but he was wide awake now and he knew it wasn't going happen again— at least not with Julian.

Julian walked back out from the bedroom ten minutes later. He wore white shoes with white socks, light blue shorts that ended just above his hairless knees, and a powder blue polo shirt. Bruce saw a gold chain around his neck that disappeared behind the shirt. He looked incredibly clean and collected, every hair in its place—everything that Bruce wasn't at the moment, or ever.

"Come on, I'll drive you back to the club. You left your car there last night," Julian said. Bruce nodded and followed him out the door.

In the end, Julian had seemed disappointed when Bruce simply got out of the car without a commitment to see each other again or a kiss goodbye. Bruce just wanted to get away without any mess and Julian wanted something more that he couldn't give. Bruce simply thanked him when he came to a stop behind the bar and jumped out without a backward glance. He felt Julian's eyes on him as he walked away, but didn't look back.

Bruce drove out of the parking lot with his window down and left arm dangling out. He felt guilty for leaving like he did, but he didn't know what else he could do. He was too broken on the inside to open up to another person, let alone be in any kind of relationship with someone. His life was just too fucked to bring another person into the mix, and what had happened last night had been wrong on so many levels. He knew he was gay. He had known that for a long time, even though he had never shared that fact with anyone, not even Father Murphy. The Catholic man in him was offended by how he felt and screamed at him all the time that he was a sinner doomed to an eternity in Hell. This inner battle between his sexuality and his faith killed him on the inside and left him hating himself.

Bruce drove over the Charter Oak Bridge from Hartford into East Hartford, looking down at the Connecticut River the whole time. All he wanted to do was get home and take a long hot shower and maybe nap in his own bed. Later, he would call Jeffrey and fill him in on what he had seen at the

Hollow the night before, but right now all he wanted to do was take a shower and change into something clean.

Chapter 19

Bruce stood outside his car looking up at a large house, wishing he were somewhere else. The driveway he stood on had just recently been resurfaced. The black tar glistened in the late afternoon light. The house was a raised rancher with an attached garage situated at the top of a dead-end street. It sat on a corner lot full of Italian chestnut trees. Tiny green husks filled the branches now, but by late October those husks would be fully grown and covered with spiney needles protecting the delicious chestnuts within.

Bruce took a deep breath and walked up to the front door of the house that was built sometime in the late sixties on what had once been tobacco land. He walked through the front door without knocking. Directly in front of him as he stepped into the house was a flight of stairs that rose up into the main living area of the house. Another flight of stairs just to the right descended into the basement. Bruce chose the stairs going up and stepped onto the bottom step, but before he could manage the next step, a small boy appeared at the top. He was a mini version of his brother Jeffrey, blue eyes, round chin, short brown hair, and a wide, toothy smile.

"Uncle Bruce," the boy cried, leaping from the top step. Bruce caught the child in midair and swung him over his shoulder. The boy squealed with glee as Bruce carried him back up the stairs.

"You're going to be too big for that soon, William," Bruce said, dumping the boy back onto the top step.

"Never!" William cried, running down a hallway to the right of the stairs. Bruce watched him duck into a doorway on the left and disappear.

"Beer," Jeffrey asked from the kitchen.

"Sure," Bruce said, holding out his hand. Jeffrey slapped a beer into the offered hand. It made the wet smacking sound of cold glass against skin. Droplets of moisture ran down the side of the bottle.

"Hello, Bruce," a woman said from behind his brother. It was Annie, Jeffrey's wife. She was tall for a woman, five foot seven, one hundred and forty pounds. She had light blonde hair, cut short, an inch above her shoulders, and bright blue eyes. Her voice was soft and welcoming. She taught elementary school. Bruce liked her at a distance, but that was as far as it went.

"Hey Annie," Bruce said, taking a sip from his bottle, licking the moisture from his lips.

"Brucie," a woman cried from the back door. Bruce looked up and saw his mother walking through the screen door. She was carrying a clear Pyrex dish of lasagna. Her steel gray hair was tied up in a babushka knotted at the back. She wore blue framed glasses low on her nose and a flowered patterned dress that she called a house dress. She lived alone across the street in a house similar to her son's house.

"Just Bruce, Mom," Bruce said. Jeffrey chuckled before taking a sip from his beer.

"You will always be my Brucie to me," his mother said in her Southern New England accent mixed with just a touch of that Italian roll. She set the Pyrex dish on the counter beside the stove.

"Okay, Mom," Bruce said, following his brother into the living room.

"Food is going to be ready in a few minutes," Annie called from the kitchen. Bruce listened as she greeted his mother and commented on how good the lasagna looked. She was a good daughter in law.

"Sox look good this year," Jeffrey said, taking a seat in a recliner beside the fireplace.

"Yeah, they do," Bruce replied, not sure if they were good or not.

"Everything alright?" Jeffrey asked, setting his beer down on an end table. Bruce set his beer on top of a coaster displaying a nighttime scene from Niagara Falls.

"Just stuff we need to talk about later," Bruce said, glancing at the kitchen. Jeffrey nodded.

"It's time," Annie said from the entrance to the kitchen before turning to look down the hallway. "William, it's time to eat baby."

"Up, up, and away to the kitchen table," William shouted, running from his bedroom with a red cape flapping behind him.

"Your hands better be clean before you come in for a landing," Annie said with a stern look. William did a quick U-turn before reaching the kitchen and ran back down the hallway to wash his hands.

"So much energy," Bruce said, taking a seat at a small table. Jeffrey sat at the end and his mother sat at the opposite end. Annie sat across from Bruce. William sat beside his uncle against the wall, his hands supposedly clean now.

"If we're all ready, I'll say grace," his mother said. Everyone bowed their heads. "Father God, thank you for this meal and the loving hands that prepared it. Thank you for bringing all of us together so strong and healthy, and I pray that we will come together again soon as family to share in the bounty you have provided. May the Blessed Mother watch over all of us. Amen."

Everyone said Amen together and looked up. Annie filled Jeffrey's plate with chicken and lasagna, green beans, and a slice of bread. Bruce served himself. William waited for his mother to prepare his plate. Everyone ate.

"So Brucie, when are you going to bring someone home for your poor old mother to meet? I would like to be a grandmother again before I die."

Bruce coughed around a mouthful of bread and grabbed his beer, taking a long swallow to clear his throat. "I don't have time for dating, Mom, let alone making a grandchild for you."

"You don't need time to make a baby, Brucie. Your father and I, God bless his soul, never needed any time for that; we just did what we did and you two came out."

"Mom!" Jeffrey cried, a slight shade of red touching his face.

"Time for what, Grammy?" William asked, looking from his father to his grandmother.

"Never you mind that, William, just eat your food," Annie said, glaring at her mother-in-law.

"Well, it's only natural, you know. Better he learns that now than at school from some foul-mouthed child," her mother-in-law said, a thin faraway smile on her face.

"Jeffrey," Annie whispered. Jeffrey sighed.

"We will be the ones to teach William about that stuff, Mom. So, no more talking about that at the table, please."

"Annie, thank you for the meal. Mom, the lasagna was amazing, as ever. Jeffrey, I'll be down in the basement when you're done," Bruce said, standing up and walking out of the kitchen.

"Did I say something wrong?" his mother asked as he jogged down the stairs. He didn't hear if anyone responded to her question.

Jeffrey entered the basement twenty minutes later with two fresh beers. He handed one to Bruce as he took a seat in front of the television. He turned it on with the remote and changed the channels until he found the ballgame. It was the Red Sox versus the Baltimore Orioles.

"You know, our killer is a Sox fan," Bruce said, sipping from his beer.

"How do you know this?" Jeffrey asked as a Red Sox player struck out. "Bitch," he mumbled.

"He wears a Red Sox ballcap to hide his features and to blend in."

"What else?" Jeffrey asked.

"He's in his mid-thirties, early forties; white male, average height, not skinny but not overweight either. He could be strong, but hides it well. He has short hair, not dark, but not blonde. He doesn't stand out from the crowd. He has a dog, I think his name is Max—the dog, not him. He's a loner, no wife, no girlfriend. He doesn't have time for any of that. He's very focused on what he's doing. He believes it's God's work that he's doing, but he's beginning to crack at the edges. Deep down, he wants to sexually assault these girls, but so far, he's held himself back. I don't think he'll be able to do that for much longer." Instead of watching the game, Jeffrey focused on Bruce as he spoke.

"Our killer is breaking down a little bit at a time, I can feel it. Right now, he thinks he's on a divine mission, but when he loses control there's no telling what he might do."

"Any idea where he takes them before he dumps them?" Jeffrey asked.

"Nothing," Bruce said.

"The feds are coming in on this tomorrow. How do you want me to handle it? I could try to keep you out of it, but they're going to figure it out sooner or later."

"Figure out what? That I'm some kind of psychic, that I can literally enter into the mind of a killer? I don't think so. If they ask, just tell them I'm a consultant."

"If they ask," Jeffrey said. "But even if they don't, they're going to want to know something about how we're getting our information."

"Maybe, we'll see," Bruce replied, draining his beer. He glanced at the television in time to see Mark Trumbo hit a ball over the Green Monster.

"Fuck a duck," Jeffrey cried. Bruce laughed.

Chapter 20

Amy opened her eyes and found herself back inside the trunk of the man's car. She wasn't sure when this had happened. All she could remember was the stomp of boots on the floor above her head. She heard someone moving about the house. She would have tried crying out to whomever it was, but the tape over her mouth wouldn't allow her to. All she could do was listen to the heavy footfalls on the floorboards overhead and the patter of small paws following close behind. She knew it had to be the man because Cujo wasn't going nuts.

As the movement continued overhead, Amy didn't know if it was day or night. She guessed night though, because she had been alone in dank, dusty silence for what felt like a long time now. The only company she had was the stink of her own piss from soiling herself, the horrible ache of her muscles, and the ticking of the old house as water passed through its pipes. She was scared and hungry and chilled to the bone. She had cried so much that there were no more tears left for her to cry. Her mouth felt like rough sandpaper. She was thirsty. Her throat felt cracked like old paint on an abandoned house. Everything hurt so much. She wished she could just move a little bit.

The footfalls above her head paused and she heard the squeal of dry hinges echoing in the stillness of the basement. It was the door opening at the top of the basement stairs. The sound was like a cat after someone stepped on its tail. It was a sound that cut through everything like a knife through crusty bread. She wanted to scream along with it but she couldn't.

A faint light leaked into the darkness of the basement after the squeal of the hinges. The light crawled across the cold concrete walls. Heavy footfalls echoed in the silence, descending the stairs to the basement floor. Amy shuddered as each hollow thump exploded like a grenade into the dank darkness.

A shadow appeared in the rafters overhead, weaving its way deeper into the basement. She heard a man's heavy breathing as he stepped off the last stair onto the cold concrete floor. His footsteps sounded dull and muted now as he approached the exam table where she lay. Her heart thudded loudly inside her chest. The need to scream, to shout, to fight, filled her.

The man stopped somewhere near her feet. She twisted her head just enough to look at him. He stood at the end of the exam table, slightly off to one side concealed in the shadowed darkness, his features melting with the lack of light. She blinked several times, trying to make sure he was real and not a ghost come to haunt her.

A bright light came to life suddenly above her head, the bulb swinging slowly back and forth on a chain. Dark after-images floated behind her eyelids and silent tears leaked from the corners of her eyes. The pain was intense after being in the dark for so long. She heard the man breathing. Each breath sounded labored and thick. She forced her eyes to open, looking up into the light. The man stood over her, his lips parted, the tip of a blood-red tongue poking out between them. There was a look of hunger on his face. He looked like a person starving for a meal. She thought he was going to attack her at any moment, but then a frown creased his face and his eyes wrinkled and narrowed.

"What a mess you have made of yourself," the man whispered through clenched teeth. Amy shook her head from side to side, wishing she could speak, wishing she could scream. The frown on the man's face disappeared and a thin smile appeared. She watched him walk away somewhere out of sight. She could hear the sound of running water filling the basement. It lasted for little more than a minute. The man returned with a blue bucket in his hand and that same thin smile on his face. "Cleanliness is always close to Godliness," the man said. Amy's eyes went wide, realizing that the man was about to bathe her.

"A baby in a tub is such a sight, she giggles and laughs with such delight, as her body is scrubbed from head to toe, her skin is left with such a glow," the man sang as he washed her body from the top of her head to the bottoms of her feet. Amy tried to twist and turn away from him, but the straps held her down so she couldn't. All she could do was listen as he sang that same tune over and over.

The man had washed and scrubbed her naked body, touching her in places that left her feeling ashamed and disgusted. He had paid special attention to her private areas, scrubbing each breast slowly, lingering over them. She saw a bit of drool leak from the corner of his mouth and noticed that his breathing was shallow and fast. He was enjoying what he was doing. She felt so completely violated.

The sponge shook in his hand as he dipped it back inside the bucket and brought it back out again. Cold soapy water splashed all over her and the exam table. She could hear it raining down on the floor below. Goosebumps covered her exposed skin. The tiny hairs along her arms stood up. She felt dizzy and sick and disgusted. She thought she might throw up.

The man's hand suddenly slipped between her legs and the world came to a crashing stop all around her. The sponge touched her vagina and she squeezed her eyes shut, praying that he would move it away from where it was, but then a sudden sharp pain filled her body. She felt the sponge being shoved up inside her. Her mind exploded. Bright flashes of white light washed out the light of the bulb above her head, filling her vision until there was only darkness. Her mind slipped away to somewhere—somewhere where there was no pain, somewhere where she might be safe.

Afterward, all she knew was that she was in the trunk of the car with her feet bound and her hands tied together behind her back again. There was a painful throbbing between her legs like something filling her, but that was all. The drive took an eternity. She felt every bump and turn, rolling painfully forward and backwards every time the car came to a stop and started back up again. Everything hurt, everything was on fire, and the ride continued.

The car finally came to a sudden stop and she slammed painfully into the front of the trunk. Bright sparks of light went off inside her head as she settled back. The engine turned off and she suddenly found herself wishing it hadn't. The trunk opened and the man stood outside. The tiny bulb looked like a star dangling from the lid. The man looked down at her with a sad expression on his face.

"This is it," she thought. "He's going to kill me now."

The man reached into the trunk and gently lifted her out. He tossed her over one shoulder before reaching back down into trunk. She saw a small doctor's bag in his other hand. She heard him sigh and close the lid of the trunk. There was a soft click and then nothing. The dog was nowhere to be seen. It was just her and the man outside somewhere in the dark. Cool night air whispered against her skin. It felt so good after being cramped up inside that trunk. The man walked away from the car.

Amy tried looking around as much as possible as the man walked. She saw a path beneath her that he was following. There were trees and bushes on either side of the path but no lights or signs to let her know where they were. All she could see were trees all around them. *A park maybe*, she thought.

Leaves and twigs snapped beneath the man's feet as he walked along the path. It was extremely dark outside, ghostly quiet, and still. Insects buzzed and nipped at her exposed skin. She thought of her mom and dad, hoping they didn't miss her too much. She thought of Patricia and hoped she didn't blame herself.

"Are you wondering where we are, child?" the man asked in a casual voice that sounded as if he had no cares at all in the world. Amy didn't respond to his question. "This is Devil's Hopyard," the man answered. "They say it got its name from a man named Dibble who grew hops here somewhere, a long, long time ago. Over time, Dibble's Hopyard somehow became Devil's Hopyard. Isn't that interesting?"

Amy listened as the man talked. It was the most he had said to her directly since kidnapping her. The tone was casual, almost friendly.

"Do you believe in the Devil, child?" he asked, still following the path. "I believe in the Devil, and I am sure he is roaming around seeking whom he might devour right now, but it won't be you. I won't allow it."

Amy heard rushing water now over the man's voice. She twisted her head to the side and saw a fence running along one side of the path. The sound of the water came from somewhere beyond the fence. The man stopped talking. He left the path and climbed over the top rail of the fence, walking out to the edge of a flat rock. The sound of rushing water filled her ears now as he set her down on the cold surface of the stone. Twigs and pebbles bit into her skin. Above her, clouds drifted past a quarter moon. A few stars littered the sky. She felt terrified and alive at the same time.

The world seemed so real and alive to her, more than it ever had before.

"So here we are, child," the man said, looking down at her. "I am the bringer of your salvation. I am here to save you from yourself before you fall into a life of sin and disgrace," he explained, squatting down beside her. He gently touched one of her small breasts with the tip of a finger. The nipple was rock hard. A shudder passed through his body. She felt it through the tip of his finger as it lingered on her breast.

"Oh God, please let this end," Amy prayed. "Daddy, where are you? I need you."

Without removing the tip of his finger from her breast, the man reached into the bag beside his leg. The movement caught Amy's eye and she followed the hand, forgetting all about the finger. The man sighed deeply and withdrew a large steel knife from the bag. The other hand fell away from her breast, but she didn't even notice. Her eyes were fixed on that impossibly large knife. In the man's hand, the knife looked like a sword from the days of knights and dragons. The blade sparkled in the moonlight as it came closer.

"Please God, please God, please God," Amy prayed over and over.

"Now I lay you down to sleep, for the Lord your soul to take and keep," the man said.

Amy felt the blade against the skin of her throat. It stung like the sting of a hornet as it bit into her flesh. Something wet, ran down the back of her neck and suddenly her throat felt like it was on fire. She saw no flames, but something white and hot clawed at her throat. She screamed around the tape, unaware she was even doing it. The pain grew and grew and then it was just gone. She looked up at the man and he seemed so far away now. She didn't understand what was happening. One second she was on the ground in incredible pain and now she felt like she was floating on air, drifting along with the wind. It felt amazing. God had saved her after all, she thought, as the world turned slowly dark. Amy slipped away peacefully from this life and into the next, believing she had finally escaped her tormenter.

Chapter 21

Bruce woke up to the sound of his phone buzzing like an annoying bee beside his head. He had fallen asleep on his stomach the night before, laying across his bed with his pants still around his ankles. Beneath his feet were a small pile of change and a set of car keys. On the floor below his head was a tipped-over bottle of vodka with a dark stain soaked into the carpet spreading out from the mouth of the bottle.

"Fuck," Bruce moaned, shoving the cellphone away from his head. "Will you shut the fuck up," he cried at the buzzing instrument, and just like that, it stopped. He closed his eyes again, exhaled, and kicked his legs several times. The pants dropped to the floor in a puddle of denim on top of the keys and change. He sighed and curled up in a ball to fall back to sleep, but before he could, his cellphone buzzed again.

"Motherfucker, will you please leave me alone," he shouted, snatching the phone from the mattress. He glared at the screen and saw that it was his brother. "Fuck," he sighed. "What?" he grumbled into the cellphone, getting up onto one elbow.

"Get down to Devil's Hopyard State Park. We got another body. It's the girl from the other day."

"Son of a bitch," Bruce mumbled. "Where the fuck is Devil's Hopyard?"

"It's in East Haddam. Google it for God sakes, but get down here before the feds show up," Jeffrey said before hanging up.

Bruce dropped his phone on the floor and rolled over onto his back. He sat up slowly with one hand on his head. His stomach felt queasy and his head hurt as he slowly glanced around his tiny apartment. *Shower,* he thought, stumbling across the room, almost pissing his boxers before he reached the bathroom.

Fifteen minutes later, Bruce was showered and dressed. A piece of burnt toast was clamped between his lips as he walked out of his apartment. Downstairs, he was thankful for the dark clouds filling the sky overhead. The muted light was bad enough, but sunshine would have killed him. He got into his car, which was parked on the grass again, and started it. The engine came to life and sounded a hell of a lot better than he felt. He rolled down the window and drove toward Main Street, turning left at the light. A few minutes later, he pulled into the Dunkin' Donuts for coffee and something tastier than the burnt toast he just ate.

Back in his car again, he pulled up Google Maps on his cellphone and typed in Devil's Hopyard. The robotic voice instructed him to turn left onto Main Street. Bruce texted his brother that he was on his way before turning left onto Main Street.

Bruce relaxed into the short forty-minute drive once he was headed east on Route 2. He leaned back in his seat and thought about the night before and the horrible news he had received. His phone had buzzed around eight-thirty that evening. It had been the wife of an Army buddy from his time in Iraq.

"Bruce Westman?" the voice had asked nervously before Bruce could say anything. He heard the tremor in her question as she spoke.

"Yes, I'm him," Bruce answered, wondering who it was. The number wasn't familiar.

"I'm Vickie Malloy. You served with my husband, John," she explained, her voice cracking.

"John, yeah," Bruce replied cautiously, knowing whatever she had to say wasn't going to be good.

"He committed suicide this morning," she sobbed. "He drew a bath and cut both of his wrists. He left a note on the floor beside the tub mentioning you."

"Oh my God," he stuttered. "Holy shit."

The woman on the other end of the cellphone cried softly before clearing her throat. Bruce heard a baby crying somewhere nearby. "He said you would understand why he had no choice, and thanked you for being his brother," she explained. "Can you tell me why? Can you tell me why he would do this to me and his daughter?" she shouted through the tears. "Why the fucking hell would he do this to us?"

Bruce allowed the woman to cry herself out. He listened as she yelled and screamed and when she finished, he promised to head down to South Carolina and explain everything about what John went through in Iraq. She thanked him and apologized for losing her shit. Bruce told her it was alright and hung up a few minutes later. After that, the rest of the night was a blur of drinking in some dark downtown bar. He had no idea what time he stumbled home. He looked down at his cellphone. "The fucking war is still being fought," he muttered at the cellphone. "That's why he killed himself."

Bruce Westman finished basic training and AIT with the United States Army in 2009. He was part of a military police detachment assigned to the 1st Battalion, 184th Infantry Regiment, Camp Falcon, Iraq. His mission there had been to patrol downtown Baghdad and Al Sadr City. The shit he had seen there left him and those he served with suffering from PTSD and other assorted ailments that the Federal Government paid them for each month tax free. It had been a roadside bomb that had finally sent him home. John had left the sand a month earlier after taking a round in the chest from a sniper. Either way, no matter how they had managed to return back home, the memories of what they had seen there still haunted them. For Bruce, it had been the PTSD and other assorted mental issues that kept him from getting hired by the Manchester Police Department.

Of those he had served with, John Molloy made three that hadn't survived the war after the war. The politicians didn't share that fact with the public. They kept it secret, but the scars ran so deep. Bruce wondered who was going to be next. He wondered if it might be him that ended up swallowing the barrel of a gun or taking a bloodbath.

The sign for Devil's Hopyard loomed ahead, snapping him from his thoughts. He followed Fox Town Road to the parking area for Chapman Falls, parking next to his brother's city-issued car. The heat outside the car fell over him as he walked away with a small notebook clasped in his hand. On the far side of the lot was a trail sign for the falls. He started that way, meeting Jeffrey before he got too far along the path.

"You awake now, dickhead?" Jeffrey asked, walking up to his brother.

"Yeah, rough night," Bruce answered.

"Want to tell me about it as we walk? We have a few minutes."

"Not really," Bruce answered.

"Okay," Jeffrey replied. "Maybe later. For now, we have the girl's body caught up at the bottom of the falls. She was found there after the park was opened by a ranger. Same modus operandi: Throat slashed, naked. No one has disturbed her yet. I wanted you to get a fresh look before everyone has a shot at her."

"Good," Bruce said, looking at the fence that ran alongside the path. Names, initials, penises, and hearts were carved into the wood. He sighed and shook his head. He could hear the falls just beyond the fence. "I guess no one saw anything, just like all the others?" he asked, stopping at the fence. He looked around for a moment. The path continued, but where he stood felt right. He stepped over the fence. Jeffrey watch and shrugged.

"He approached the falls from here," Bruce said, walking slowly to the edge of the stone outcropping that overlooked the falls. A small pool of dried blood coated the stone. "But I guess you figured that out," he said, looking over the edge at the girl. Even with all the water rushing around her he could see that she was very dead. Her head hung down, her eyes wide and blank staring up at him. The water tugged at her feet wanting to take her further downstream, but something held her up. He looked closer and saw that she was stuck to the rock she landed on. From where he stood, Bruce could see the ugly slash across her throat. It looked nasty and ragged. There was exposed tissue and bone.

"Fuck me," Bruce whispered, making his way down the falls now. He worked his way as close as he could to the girl and stopped. Her lifeless eyes held him. He looked into those eyes. "Talk to me," he whispered, kneeling down and placing a hand on the stone where she came to rest. He closed his eyes and waited.

The drift came and he saw the killer with the girl, except they weren't at the falls. They were in some kind of concrete room. "Maybe an unfinished basement," he thought. A single light lit the room. The girl was secured to a table of some kind and the killer was washing her. He held a large brown sponge that he kept dipping into a blue bucket. Over and over, he dipped the sponge and applied it to her exposed body, washing and scrubbing until her skin turned pink.

She was naked and scared. He could see the fear in her eyes. Gray tape covered her mouth, but he could hear the muffled cries from behind it. She looked so frightened, so fragile. He wanted to scoop her up and save her, but he knew he was only an observer of things that had already happened.

The killer stood over the girl humming a tune that Bruce had never heard before. He saw the excitement on the killer's face as he went about his task. His hands were shaking, his eyes wide and unblinking. The hand with the sponge suddenly disappeared between her legs. The girl screamed from behind the tape, her eyes bugging out, her face turning bright red. Snot ran from her nose. Tears fell from her eyes. The pitch of the scream rose and then she passed out. The hand reappeared. The sponge was missing. Bruce turned away and looked around.

A basement, he thought, wishing he hadn't seen what he had seen.

The killer stepped away from the table and Bruce saw that it was an exam table, like what you might find in a doctor's office. The killer took several steps away until he stood in one of the dark corners of the basement. He let his pants fall to the floor, puddling around his ankles, and masturbated. He finished with a pained cry, leaning back into the exposed concrete. On the floor, just in front of his pants, a wet stain spread.

"Who the fuck is that?" a voice shouted from above, snapping Bruce back. He looked over his shoulder to where his brother stood and saw an African-American male standing beside him waving his arms and pointing. Bruce stood and climbed back up the falls.

"You can move her now; I got what I needed," Bruce said, ignoring the very angry looking man standing beside Jeffrey.

"You got everything you needed. You just fucked up my crime scene, asshole," the man said, jabbing a finger into Bruce's chest. "Who the fuck let you down there?"

"Look, Agent Shelby, like I told you, he's a consultant with the department."

"I don't give a fuck if he's the fucking Pope of America. Your fucking department was told to simply hold the scene until I arrived," Agent Shelby growled.

"Your scene is completely intact. I touched nothing, disturbed nothing. Now if you don't have any questions for me, I'll be on my way," Bruce said, trying to step around the agent, but before he could manage a few steps, Agent Shelby grabbed his arm and forced him to turn back around. Bruce looked him in the eyes, barely holding back the anger that wanted to explode. Bruce took a deep breath, never looking away from Agent Shelby. "Unless you want to lose that hand, Agent Shelby, I suggest you remove it from my arm," Bruce growled. Agent Shelby let the arm go and took a step back. Bruce held his gaze for a moment.

"You're not going anywhere," Agent Shelby said, looking away from Bruce. "When I'm done here, I'm going to want to talk to you and Officer Westman."

"Fine, I'll be in the parking lot leaning against my car," Bruce said, walking away. He headed back down the path he had taken to the falls. Halfway back to the parking lot, Jeffrey caught up with him. Several other FBI agents dressed in white protective suits passed them going in the opposite direction.

"What an asshole," Bruce said as they kept walking to the parking lot.

"He's just trying to do his job," Jeffrey said. "He sucks at it, but that's all he's doing."

"Screw that. He could have handled things better than he did. I hate the fucking FBI. They come in like they're knights in shining armor. They ain't no better than you and me."

"It's not a big deal," Jeffrey said, watching Bruce walk up to his car and lean against it. Jeffrey leaned beside him. "Lunch later after we're done here?" Jeffrey asked. "The ranger said High Tides on Main Street is good place to grab a bite."

"Sure," Bruce said. "You're buying."

"So, you going to tell me what you saw before Shelby interrupted?"

Bruce looked down the path and sighed. "You're going to find a sponge inside her. At least I think so. He washes them before he brings them to wherever he's going to kill them," Bruce explained. "Before that, he keeps them tied down to some kind of exam table in a basement somewhere. It can't be too far away. He has to live in East Hartford or Manchester or Glastonbury maybe. Wherever he lives, it has to be somewhere close." Jeffrey wrote everything that Bruce said in a notebook. He looked up after Bruce stopped talking.

"Anything else?" Jeffrey asked, his pen poised above the paper.

"What he did to her, with the sponge. He's slipping over the edge little by little now. When he goes completely over, God help whoever he has. He's not far now. We have to catch him before he completely loses his shit." Jeffrey nodded, shoving the notebook in his breast pocket.

"I wish I still smoked," Jeffrey sighed, focusing on the path with his brother. Together, they waited for Agent Shelby to appear.

Chapter 22

The restaurant where they met was a small building in what passed for downtown East Haddam, Connecticut. It was a family owned establishment that gave off a sixties hippy, bohemian, Greenwich Village vibe. A large grease board just inside the door, covered with bright florescent letters written in large script, listed the specials of the day for the arriving lunch crowd. The sign above the entrance door advertised the restaurant as a coffee house and art gallery. Inside, the lower level was an eatery with a small stage in one corner where people set up to entertain the customers on open mic nights with slam poetry or music. The atmosphere was very laid back and casual. A customer could fit in wearing shorts, sandals, and a tie-dye t-shirt just as easy as someone wearing a business suit with five hundred dollar shoes. Bruce liked the restaurant immediately after walking through the door. Jeffrey appeared a bit uncomfortable.

"Over by the window," Jeffrey said, nodding his head in that direction. "I have to use the restroom." Bruce nodded and took a seat at a table beside one of the street-facing windows. On the other side of the glass, he watched as the afternoon traffic passed by.

"Can I set you up with something to drink?" a girl in her late teens wearing a short-skirted pink outfit asked. She was light skinned, most likely mixed African American. Her hair was straight, cut short just over her shoulders and pulled back in a tight ponytail. She was tiny, very thin, not much older than eighteen. Her smile was full of energy and infectious, and Bruce couldn't help himself: he smiled back at her as she stood there with pen and paper in hand.

"Water, please, and a black coffee for my brother," Bruce said, pointing at the empty chair across from him. The waitress wrote the drink order down and walked away. Jeffrey sat down a few minutes later just as the waitress came back with the water and coffee.

"I ordered you a coffee," Bruce said, glancing out the window as she set it down in front of Jeffrey.

"Give us a few minutes, please," Jeffrey said, sipping at his coffee. The waitress smiled and walked away. Jeffrey watched her go.

"She's too young for you," Bruce said, grinning at his brother.

"Just because I can admire her doesn't mean I'm interested in her," Jeffrey said, running a finger over the rim of his cup.

"Whatever," Bruce replied, picking up the menu. Jeffrey did the same. The waitress returned a few minutes later.

"So, have the two of you decided?" the waitress asked. Jeffrey squinted at her nametag.

"Laney," he said, smiling. "I'd like one of your house special burgers minus the onions, fries, and a coke." Laney smiled back and wrote down Jeffrey's order before looking over at Bruce.

"Same for me, but you can leave the onions," Bruce said, setting his menu down on the table.

Laney repeated the order back to the two of them and left the table to turn it in. Jeffrey watched her go, smiling as she disappeared in the back. "She's sure something to look at," he said, grinning. "I bet you could hit it if you really wanted to." Bruce looked up, wondering what his brother would say if he told him the truth about himself.

"Yeah, sure, and I could ask her to the prom afterward," Bruce said. Jeffrey laughed, and Bruce joined him.

The waitress came back several minutes later with their food and the two of them ate. The burgers were heavenly, just the right amount of grease, and the fries were crispy without being overcooked. Bruce ate his quickly and Jeffrey took his time.

"So, what's the story with this Shelby?" Bruce asked after Jeffrey swallowed his last bite of burger.

"He's your typical uptight fed. He thinks the work begins and ends with the FBI and anything in between can just fuck itself."

"Please, don't hold back, it's not healthy just after you eat," Bruce replied, grinning at his brother. Jeffrey laughed before polishing off the last of his fries.

"That was good. It was really good," Jeffrey said. "Your treat, right?"

"Not today, rich man," Bruce said, getting up from the table. "I'll leave the tip and you can get the bill." Jeffrey flipped his brother off but snatched the bill from the table. Bruce dropped a five and three ones on the table, setting a saltshaker on top before walking out the door. Jeffrey came out a few minutes later.

"Drop me off at my car," Bruce said. "You can deal with Agent Shelby after I'm gone."

"Thanks," Jeffrey said, opening the driver's side door.

"How are we going to handle this now that the feds are involved and not all that friendly? I don't think Agent Shelby is going to be all that open to how I get things done," Bruce said.

"Yeah, can you imagine that conversation?" Jeffrey said. "So, you see, my brother here was in the war in Iraq and got himself blown up by a roadside bomb, and ever since he woke up three months later, he's been able to literally get inside people's heads. The more insane they are, the better."

"Yeah, I'm sure that would go over really well," Bruce replied. "And for the record, I didn't get blown up. No one had to put me back together, and I didn't lose any body parts. I was just really close when that IED went off."

"Ask your mother. She says, and I quote, 'My Brucie was blowed up by one of those nasty sand niggers.'" Bruce cringed. He hated to hear that word, but he knew his mother used it to describe what happened to him.

"I can't change how she thinks, but I expect better from you," Bruce said. Jeffrey reached across the seat and slugged him in the arm.

"Now you're just asking too much of me," he said, laughing at his younger brother.

"Asshole," Bruce said, looking out the passenger side window as they drove back to the park.

Chapter 23

Two days later, Bruce found himself standing in the parking lot at 239 Middle Turnpike East. The lot was the public parking lot for the Manchester Police Department. He parked close to the street beneath the arm of an old elm tree and the meager shade it offered against the summer sun. The police department was a modern government building made of red brick with a white stone façade wrapped around the front, sort of like a racing stripe. Bruce thought the façade made it appear that the building was glaring at all who entered through its tinted double glass doors.

Bitter memories flooded back as he approached those doors. With each slap of his shoe upon the hot asphalt he was reminded that he wasn't good enough to be counted as one of their officers. The guilty fact in America was that everyone liked to say that today's soldiers were welcomed back as heroes after fighting in Iraq or Afghanistan, but Bruce knew the truth. Just like the wars of yesterday, Korea and Vietnam, most people simply wanted to forget that they ever happened, and that the soldiers who fought there simply didn't exist. He was good enough to fight thousands of miles away from home, but not good enough to be hired for anything that he wanted to do. The war on terror never stopped for those who fought it.

Bruce stepped through the double doors, walking up to a safety glass-enclosed front desk. He eyed the Public Service Officers seated behind the glass. They sat at a desk that ran the length of the room. He recognized one of the officers seated there but not the other. "She's new," he thought.

"Hey there, little Westman," a white shirted older gentleman said from the other side of the safety glass.

"Hey, Mr. Watson," Bruce replied, forcing a tight smile.

"You here for that big meeting with the muckety-mucks?" Mr. Watson asked as he dug a visitor's pass out from a drawer.

"Yeah, I guess so," Bruce answered, signing the visitor's log.

"Angela," Mr. Watson said to the younger girl sitting beside him. "This is Bruce Westman, a real-life war hero. His brother is Officer Jeffrey Westman. You let him in whenever he visits."

"Nice to meet you, sir," Angela said, barely looking up from her cellphone. Bruce couldn't see what she was looking at on the tiny screen.

"Kids. What ya gonna do?" Mr. Watson asked, raising an eyebrow as he slid the pass through a small opening in the safety glass. Bruce clipped the pass to his shirt and stepped through a buzzing door to his right. He followed a short hallway on the other side of the door and down to the rollcall room.

The rollcall room was a standard classroom-sized room with desks lined up from the back to the front. A four-foot-wide aisle ran down the center of the room, which was tiled in industrial green tiles that screamed junior high school. Officers and brass were seated at most of the desks. Up front, facing out into the room, was a dark wooden podium with a mic poking up from the center. Agent Shelby stood at the podium as Bruce walked into the room. Behind him was a map of the state with a wide red circle around the towns of Manchester, East Hartford, and Glastonbury, and a smaller red circle around East Haddam. Bruce quietly took up a spot against the back wall.

The captain over Support Services sat in the front row along with a commander from the State Police and officers and detectives from several other outside agencies. His brother sat beside the captain with two other officers from the department that he recognized. Across the aisle and still in the front row sat two men all by themselves dressed in dark suits. Bruce figured they were more agents from the FBI. The lieutenant over investigations, an acquaintance of Bruce's and a veteran of the first Gulf War, sat with several officers from the department in the row behind the agents. Behind them sat more officers from outside agencies wearing varying uniforms or plain clothes.

Agent Shelby eyed Bruce from the podium. Bruce noticed his glare and smiled at him, leaning back against the wall. Agent Shelby cleared his throat and continued speaking.

"As I was saying," Agent Shelby continued, trying his best to ignore Bruce grinning up at him from the back of the rollcall room. "The Behavioral Science Unit has come up with a preliminary profile of our unsub." The smile slipped from Bruce's face. Agent Shelby had his interest now. The rest of the room had gone silent as well. Bruce listened.

"The unsub we're looking for is a white male, in his middle to late thirties. He's most likely married, but they believe childless. They think this might be because he is unable to produce any children or because of a medical condition that embarrasses him and makes him feel like less of a man. Socially, he puts on a mask and forces himself out there as to blend in with everyone around him. He most likely has a job, perhaps middle management, but nothing greater than that. He's educated, smart. He fits in wherever he works, but he doesn't advance because either he doesn't want to or because as much as he tries to fit in, he seems off somehow to others."

"You're wrong," Bruce said from the back of the room, leaning away from the wall.

"Excuse me," Agent Shelby said, frowning.

"I said, you're wrong," Bruce said. "The only thing you have right is that the guy is white, and he might be in his thirties, but could be in his forties." Agent Shelby's frown turned into a snarl. His upper lip curled up on the left side, making his nose wrinkle.

"You're that guy from the other day screwing up my crime scene. The consultant, right?" Agent Shelby said, stepping around the podium. He wore a dark FBI-issued suit complete with a tie. He had thick dark eyebrows that wiggled like worms every time he spoke.

"Yes," Bruce replied, stepping up to the last row of chairs and desks ready to confront Agent Shelby who stood in front of the podium.

"Well, Mr. Consultant, why don't you let the professionals do their jobs, and you can find something else to consult on," Agent Shelby said, giving Bruce a hard stare that dared him to say anything else.

"I would, believe me, but then another girl is going to die because your profile is totally fucked up."

"Mr. Westman, that's enough," the captain beside Jeffrey said.

"Westman?" Agent Shelby asked, looking over at Jeffrey as he stepped into the aisle. "A relative of yours?" he asked, without really looking at Jeffrey now.

"Yes, sir," Jeffrey replied, looking at Bruce, pleading for him to stop.

"Well, isn't that just perfect," Agent Shelby said. "Now you listen here, Consultant, I don't want you anywhere near my investigation. If I so much as see you anywhere near one of my crime scenes again I will have you charged with obstruction of justice. Am I understood?" Agent Shelby said, his right hand resting on the butt of his gun. Bruce wondered if he was aware of where his hand was resting.

"Your guy is average height, average weight. He is not sociable. He most likely works out of his home or has some kind of business that he can ship things from. He likes as little interaction with people as possible," Bruce said, talking fast. "But when he's hunting, when he's looking for his next victim, he blends in so no one notices him."

"Get him out of here," Agent Shelby shouted.

"He may have had some medical training and grown up in a strict church family. He could be military but that's just a guess, and he has a dog," Bruce added before Jeffrey grabbed him by the arm, dragging him from the room.

"Go home," Jeffrey said once they were outside the station.

"Fuck that asshole," Bruce shouted. "He's going to get another little girl killed because his profile is wrong, and you know it."

"I get it, you're the smartest one in the room, but you can't go after them like that," Jeffrey explained. "This is their circus now and we're just along for the ride."

"Fuck him and his mightier-than-God attitude. His arrogance is going to get a child killed."

"Go home, brother."

"Whatever," Bruce said. "He's going to feed the public and the press that load of bullshit, and you know it," Bruce shouted, storming across the parking lot. He yanked on the driver's side door to his car and it opened. He looked back over his shoulder in time to see Jeffrey walking back into the station. He felt sorry for his brother having to deal with the repercussions of his outburst. Disgusted with himself for having no self-control, Bruce jabbed the key into the ignition and started the car. He wanted to mash down on the accelerator as he backed up, but managed to control himself enough to resist that urge.

Thirty minutes later, Bruce found himself sitting in the parking lot of Globe Hollow. Though it was just before noontime, the lot was only half full. Mostly minivans and sport utility vehicles. The bike rack to the left of the gate was full of bikes of varying colors and styles. Inside the fence several teenagers, milled around puffing on cigarettes or vapes, talking to each other or on their cellphones. Blankets and towels covered the grassy hillside populated by sunbathing girls, gawking boys, and mothers gabbing with each other over the latest gossip. The sounds of children having fun in the water and whistled warnings of lifeguards filled the air. Bruce parked in the shade beneath the oaks at the back of the lot and rolled down his window. Turning the car off, he leaned his head back against the seat, closing his eyes, wishing the world to go away.

"Hey, Mr. Westman," a young voice said into the open window of Bruce's car. Bruce opened one eye and glared at the owner of the voice for disturbing his meditation. It was Matthew, sitting astride his bike beside the car. A towel was draped over his shoulder, his hair was all spiky, and his eyes were a deep shade of pink as if he had just come out of the water.

"Hey, kid," Bruce mumbled, sitting up.

"You still working on that girl's body?" Matthew asked, glancing back at the pool.

Bruce smiled at how he put it. "Yeah," he answered, resting an elbow on the window.

"Cool. You need any more help?" Matthew asked, looking hopeful.

Bruce looked at Matthew, wondering why he wasn't playing with the other kids. He seemed out of place somehow sitting all by himself on his bike. He felt sorry for the boy. "Not right now," Bruce answered, leaning across the seat and popping the glove box open. He reached in and took out a small box, shaking a card out from inside. "Here, take this, and if you hear anything or see something, call me."

Matthew's face lit up as he took the business card from Bruce. He looked at it for a moment before shoving it into a pocket. "I'll do that," he said, smiling broadly. Bruce wondered if he had any friends.

"And if you find out anything good that helps me, I'll pay you," Bruce added, jamming the box of business cards back into the glove box. Matthew's face lit up even more. He looked as if he were about to pop. Bruce smiled, glad he could make the kid happy. "Don't go getting yourself hurt, hear me? Just keep your eyes open for shit happening and call me if it does."

"Yes, sir," Matthew said. Bruce nodded and leaned back against the seat again. Matthew pedaled away across the parking lot toward the street. At the entrance, he stopped and glanced back at the car, wondering if he should go back and tell Bruce about the man with the dog that he had seen the other day while walking with his sister. There had been something off about that guy, and the way he reacted to Mary taking a picture of his dog. *Don't be stupid*, he thought, rolling out to the street. *The guy was just a creep and nothing more.* Matthew pedaled away down the street headed home. Bruce opened an eye just in time to see Matthew disappear.

You're going to get him hurt if you're not careful, he thought, looking back at the pool. He noticed a few of the mothers looking in his direction. They looked concerned, worried, and he realized it was because he was just sitting there in the parking lot. "Fuck it," he whispered. *I better scram before someone calls the cops thinking I'm the killer.*

Chapter 24

Bruce left Globe Hollow and headed out to Devil's Hopyard State Park. The afternoon traffic was light, so the trip out there was short. He parked close to the trailhead that led out to the waterfall. It was still taped off with yellow crime scene tape, but there was no one present to stop him. Ducking beneath the tape, he followed the trail out to the falls. Even though the sun was high overhead, the trees that enclosed the path dissuaded all but the most persistent rays of sunlight from getting through. Long shadows covered the pine-needle-carpeted trail as he walked slowly along enjoying the solitude.

A sign was posted on the fence that separated the trail from the falls stating that the area was closed until further notice. Bruce ignored the sign and stepped over the fence. The top rail caught him between the legs as he straddled the wooden beam, causing a sharp intake of air. On the other side of the fence, he walked over to the same flat rock the killer had used to slay his victim and sat down. His feet hung over the edge as he gazed down at the water. If he hadn't known what had happened there just the other night, he might have enjoyed the view that he had all to himself, but now it only saddened him.

The sun beat down on his shoulders. It was hot and persistent. There was no breeze to break up the heat of the day. The sound of the waterfall was relaxing, calming. He wondered if it had had that effect on Amy before she died. He hoped so.

Bright sparkles of sunlight danced off the cascading water as it splashed down on the rocks below, the same rocks where Amy's body had come to rest after the killer had finished with her. He looked down and a vision of her sprawled upon the stones flittered through his mind. It wasn't a pleasant image to have stored there in his brain up on the shelf with so many other unpleasant images.

Bruce sighed. *It's pretty here*, he thought, despite all the morbid thoughts filling his head. He could see why so many people came here during the spring, summer, and fall. He imagined that there would have been people all over the place today if the trail hadn't been closed. If the killer hadn't decided to pollute the waters of this park with his poison.

Bruce took a deep breath to clear his head. He let the breath out slowly as he placed the palm of one hand to the surface of the rock. It was warm from the afternoon sun. The heat bit deep into the palm of his hand. The stone was abrasive like sandpaper. He felt each imperfection as he pressed down. The stone bit painfully into the flesh of his hand as if it were hungry for another victim. Bruce closed his eyes and waited for the drift to come. It didn't take long.

The drift took him along on a dark gentle trip until he finally settled down in a place he knew right away. It was dark outside, but he knew he was at Devil's Hopyard on the night that Amy died. She lay on the stone where he was sitting in another world beneath the light of the moon. Her body was naked and bound at the feet and hands. In the light of the moon her skin looked like warm milk in a familiar cup on a sleepless night. She looked so young and fragile. Even from where he stood just on the other side of the fence, he saw the tears falling from her eyes. They ran down her cheeks like tiny diamonds sparkling in the moonlight. He heard her mumbled pleas from beneath the tape covering her mouth.

Above Amy stood the killer oblivious to her cries and tears. He stood in complete focus now. Bruce could see his whole face. Nothing was hidden from him now. The killer wore the same Red Sox ballcap on his head, a black t-shirt, and long dark pants. He hadn't shaved that day. A dark stubble covered his face. There was a scabbed-over scratch on the side of his throat and Bruce wondered if Amy had gotten in a lick. He hoped so. The dog was nowhere to be seen.

Bruce watched the killer reach into what looked like one of those old-fashioned medical bags that doctors use to carry with them when they made house calls. The killer took a long silver-bladed knife from the bag. It looked so incredibly sharp in the pale moonlight. The killer brought the knife down and drew it across Amy's throat, separating the flesh easily. Blood sprayed out from the cut in a shower of crimson splashing on the killer's hands. He rubbed those hands together like a man washing his hands beneath the flow of a faucet.

Bruce tried to turn away, but every time he did, he found himself forced to watch. The spray of atrial blood slowed to a trickle. The killer smiled and stood, lifting Amy's lifeless body over his head like a rag doll before tossing her out over the edge of the rock like so much trash to be discarded.

Bruce watched the killer turn slowly away from where Amy's body was gone. There was a grin on his face. His features appeared beastly. Only the eyes looked human. He stared down at the spot where Bruce stood, and Bruce wondered if the killer saw him standing there. He looked into the eyes that were nothing more than black slits of death now. Chills raced through his body as he studied the killer and then suddenly he felt himself being drawn into the killer's mind of madness. They were connected somehow. Bruce felt his blood freeze. He wanted to look away from those eyes of death and destruction. His mind screamed for him to get the hell out of there, but the drift held him where he stood.

"Who are you?" the killer asked in a hushed voice, placing a hand on each side of his face.

He feels me, Bruce thought, repulsed by the man's presence inside his own mind.

The killer drew his fingers down along the sides of his face, leaving trails of blood on his skin. The dark lines made him look like a warrior preparing for battle. "You won't stop me," the killer seethed. "I am doing the work of God. I am saving these children from themselves."

Bruce trembled and recoiled in fear at the foreignness of that voice speaking inside his head, but somehow managed to make himself speak. "No, you're not," he whispered in a shaky, frightened voice. He felt his bladder release.

"But I am. I am saving the children before they become lost," the killer explained in an emotionless voice that felt like lizards crawling around his mind. Bruce's heart thudded loudly in his chest. He had never experienced anything like this before and he had no frame of reference to make sense of it. All he knew was that he wanted out from this nightmare more than anything he had ever wanted before in his life. He wanted to escape this drift, but something held him there, forcing him to listen to the madness being spewed in his mind.

"You will never stop me, demon," the killer growled, lifting his knife into the air and pointing the blade at Bruce.

"You're the one who's evil!" Bruce shouted, his paralysis breaking. He reached out to take hold of the killer, but the man disappeared like smoke in a glass jar. His arms closed around nothing but emptiness and shadows.

Bruce swung his head around to find the killer and suddenly found himself falling. The drift released him. He opened his eyes. The world shifted and he fell over to the side, throwing up; he tumbled from the stone, falling out over the water. He landed in a shallow pool of water beneath the flat rock. His shoulder slammed into the bottom, ending in a painful pop. He felt bones grind as it dislocated. He screamed underwater, drawing in a mouthful of dirty tasting liquid. Choking and gagging, he clawed for the surface with one arm, his injured arm useless. His head broke free, and he swallowed a lungful of air through choking coughs. Slowly, he made his way over to the mud-slick bank and dragged himself ashore.

Lying there in the afternoon sunlight, he gazed up at the sky. "Motherfucker," he mumbled, turning over and vomiting into the weeds growing along the stream beneath the falls. When he finished, he sat up uncomfortably, trying not to use his injured shoulder. He stood, holding onto his right arm, keeping it pressed tightly against his body. Stumbling over to a large oak tree that grew close to the falls, he leaned his forehead against the rough bark. It crumbled beneath the weight of his forehead. Silently, he counted to three. On three, he slammed his right shoulder into the tree as hard as he could. The shoulder ground back into position as his scream split the silence of the state park. He passed out.

Bruce woke later—much later. His shoulder was back where it needed to be. He wasn't sure how long he had been out. The arm hurt like a son of a bitch, the pain sending spikes of agony through his body, but he managed to stand and walk. As carefully as possible, he walked away from the falls, looking for a path that led up the hillside and back to the parking lot.

Bruce reached the parking lot a half-hour later, much longer than it should have taken him to get there. He fell into the driver's seat of his car and sighed. His socks and shoes and clothing were wet, but he was in too much pain to bother getting a towel from the back. Instead, he leaned slowly across the seat and gingerly opened the glove box. His right hand shook from the effort like a person suffering from

Parkinson's. His fingers felt numb. He wondered if he had caused more damage to his shoulder than he was aware of.

Lightning bolts of fire ran up and down his arm as he clawed inside the glove box with his near useless fingers. He found what he was looking for and pulled his hand back. He held a small pint bottle of vodka. He dropped the bottle between his legs, and with his left hand, unscrewed the cap. He picked the bottle back up and drank. The vodka burned on the way down, but felt wonderful. He drank again, and then a third time before resting the bottle back between his legs. From the center console he fumbled out a white plastic bottle of Ibuprofen and swallowed four, chased by another slug from the quickly emptying bottle of vodka. He leaned back against the seat and closed his eyes, waiting for his pain to subside.

Chapter 25

Bruce woke the next morning in incredibly horrible pain. His arm felt like someone was trying to twist it from his body. The right shoulder was a solid purple and black bruise that went all the way down to his elbow. He tried to move the arm away from his body, but the effort only caused him to scream into his pillow. Tears dribbled from his eyes, leaving wet stains on the cotton pillowcase. Using his good arm, he pushed away from the pillow and sat up. When he was ready, he placed his feet on the floor and padded uncomfortably across the room to the bathroom. He peed hands-free into the toilet, not bothering to flush after he finished. He sat carefully down inside the clawfoot tub next to the toilet, using his toes to turn on the water. The cold chipped enamel warmed quickly beneath his skin. He allowed the hot water to rise around his body like an old comfortable blanket. It felt wonderful. He stayed there in that tub until the water ran cold.

Bruce could move his arm some after his soaking, but knew he would need something other than hot water, ibuprofen, and alcohol for the pain. His body felt like he had been hit by an eighteen-wheeler and left for dead on the side of the road. It was a minor miracle that he had been able to walk out of that park on his own and make his way home, though he had no memory of how he had accomplished that.

Bruce stood naked in front of the medicine cabinet looking at his reflection in the mirror. He didn't look good. Black circles ringed his red swollen eyes. His shoulder looked like someone had used it for a punching bag. The right side of his chest was scraped raw as if he had gone over it with a sheet of eighty grit sandpaper. As best as he could figure, he must have scraped it up in the fall, but he couldn't remember.

"Fuck it," he mumbled, walking out of the bathroom and back across the room to his bed.

Somehow over the next thirty minutes he managed to dress himself. He grabbed his cellphone and car keys from the bedside table and left the apartment without hating the world too much. Downstairs, he found his car parked up on the curb again. The rear end was sticking out in the street so cars driving by had to swerve to miss it. He shook his head and walked to the driver's door, forcing his key into the lock. The door opened with a pained squeal and he cursed the universe.

"You should see someone," a voice said from across the street. Bruce swallowed and looked over his good shoulder. He saw Mr. Davis, a fifty-something African American with snow colored hair and thin mustache. He wore a blue Yankee t-shirt, white shorts, and bright white sneakers. His socks, also white, sagged just below his knees. An unlit cigar was perched in the corner of his mouth.

"It's fine, I'm fine," Bruce said dropping down into the driver's seat. A bolt of pain assaulted his body. He sucked in a deep painful breath and let it out slowly instead of screaming like he wanted to.

"You're lucky you haven't killed someone, young man," Mr. Davis said, wagging a finger at Bruce as his tiny Chihuahua took a dump in the grass between the sidewalk and the street. The dog eyed Bruce from across the street as if it were embarrassed that Bruce had seen him shitting in the grass.

"You should do something about that," Bruce said, pointing at the dog before closing his door carefully with his left hand. Mr. Davis looked down and shook his head at the animal. Bruce smiled, squinting his eyes at the sunlight pouring in through the windshield. and drove off. In his rearview mirror he saw Mr. Davis picking up the dog shit with a green plastic bag wrapped around his hand. *Good for you, jackass*, Bruce thought, turning onto Park Avenue.

Bruce stopped the car in front of a three-story red brick building on Burnside Avenue in East Hartford not too far from his office. He parked along the curb in front of a sign that read "no parking anytime." Reaching up, he removed a placard from the sun visor and tossed it on the dashboard. Official Police Business was scrawled across the front in black block letters. A woman exiting the building with a small child in tow shook her head at him as he crossed the sidewalk to the steps. Bruce forced a smile as she stomped passed him, dragging her child with her. He felt sorry for the kid as he started up the steps. The woman paused at his car and read the placard left casually on the dashboard. She wrinkled her nose as if she had sniffed something rotten and then continued down the sidewalk, the child squalling behind her as she went.

Screw her and the horse she rode in on, Bruce thought as he entered the building, the door closing silently behind him. The blast of A/C as he walked through the door felt wonderful. He paused, eyes shut, and simply enjoyed it.

"Can I help you?" a young woman with blonde hair asked from behind a reception desk. Bruce opened his eyes and stared at her, and the pair of pink glasses perched on her narrow pointed nose. She was new. He despised her already.

"Veronica," Bruce said, walking up to the desk and leaning against it for support. He was in no mood to waste words. His shoulder was on fire and each breath he took felt like needles punching through his skin.

"Do you have an appointment?" the woman asked, knowing that he didn't because he was a child, and he didn't have a child with him.

"Just tell her Bruce Westman is here. She'll see me."

The woman behind the desk gave Bruce a look that said she was one step away from calling the police, but she stood just the same and walked through a doorway to her right. She came back out a few minutes later and told Bruce to take a seat in the waiting room. Bruce smiled at her and did as she asked.

The waiting room was a new special level of hell that most people never have to experience, if they're lucky. It smelled like a combination of shit, piss, puke, and baby formula. Tiny humans ran everywhere while a purple dinosaur laughed way louder than was necessary on a television mounted to the wall. The noise in the room was made even louder as mothers had to shout at each other to be heard above their children. It all caused Bruce's arm to hurt even more and his head to join in on the party. He took a seat as far away from the action as possible, though distance was all relative in such a small space.

A tall brunette stepped through the door beside the front desk a few minutes later. She wore a tan knee-length skirt and a white blouse. A stethoscope hung around her neck. Her hair was pulled back in a tight bun that made her appear stern. Stylish glasses sat on her nose; a silver chain wrapped around the back of her neck. She smiled a perfect smile at Bruce as mothers in the waiting room looked on, hoping it was their turn to go back.

"Bruce Westman," the doctor said, holding out a hand to him. Bruce took the hand in his left hand and held onto it affectionately. He stood slowly.

"Can you see me, Veronica?" Bruce asked, trying to hide how much pain he was in and doing a lousy job.

"Of course," Veronica said.

"Thanks," Bruce replied, following Veronica back through the door.

Veronica led Bruce back to an exam room at the end of a short hallway. There was an exam bed, two chairs, a small desk, and a computer in the room. On the walls were pictures of ducks and puppies and kitty cats playing with balls of yarn. Another poster warned that the flu was not to be taken lightly. Veronica was a pediatrician. Her normal patients were small children and on that rare occasion, Bruce Westman.

Bruce and Veronica had met in high school and became quick friends. They had gone out on a few dates but decided they weren't right for each other and simply remained friends. In their senior year, Veronica had started dating one of the linebackers on the football team. He was tall, big, and strong. He had shoulder length blonde hair and blue eyes that most girls fell hard for. He was the kind of person used to getting his way and when Veronica refused to give in to him one night, he forced himself upon her. She told Bruce what had happened that night a month later when they were well into a bottle of Seagram's. They held each other as tears spilled. Bruce's heart broke.

After that night, Bruce had made it his mission to learn everything he could about Todd Casamino, linebacker and rapist. He followed the shithead after practices and games. He found out that he worked at the K-Mart in Manchester and that Todd Casamino liked to smoke pot behind that K-Mart on his breaks and after work.

Bruce waited for the perfect time to confront him, and it came one evening when Todd had to work late. As the lights dimmed inside the store, Todd came out the front doors, walking over to his cherry-red Mustang that his parents had bought him on his last birthday. Todd drove the Mustang around to the back of the store and parked away from the security lights. Bruce watched from a stand of sumac trees that grew beside the drainage ditches behind the K-Mart. He had an unobstructed view of the car and its occupant.

Another car joined Todd a few minutes later, its headlights washing over the fields behind the store. Two kids exited and joined Todd beside his Mustang. The skunky smell of marijuana quickly filled the air. Giggled laughter followed. The sound of farts and burps filled the gaps of conversation about how this one wanted to fuck this girl or how that girl had blown one of them behind the gym. It was all rather boring and totally unbelievable.

Todd's friends left an hour later, leaving him stoned and sitting atop a drainage pipe facing away from the back of the store. Bruce snuck up on Todd with a baseball bat in his hand and a ski mask pulled down over his face. His approach was silent, and Todd had no idea he was there until Bruce tapped the end of the bat against the pipe. It made a hollow thunking sound and Todd turned around slowly, too stoned to understand what was happening. Confusion filled his eyes as he studied Bruce standing in front of him with a baseball bat in his hands, his face hidden like something out of a horror movie.

"Who the fuck are you?" Todd slurred, his eyes half closed.

"Don't worry about who I am," Bruce answered, lifting the bat to his shoulder. "Just know that your career as a football player is finished, dickhead."

Bruce brought the bat down with all the force he could muster onto Todd's right knee. It exploded like a grape beneath a shoe. Todd screamed and grasped at the injured knee as he fell from the drainage pipe. Bruce drove the bat down again on his left knee and Todd screamed even louder. His pants were soaked in blood as tears and snot covered his face. He tried to crawl along the dirt and weeds. Bruce drove the end of the bat into Todd's groin, and he curled up into a ball, cupping his balls and begging for Bruce to stop. Bruce smiled beneath the ski mask.

"If I ever hear that you've touched another girl against her will, I'll fucking kill you, asshole. Do you understand me?" Bruce asked, bringing the bat up again as if to swing it.

Todd screamed a high-pitched cry of pain, nodding his head that he understood. He tied to crawl away again and Bruce lunged at him. The former linebacker screamed again in terror, sounding like a little girl instead of a boy on the verge of becoming a man. The smile beneath Bruce's ski mask spread even wider.

"Fucking pussy," Bruce whispered through the mask, his breath hot and steaming. He turned and walked off into the high grass behind the K-Mart. Todd lay there in the dirt in front of the drainage pipe, crying. Bruce didn't bother to look back as he walked away whistling a tune through the ski mask.

He never told Veronica what he had done that night, but suspected that she knew. In truth, he loved her like a sister and would do anything to protect her, and he suspected that she knew that, too. He always felt so safe coming to her because he knew he wouldn't have to answer any questions about what had happened. The VA would have treated him for free, but that treatment would have come with questions that he didn't want to answer. They already thought he was fucking nuts, so he didn't need to add to it.

"So, you look like shit," Veronica said as she sat down in one of the chairs. Bruce sat on the end of the exam table.

"I need something for my shoulder," Bruce said, struggling to get out of his shirt. Veronica jumped up and helped him. She gasped when she saw the shoulder.

"Oh my God, what happened?" she asked as she set the shirt down.

"I fell down a waterfall," Bruce said.

"Really?" she asked as she began to examine the shoulder. "Did you dislocate it again?"

"Yeah, but I think I managed to pop it back in."

"What a dumbass," Veronica muttered. "You should have gone straight to the emergency room. One day you're going to try that and really fuck yourself up."

"Look, I just need something for the pain to get me through the day," Bruce explained.

"Let me clean those scratches up for you," Veronica said, pointing at the nest of red welts covering his chest and back. "You might have cracked a rib." Bruce nodded, letting her get to work. She finished a short time later, wrapping gauze around his chest to cover the scrapes and cuts. She placed his right arm in a sling that kept it close to his body and gave him some free samples of Hydrocodone.

"No more than two of those," she explained. "And no drinking while taking them."

"You're no fun," Bruce said, bringing his shirt over his head. "How long should I wear this?"

"Keep it on for a few days, but try to move your arm around every now and then. If the pain gets worse, or you have too much difficulty breathing, I want you to go the emergency room at Manchester Hospital."

"Sure," Bruce replied, knowing he wouldn't.

"I'm serious, Bruce. Without x-rays, I have no way of knowing if you did anything on the inside. You could have messed something up in there really bad," she scolded.

"I got it, emergency room if it gets worse," Bruce said, standing up from the exam table.

"You just be careful, Bruce Westman. You're one of my very best friends and this world would be so much sadder without you."

Bruce brushed the side of her face with his good hand guiding her toward him. He kissed her softly on the cheek.

"Same goes for you, lovely lady," Bruce said. Veronica opened the door and he stepped out of the room, walking down the hallway and out into the reception area. A quick glance into the waiting room informed him that hell was well populated. He cringed and went to the entrance. Behind him he heard Veronica speaking.

"Ashley Williamson," she said. Bruce smiled and walked out into the sunlight.

Never in a million years, he thought, walking down the steps to the sidewalk.

Chapter 26

The killer sat in his old worn recliner looking out the picture window of his home at the street beyond the living room. The recliner was a familiar place of refuge for him while looking at the outside world from the safety of his house. He had little interaction with what he saw on the other side of the glass, but at times he enjoyed watching what took place beyond the shelter of his living room. It allowed him to feel like he was part of the world instead of someone destined to be separated from the world. He imagined that that was how all the prophets of God felt.

A tall glass of iced tea rested beside him atop a ring-stained coffee table. The table had once belonged to his mother, but now it was his coffee table. Beads of moisture ran down the glass, spreading out over the coffee table, weaving an intricate web of water between the forgotten rings. The glass he drank from belonged to his mother as well, but like all her things, it now belonged to him.

The view outside the picture window was an obstructed view of the street in his quiet neighborhood. Shrubs grew beneath the window, hiding the front of the house from anyone passing by. The shrubs also provided excellent cover for the basement windows along the front side of the house. Similar shrubs grew along the sides and back of the house as well, covering those basement windows from prying eyes, even though they were all boarded over in case someone should want to snoop. In the front yard, two full grown maples grew with their wide reaching limbs casting twisted shadows over the grass. The trees worked to keep the house secluded from the rest of the neighborhood like

Templar Knights standing guard over everything while the killer went about his work safely tucked away inside. At night, if it was windy, the shadows cast by the branches looked like the gnarled hands of ancient giants scratching at the interior walls of the house. The killer enjoyed sitting in his recliner during those times as well, watching as the ancient limbs danced around the living room.

Max lay sprawled in his master's lap trying to sleep, his soft snores and occasional dog farts interrupting the silence of the house. He could sense that his human was anxious, and this anxiousness caused Max to be alert. He knew the cycles of his master, and he knew that soon they would go outside and search for other humans to bring back home.

The killer glanced down at his dog as the animal cut an especially loud fart. He wrinkled his nose at the smell and waved his hand over the dog's body. Max's tail wagged back and forth as if he were proud of what he had just done. The killer shook his head and looked back out the window. He knew it wouldn't be long now before God provided the next child for him to save. He could feel it racing through his body.

It was like a nagging itch that began in his head. It spoke to him from outside his mind, whispering that the time for salvation was coming soon. Whispering that he needed to hunt, to capture, to kill. Soon the itch would become a fire that was all consuming and the only way to extinguish that fire was to save someone. He knew that somewhere out there beyond the walls of his home was a girl in need of saving before she was lost forever.

The world was full of such children, so lost and in need of being found. The killer smiled, absently stroking Max's exposed belly as he continued to stare through the picture window. The dog's tail wagged, and his eyes split apart. Max gazed up at his owner and the killer smiled down at his dog.

He was so ready to hunt again. He could feel it inside his body now like tiny bolts of electricity just sparking beneath his skin, crawling around like so many insects in his brain.

It hadn't always been like that for him, this itch, this need, to do God's will. It hadn't always been a part him, living there just beneath the surface like some soulless creature beneath the waves. In the beginning, it hadn't even been something he had been aware of crawling around inside his mind like thousands of tiny little annoying ants chewing on the tiny bits and pieces of his brain. In fact, that first time he had taken a life, the itch hadn't even existed, but maybe that was because the life he had taken hadn't even been a real human life.

According to his mother, the life he had taken had been nothing more than an animal, undeserving of life. Nothing more than a speck of dirt on the bottom of a shoe needing to be scraped off like dogshit on a curb. The life that he had taken counted for nothing.

The killer had grown up in Enfield, Connecticut, in a small neighborhood of World War Two built homes. These houses were on the small side: two bedrooms and a master, galley-style kitchens, one bathroom, and a family room up front that always faced the street. The basements were all unfinished unless the owner of the house had the money to finish them, but most didn't because this was a working class neighborhood. His mother hadn't had any money back then because it had been just him and her. His father had run off before he had been born and had never been a part of his life.

The basement in their house was a cold dank place full of monsters and ghosts and creepy crawlers that scuttled over the walls. It had been all exposed concrete, chipping and crumbling away in places. The smell down there was dirty and dusty. It smelled like death and decay and mold. The basement in his house was a place for the furnace, the hot water heater, and the few Christmas decorations that they had. It was not a place where someone wanted to be forgotten like used clothing or boxes of pictures of long-gone relatives.

The house in Enfield was what they called a starter home, something to be used for a short time by families of little means until they could afford something better. His father had bought the home on credit for his mother while she was pregnant, but he had left a short time after that with no explanation and no forwarding address. So, it was just him and his mother surviving together, scraping by as best as they could.

At the age of eight, his mother had to move from that house to a tiny two-bedroom apartment above a bakery at the border of Hartford and Windsor. The bank had taken the house from them because she hadn't been able to afford to pay the mortgage. He had a distant memory of holding his mother's hand standing on the sidewalk while men carried their belongings outside.

His mother worked the counter of the bakery below their new home six days a week while he sat upstairs watching television, reading old comics, or doing homework. At the end of her shift, she always brought him a Danish and a pint-sized carton of milk. One of his happiest memories of growing up was sharing an apple Danish with his mother at their tiny kitchen table in that apartment above the bakery, but sadly not all the memories from that apartment were happy ones.

The truth was, he really didn't have many good memories of growing up. He didn't get to play catch with his father or go fishing on a pond or lake. Other children his own age hadn't liked him very much. They made fun of him all the time because he had been so skinny and uncoordinated. He was always the last kid picked for games in gym class. From the start of kindergarten, children had picked on him something fierce. Once a week someone chased him home or beat him up if he was too slow to escape. The only kind person in his life had been his mother.

As bad as most of this had been, they were not the worst memories of his young life. Those memories, the real bad memories, made all the bullies who spit on him, knocked his books in the mud, smashed his bagged lunches into mush, or beat him up for no other reason than just because they could seem like happier moments. The worst memories, the real bad memories of his young life, involved the parade of men that came and went through that apartment he shared with his mother above the bakery. He hated them so much and all the strange sounds that bled through the walls of their small apartment at night. He hated having to listen to the moans and grunts coming from his mother's bedroom. He hated the idea of all those strange men touching his mother in ways that they shouldn't have.

If he was lucky, most of the men only spent a night or two, taking advantage of his mom, but a few had stayed longer. Of these, only a couple had tried to be nice to him, but most of them could have cared less if he lived or died, and they did little to hide how they felt. They were assholes for sure, but even they were not the worst. There were two men who stood out above all the others earning the title of major assholes.

He met the first man when he was nine. He looked much older than his mother. He had gray sideburns and a salt and pepper mustache above his upper lip that looked like a mutated caterpillar. The top of his head was bald and littered with brown freckles. The little hair that he had circled his head like a lopsided horseshoe. He always wore bright shirts with the top three buttons unbuttoned so his hairy chest sprang out like tangled wires.

This man just appeared one night when his mother came home from work. He walked through the door with her on his arm as if he already owned her, and he didn't leave the apartment the next day like all the others when she went back to work. She called him Sid, but he was nothing more than a stranger, and yet she allowed him into their home.

Sid hadn't been a mean person. He fixed dinner for the two of them and sat down to watch television after they finished eating. Sid always wore a pair of stained white underwear and a matching white t-shirt while watching television. When his mother wasn't home, Sid always told him to lose his pants and relax like a grown up.

One night, Sid had him sit in his lap while they watched television. Sid wore his stained white underwear, and he wore a pair of Spiderman Underoos. During a commercial, Sid's hands settled against his stomach. They felt rough and hard against his soft skin and even tickled. Sid's hands hadn't become uncomfortable until his fingers began to dig and knead at his skin. He tried to get off of Sid's lap, but Sid held onto him with one hand while the other hand pushed down on his Underoos. The Underoos slid down his legs and fell to the floor. Sid's hand dropped into his lap, brushing against his tiny nine-year-old penis.

A scream interrupted what was happening inside the apartment between him and Sid. He looked around and saw his mother in the doorway, her work apron bunched in one hand, a box of Danish in the other. Sid stood quickly, knocking him from his lap. He fell painfully to the floor and cried out, landing on top of the discarded Underoos. His mother screamed again and dropped the box of Danish. She flew from the doorway with a bloodcurdling scream. He looked up at Sid and saw that his penis was pushing against the stained fabric of his underwear. It looked so large hidden behind the cotton underwear. He looked down at his own penis and saw that it was stiff as well but nowhere near as large as Sid's.

His mother reached Sid still screaming. He wondered absently if she had even taken a breath from the door of the apartment to the living room. She raked her fingernails across Sid's face. Red lines of blood rose up where the nails had just been. His mother's screams finally paused as she swallowed a mouthful of air. Words poured out from her mouth, all jumbled together but he understood what she said just the same. "I'll kill you, I'll kill you, I'll kill you, motherfucker. Get out, get out, get out, get out!"

Somehow, Sid managed to gather up his pants from the floor while under a constant barrage of punches and slaps and slashes. He fled the apartment with his mother at his back, running down the hall.

"I'll kill you if I ever see you again!" she shouted as Sid ran down the stairs at the end of the hall. The door slammed shut. She locked it and turned around, falling back against the door. She looked down at him and burst into tears, covering her face with her hands. He ran to her now, crying, thinking that he had done something wrong.

"Don't cry, baby," she said, scooping him up in her arms. "That was nothing but an evil man, you understand me, baby? An evil man bent on making you sin, but I stopped him. I saved you from that sin. Do you understand what I'm saying, baby?" He nodded, looking over his mother's shoulder at the locked door. "And if I ever see him again, I'll kill him, I promise you that. I'll kill him dead because evil doesn't deserve to live in God's world," she explained, hugging him tighter. He nodded again and hugged his mother back just as tight as she was hugging him.

The next time he met someone evil like that was when he was eleven years old. This man hadn't been any different than all the others before him. His mother had come home from work as she did every evening, except this time she had a man with her. This was a man he had never seen before and one that left him feeling uneasy. If someone had asked why he felt that way, he would not have been able to say, but now, so many years later, he knew. He understood evil, and that man was evil.

The man was tall with dark hair swept straight back. He stood several inches taller than his mother, who was tall for a woman. He had a lean build that said he might be a whole lot stronger than he appeared. He felt dangerous, unpredictable. His eyes were the deepest blue he'd ever seen before. They looked as if they had been painted on him like the eyes of a doll. They looked empty and lifeless, as if love and emotion had never existed in them before.

The man and his mother sat at the kitchen table drinking coffee and talking that night while he watched television in the next room. Every so often he caught the man looking his way, glancing into the living room with those lifeless eyes. Those glances left him feeling dirty and frightened. He wanted to tell his mother to send the man away. He wanted to walk right into that kitchen and warn her, but those horrible, haunted eyes kept him away. At ten o'clock he went to bed while they still sat talking. He was glad to go to bed for a change because it allowed him to get away from those eyes.

Later that night he woke from what he believed had been a nightmare. For a second, with his eyes open, he believed he was still dreaming because he heard the muffled sounds of his mother crying in the next room. Her cries weren't the ones she made when she had a man with her, and they were doing it. He lay still beneath his dark ceiling listening, making sure they weren't the sex sounds he was used to hearing.

The cries he heard through the wall of his bedroom frightened him. They sent shivers up his spine and goosebumps crawling across his skin. Sitting up slowly, he eased himself out of his bed and made his way to the door. He paused at the door to listen. The cries were fainter here at the door, but he was sure that they weren't the normal sex sounds his mother made. She sounded scared and frightened. He stepped out of his room and crept down the hall to his mother's doorway. The hallway, short as it was, was full shadows cast by the streetlights in front of the apartment building. The shadows looked like hungry monsters hunting for flesh to feed upon.

A cold sweat covered his skin as he stood there in front of his mother's door, hand hovering above the doorknob. It sounded like his mother was crying into a pillow on the other side of the door. He twisted the doorknob. The door opened just enough to see through the thin crack between the door and the jamb. What he saw through that crack in the dim light of the bedroom both scared him and confused him.

His mother was naked, flipped over on her stomach. The milky white skin of her ass looked pale in the moonlight that filtered in through the bedroom window. For a moment he thought she was dead, and that he was looking at her ghost. The man that had come home with her that night was on his knees behind her, positioned between her legs. He was naked as well. His skin was darker than his mother's. He looked like one of the shadow monsters in the hallway crawling along the walls.

The man had a hand pressed against the side of his mother's face, forcing her head down into her pillow. She made soft painful groaning sounds as the man clawed at her legs, forcing them apart, forcing her butt further up into the air. He was making deep grunting noises while slamming his body into her upraised ass. His mother screamed a muffled scream into the pillow. The man was hurting her. He grabbed a handful of hair and yanked her head up, leaning down as he did so.

"You better shut the fuck up and take this like the whore that you are, or I'll kill you when I'm finished and then fuck your little boy in the ass before I kill him too," the man growled, letting go of her hair. He punched her in the back of the head and her face fell back into the pillow as he thrust against her again.

On tiny, silent bare feet, he stepped into the bedroom. The floor was cool beneath his feet. It felt like ice on a pond during the winter. He crossed the room as the man continued to thrust against his mother. He never saw him walk into the room, but his mother had. Her eyes were wide and terrified as she followed him without moving her head. The man slapped her hard across the ass, first with one hand and then the other. The sound of the slaps echoed loudly in the room. Twin red handprints marked where he had struck her. Tears fell from her eyes. He could see them glittering like stars in the meager light leaking in through the window. The image pained him and fascinated him at the same time.

"You fucking bitch whore, you better let me fuck you all I want or it's only going to get worse," the man growled, punching his mother in the back of the head again while ramming himself up against her.

He forced himself to look away from his mother. On silent feet, he made his way toward the dresser against the wall.

He opened the top drawer, the squeal of dry ancient wood filling the room. The man stopped what he was doing to his mother and looked over his shoulder. His insides turned to ice as the man's cold lifeless eyes fell upon him. Knowing he had only seconds now, his fingers scrambled inside the drawer, searching for what he wanted. Searching for what he knew should be there because his mother had shown him that it was there.

"What the fuck are you doing in here, freak?" the man shouted, pulling away from his mother. He tried to ignore the man as his fingers swept back and forth feeling around the drawer. Finally, he felt cold hard steel beneath the tips of his fingers. He grasped the gun in his small hand and brought it out from the drawer. It was the snub-nosed Smith and Wesson 38 revolver that his mother kept there in case of an emergency. He held the gun in both of his hands, pointing it at the man as he started to get off the bed.

"You better put that back, shit stain," the man grumbled, his stiff dick bouncing up and down in the light from the window, pointing at him just like the gun he pointed at the man. Unable to stop himself, he wondered which of them would fire first.

Behind the man, his mother sat up. She grabbed the man from behind, digging her fingernails into his flesh. The man spun and slammed his fist into her face. Blood exploded from her nose and she fell back against the headboard. The man turned back around. His face was red with rage, and his eyes, large and vicious looking, cut through him like knives. He wanted to crawl away and hide in a closet somewhere, but somehow, he managed to stand his ground.

His mother sat up on the bed again. Blood ran down from her face, soaking into the sheets and blanket. She looked dazed and hurt. Fury filled his mind at the sight of his mother.

His heart broke. He gripped the gun even harder, slipping his index fingers over the trigger. He began to squeeze. Something clicked beneath the pad of his index finger. He squeezed a little harder and then everything slowed down to a crawl.

"You going to shoot me or what, fuck wad?" the man asked, taking a step toward him, his cold, cold blue eyes blazing like liquid ice.

The gun roared in the small room like unexpected thunder on a hot summer's night. A bright yellow flame shot from the barrel as dust and dirt burned away behind the flight of the bullet. A small round hole appeared in the man's chest just below his right nipple. A thin ribbon of blood ran a crooked path down from the hole and over the man's stomach. The man looked down at the hole in his chest, shock and confusion replacing the look of rage and fury that had just been on his face. Slowly, he dropped to his knees. That cold, hurtful lifelessness left his eyes now, replaced by fear and uncertainty.

His mother screamed. Her hands covered her face, smearing the blood there so it looked like a horrible mask one bought on Halloween. She looked terrified.

He pulled the trigger again without knowing that he had, and a second hole appeared in the man's chest just to the left of the first. Blood pumped out from that hole in a steady stream instead of just a trickle. The man coughed once and fell face first to the floor with a wet smack. More blood seeped from beneath his body. His fingers flexed; one leg spasmed, smashing his toes into the floor.

The gun clattered to the floor making an awful sound inside the bedroom. He looked down at his hands, at his fingers, turning them over as if they belonged to someone else. His mother appeared out of nowhere sweeping him up in her arms. She took him from the bedroom squishing his face to her naked breasts. He had to fight to breathe because she was holding him so tightly against her. She didn't let go until they sat down on the couch.

"You stay here, Michael," she said, standing back up. "Don't you move from this spot, my special little boy." He nodded and stuck his thumb in his mouth, something he hadn't done since he had been a very, very young child. He watched his mother go back into her bedroom with wide frightened eyes. She returned a few minutes later with the gun. Her blood was smeared on the handle and the barrel.

"It's going to be okay, Michael," his mother said as he continued sucking on his thumb. "He was nothing more than an animal, do you understand me? Nothing more than an animal trying to hurt your mother, and you protected me. He was trying to make me sin and you saved me from that sin. You kept me from sinning like an angel sent from God." He smiled around his thumb, nodding. He held onto those words from his mother as she disappeared back inside her bedroom, taking the gun with her. He didn't move from the couch. Eventually he lay down, curled up in a tight ball, thumb still in his mouth, and slept. Visions of angels filled his dreams.

Chapter 27

Michael stood up from his chair and walked to the picture window. He looked out at his quiet street in his quiet neighborhood. It was still early afternoon, not much after twelve, and the sun was shining bright with only a few puffy white clouds in the sky to mar the perfect blue. It was a typical summer afternoon in Southern New England. *Just the right kind of day to begin a hunt*, he thought.

The street outside the window of his modest house was empty. There were no neighbors outside doing yardwork or checking mailboxes for junk mail and bills. It was so quiet. The kind of day Michael Abernathy, an angel of God, liked so much. He smiled broadly, focusing on his reflection in the glass. He liked what he saw there in the reflection. He looked so normal.

It's such a good day to be alive, he thought, taking Max's harness from a hook on the wall. The leash, still attached to the harness, dangled down from its silver ring. "Come on, Max," Michael said, holding the harness out. Max jumped from the chair, excited to leave the house. His tail wagged back and forth like a fan on a hot afternoon as he rose up on his hind legs so his owner could place the harness over his head.

In the kitchen, Michael placed his Red Sox ballcap on his head and his sunglasses over his face. He paused at the back door with his keys in one hand. "I need to deliver something before our walk today, Max," he said, lifting a small package from the floor. It was addressed to a place in Florida and contained a handmade doll that looked like the child it was going to belong to soon. The eyes were blue and the hair all blonde curls. The lips were red and puffy, the nose tiny. The doll wore a flowered dress that matched the dress the child wore in the picture her parents had sent.

With the package tucked under an arm and Max at his heel, Michael walked out the back door of his house, making sure to lock the door behind him. He gave the doorknob three quick twists to the right and then three to the left. He always did this the same way every time when he left the house. It was always better to be careful than to be caught because of a mistake. At the driveway, he opened the driver's side door and Max jumped into the car ahead of him. The vehicle was parked safely beneath an old oak tree, the branches spreading out in all directions, covering the driveway and the detached garage in a cave of shade and shadows. Max sat in the passenger seat of the car while Michael placed the box in the backseat before getting behind the wheel.

"Are we ready, Max?" Michael asked, looking over his shoulder as he backed out of the driveway. He never used the backup camera on the car because he didn't trust it. His mother had always said, "Cameras lie, Michael. Never trust a picture of something that you can see with your own eyes. Bad men can do all sorts of thing to a picture."

Michael backed slowly down the driveway and out into the street, pulling away slowly, mindful to obey all the traffic laws. "You never get in trouble for doing what's right," his mother had said many times while he was growing up.

Never never ever ever hunt in your own backyard, he thought, driving down the street. "I'm much too smart for that, too smart by half," he whispered over the steering wheel as he came to a complete stop at a stop sign. "Mama always said that about me, Max. She always said I was too smart by half." Max wagged his tail and looked out the passenger side window as the car rolled away from the stop sign.

Michael pulled into the post office on Silver Lane in East Hartford, parking beside a blue Chevrolet Cruz. He cracked the driver's side and passenger side windows for Max and walked into the building to take care of his business. He came back outside five minutes later and drove away singing. "A hunting we will go, a hunting we will go, hi ho the Derry-o, a hunting we will go." Max wagged his tail excitedly.

Twenty minutes later, Michael parked his car across the street from the old Marco Polo restaurant on the East Hartford Manchester town lines. The family that had owned the restaurant sold it several years ago and the name changed, but to him it would always be the Marco Polo. He had never been inside the restaurant because his mother could not afford such an extravagance like that, but it did hold a special place in his mind.

Every winter his mother took him sledding at Wickham Park and they would always park across the street from the Marco Polo, so they could cut through the trees at the bottom of Wickham Hill. Back then, in those far away memories of childhood, Wickham Hill had seemed like the next best thing to climbing a mountain. It went up and up into the gray winter sky, a hill without end, and when he came back down on his saucer, he felt like he was flying.

Michael set Max on the ground, making sure the leash was secured, and locked his doors. They cut through the trees just as he and his mother had done so many years ago. The ground was soft and squishy beneath his feet as he picked his way through the thin pines and stunted maples. Skunk weed and palm fronds covered the ground, leaving an odor of decay in the air. He tried to breathe through his mouth as much as he could as the two of them walked through all that muck. Max didn't even try to pee on anything as they cut through to the grass-covered hillside. Looking up, Wickham Hill didn't seem so intimidating now. It no longer reached the sky or was a hill without end. It was just a hill.

Wickham Park is a 130-acre private park on the East Hartford Manchester line just off Burnside Avenue. It was originally owned by Clarence Wickham who left the property to his wife under the condition that it become a park upon her death. Edith Wickham died in 1960 at the age of eighty-eight. The park opened officially on July 1, 1961, one year after Edith Wickham's death. Today the park is used by people from all over Connecticut for weddings, family reunions, baseball games, disc golf, and sledding in the winter. Teens from East Hartford and Manchester use the park as well as a gathering place for hidden parties driven by drugs and alcohol during the summer and sexual encounters under the trees or beneath the stars up on the hillside any time of the year. It was not unusual for park security to catch kids engaged in sexual acts on top of blankets after the sun had gone down or to find several gathered around the fireplace beneath the pavilion after the park had closed consuming alcohol or smoking weed.

Michael and Max climbed to the top of the hill and paused to catch their breath. Michael looked out at the Hartford skyline in the distance. City Place and Travelers Tower dominated the view. Max ignored all of this and peed on a clump of grass. Michael looked away from the view and eyed his surroundings through the dark lenses of his sunglasses. The top of the hill was empty. There was nothing here to hunt. He sighed and continued walking, following a path into the trees that led down to the ball fields.

Michael and Max returned to the car an hour later and drove away from Wickham Park, heading down Burnside Avenue back into East Hartford. Nothing in the park had presented itself as something that was in need of saving. He was disappointed that God hadn't provided anything, but

Michael was not discouraged. He knew God would provide someone eventually—He always did—and until then he would continue the hunt.

At the light at Forbes Street, Michael stopped and looked to the left and to the right. A young child sat on a silver and black bike with a banana seat at the curb studying the traffic for the right moment to race across the street. He was eleven or twelve years old, wearing a filthy white t-shirt that had given up trying to be white a long time ago, ripped blue jean shorts, and Converse sneakers that had seen better days. His socks pooled around his ankles just below his scabbed knees. Max growled at the boy from the backseat when he crossed in front of the car.

"Hush, Max," Michael said, following the boy to the opposite side of the street. Max huffed his displeasure and went back to watching the world on the other side of the passenger side window. Michael sighed and shook his head, pulling away from the light after it turned green. He drove the speed limit in the right-hand lane even though the traffic was light. He never passed anyone or changed lanes, and always came to complete stops at the traffic lights even when they were only yellow. He did nothing to draw attention to himself as he drove down the road, always keeping an eye on the sidewalk for any possibilities. He never knew when God would send a sign. As he passed the Newkirk and Whitney Funeral Home, he slowed so he could turn left into Martin Park.

Martin Park was a small park in East Hartford. Stories abound about the ghosts that prowl the park spooking the living. Many kids have told stories of seeing things in the park around the Huguenot House. Lights in the windows, the ghosts of a man and woman walking around the grounds. The house was built in 1761 by Edmund Bemont and originally stood on Tolland Street until the town of East Hartford had it moved to the park and set up as a museum.

The Bemont family was said to have suffered many tragedies through the years until the house was finally sold to an outsider. Today, for reasons unknown, the house is known as the Huguenot House. No one alive knows why, and no one by that name ever lived in the house, but that is what it's called. Ghost sightings had been reported over the years by those who restored the house and by those who work in the museum. The Historical Society of East Hartford decided to move the house to where it stands now and have it restored to its former glory.

Today, Martin Park attracts many children to its shaded hills, skate park, ballfields, and town pool. The stories of ghosts haunting the property only added to the attraction of the park. Many teenagers over the years have spooked themselves with real or imagined sighting of ghosts.

Michael parked his car near the pool and got out with Max. He walked around to the back of the car and removed a small backpack from the trunk. Inside the backpack was a false bottom that hid a roll of tape and two four-foot lengths of rope. On top of the false bottom was a bottle of water, a small bowl, and small amount of dog food in a Tupperware container. Michael shouldered the pack and walked with Max beneath the tall oak trees that littered the park. He paused while Max peed and glanced at the pool. He saw children swimming, running around the pool, and diving and jumping into the water, but nothing really drew his attention. He turned his eyes to the pavilion across from the pool and saw several teenagers sitting on top of one of the picnic tables beneath there. There were four boys and a girl sitting and chatting as if nothing in the world could harm them.

Michael's nose flared and he felt the itch quicken beneath his skin. It was like a bolt of electricity rolling just under the surface. He closed his eyes and let it take him for a moment before opening his eyes again and continuing to watch the children through the lenses of the dark sunglasses he wore.

Michael walked slowly, allowing Max to sniff and pee wherever he wanted as he studied the girl without making it look too obvious that that was what he was doing. The girl was young, maybe sixteen or seventeen. She wore a loose-fitting top that showed just a flash of breast every time she leaned forward and a sliver of pale stomach each time she leaned back. She wore matching white shorts that were much too short, only an inch or two beyond the split of her legs. Her hair was medium length and looked quite dark beneath the shadows of the pavilion.

"She might do, Max," Michael whispered as Max peed on an old oak tree, its branches twisted and bent overhead.

Michael smiled and nodded before continuing down the uneven sidewalk in the direction of the skate park. Boys and girls worked the concrete ramps and walls of the park on their skateboards risking life and limb. Everyone wore knee pads, elbow pads, and helmets like good little children, but the risk was real. Michael sat on a bench and watched, even though he really wanted to go back to the pavilion.

"The Lord will provide a way," he whispered at Max. The dog glanced up for a second before going back to sniffing the ground for left-behind messages from other dogs.

Michael stood after a few minutes and forced himself to walk deeper into the park toward the ballfields in the hopes that something would present itself to him. He regretted the decision immediately when he saw the crowds of parents cheering on their little leaguers. He felt so out place among the mothers and fathers. He imagined that he didn't look out place walking his dog, but that didn't change how he felt. He worked so hard at fitting in whenever he stepped outside his house, but he knew in the ways that really counted he didn't fit in with the world. He was the wolf among the sheep and the sheep always knew when a wolf was close. They might not see the wolf, but they always sensed it when it was nearby. A mother glanced his way as he and Max walked close to the short chain link fence. He knew she sensed something dangerous about him. He tugged at the dog's leash and Max followed back toward the pavilion. The woman watched the two of them walk away, unsure what it was about the man in the ballcap that had set off her radar.

As Michael crested the short hill behind the pool, he saw that three of the boys had left the pavilion and only the girl and one boy remained. The itch beneath his skin went into overdrive. It felt like lightning surging through his body. Every nerve was alive and on fire, every one of his senses heightened. He could smell the leaves rotting in the dirt beneath the trees. He saw the fractured rays of sunlight piercing the canopy overhead. He held the leash in a tight fist, bringing Max into the cover of the trees on the other side of the sidewalk. He knew it was dangerous now for anyone to notice him. He bent to tie his shoe while keeping an eye on the boy and the girl.

The boy that sat with the girl smoked a cigarette. Michael could see the cloud of gray smoke curling over his head. The boy looked older than the girl, eighteen or nineteen. He had short hair, cut close to his head in a buzzcut. He wore a black t-shirt with something on the front that Michael couldn't make out, torn blue jeans, and black boots. The girl smiled and giggled at the boy, pretending everything he said was funny or interesting. She even took an uncomfortable drag off the cigarette when he held it out to her to show that she was just as cool as him.

He's a wolf, Michael thought. Cocky and sure of himself, ready to pounce on his prey, and the girl was definitely his prey. Michael knew this about the boy just as he knew that God had provided the girl for him to save. She would be his now because even though the boy was a wolf, he was a very young and inexperienced wolf and Michael was doing God's work.

Michael studied the pair in the growing shadows stretching across the park. It was early evening and the sun was just beginning to set. He glanced up at the branches overhead as he straightened. *Does she need saving, or is she already lost?* he wondered. His body was on fire and he knew it no longer mattered because the need to act was about to take over. *Fight it*, he thought. *Wait for the right moment.*

Max tugged on the leash forcing Michael to look away from the two teenagers. "What?" he hissed down at the dog, afraid he might lose sight of the two teens. Max tugged harder on the leash, wanting to sniff at something just outside his reach. "Patience, Max," Michael said, looking over the rims of his sunglasses. "We all have to wait for the things we really, really want." Max tugged at the leash again, and Michael allowed the dog just enough slack to sniff at whatever it was that had his attention. Sighing, Michael looked back over at the pavilion and the boy and the girl were gone. He spotted them walking away, holding hands, the girl leaning up close to the boy. Michael's eyes narrowed. The boy casually flicked his cigarette into the trees. Michael's lip curled into a snarl, his dislike for the boy growing.

"Come on, Max," Michael whispered, tugging on the leash. Reluctantly, Max followed after the man. They walked slowly through the park, always keeping a safe distance from the two teens. They walked behind the pool between a couple of cars parked there and into the trees beyond. Michael smiled. God had provided an opportunity for him to act before it was too late.

"She needs to be saved, Max," he whispered at the dog, cutting behind the pool and entering the woods several minutes behind the boy and the girl.

Chapter 28

"I really need to head home, Steve," Ashley said, while allowing herself to be led deeper into the trees. Somewhere in the back of her mind her mother's warning about girls being attacked by some creep played in her head.

"Everything is going to be fine; don't worry, Ash," Steve said, holding onto her hand tightly so she couldn't get away. "We're just going down to the Hockanum River to watch the sun go down. Trust me."

"I can't be late again; my parents will kill me," Ashley replied, drawing even closer to Steve as they cut through the trees and brush. Long shadows spread across the forested floor like ghosts escaping from their graves as the sun fell lower in the sky. Birds and bugs competed with each other to see who could make more noise. The woods along the river were alive with life and energy, and the sexual tension passing between the two teens only added to it.

"It's going to be okay, Ash, I promise," Steve said, picking his way through the thick growth. Ashley sighed, continuing to walk alongside her friend. She knew she should leave but she didn't want to disappoint Steve or be thought of as a little girl afraid of her own shadow.

"I don't want you hanging out by yourself, Ashley," her mother had said as she walked out the door that day.

"I'm just going to the park, Mom," she had replied as she stepped out the door, her mother's worried eyes following her.

At the edge of the Hockanum River, Steve stopped and smiled at Ashley. His brown eyes flashed in the light of the setting sun. "See? I told you we weren't going all that far."

Ashley smiled and leaned into Steve's shoulder, hugging his arm to her body, pressing it tightly to her chest. She looked out over the river thinking how pretty it looked as dusk slowly settled over the forest. Everything felt alive and perfect. She forgot all about her mother's warning about those other girls whose bodies were found.

Behind the two teens, Michael quietly picked his way through the woods. He couldn't see them any longer, but he had an idea which direction they went. Max trotted along beside him, peeing and sniffing at trees and bushes as he went. Michael knew why the boy had led the girl down to the river. He wanted to make her sin, and Michael was the only one who could save her before it was too late. The boy was the evil that stalked the land and he had to be stopped or the girl would be damned forever. It was Michael's job to stop him and save her.

"Let's sit down over there," Steve said, drawing Ashley to a clear spot beside the water's edge beneath the branches of a tall weeping willow tree. The branches hung down like curtains forming a green web around them that only allowed the thinnest beams of the setting sunlight to penetrate. It was lovely under there, like something out of a fairy tale.

They sat in the weeds beneath the tree leaning into each other, holding hands watching the water drift lazily by. Steve turned slightly and kissed Ashley softly on the lips. She kissed him back. They fell slowly to the ground, kissing and touching each other, forgetting all about the setting sun and the slowly flowing river in front of them. The world collapsed all around them until they were the only ones left alive.

Michael reached the Hockanum River and paused. He listened to the gurgling water as it slowly flowed over rocks and stones. Mosquitoes flew around him, buzzing in his ear, nipping at his skin. Max strained on the leash to get at the water, but Michael held him back. He looked around for the two kids, thinking he might have lost them somewhere beside the muddy water of the Hockanum River.

"I can't," a soft voice whispered off to his left. Michael's head turned and looked that way. He saw the shadows of the boy and girl sitting in the grass beneath the branches of a weeping willow tree. The girl's shirt was off, but she still wore her bra. The boy was trying unsuccessfully to unsnap it with his clumsy inexperienced fingers, and she was telling him no. She was telling him to stop. It wasn't too late to save her. A smile crept over his face.

"Stay here, Max," Michael whispered, wrapping the leash around a fallen limb. Max sat in the tall weeds that grew beside the water's edge and watched. Michael crept along the bank of the river on silent feet, always keeping an eye on the two teenagers beneath the tree in case one of them saw him.

"I said no, Steve," the girl cried, pushing the boy away now, her voice more forceful than it had been a moment ago. Michael's smile grew, positive that he was right where he needed to be, where God had chosen him to be.

She wants to be saved, he thought, closing the gap quickly. He slipped silently through the hanging branches of the willow tree, reaching down and grabbing a handful of the boy's hair, lifting him up off the ground by his head. The boy, Steve, stood on his tippy toes with both of his hands clamped down over Michael's hand. "You will not make her sin!" Michael growled into the boy's confused face.

Steve cried out, struggling to free himself. Michael smashed his confused face into the trunk of the weeping willow tree over and over until there was no life left in that face. The thin bark around the trunk of the weeping willow tree was stained a dark shade of red. Blood ran down both sides of what was left of Steve's face from a large gash across his forehead. It soaked into his ratty t-shirt, dribbling to the ground like crimson tears.

The girl at Michael's feet unleashed a bloodcurdling scream that echoed out over the river. Max barked excitedly, poking his head up over the tall weeds. Michael wasted no time. He tossed the boy's lifeless body into the river. It splashed and bobbed up and down several times before settling down and floating away. He turned back to the girl who was still sitting there at his feet, shirtless and screaming. He slapped a hand over her mouth and shoved her head down into the weeds beneath the tree.

"Silence," Michael growled into her frightened face. She stared back at him with wild eyes full of absolute fear. Michael smiled. "I'm here to save you; you don't need to be afraid," he whispered, trying to sound reassuring. The girl screamed into the palm of his hand, her cries muffled, her tears running over his fingers. Michael smiled again and slammed her head into the ground just hard enough to knock her out, but not so hard that he killed her.

Once the girl was still, Michael looked around his surroundings, making sure they were still alone. He saw no one except Max, up and alert, straining to join him. Everything else alongside the river was just as it had been a few minutes ago—before he had interrupted the boy trying to force himself upon the girl. Michael smiled again and rolled the girl over onto her back. He drew the tip of a finger over the outside of her bra. A shiver of pleasure burned through his body. He felt himself stirring and looked up through the branches guiltily.

"No, no, no, we mustn't play with our toys," he mumbled, standing so he couldn't touch her again. "We have to leave her here, Max. We'll come back later and collect her." Max wagged his tail and strained against his leash. Michael took his backpack off and reached inside. He removed the bottle of water, the bowl, and the food from the backpack. He reached back inside and pulled at a string on the bottom of the backpack and the false bottom lifted up, revealing the hidden compartment. He removed the roll of duct tape and the three-three-foot lengths of rope he carried. He tore a piece of duct tape free and slapped it over her mouth. He tied her hands together behind her back and her feet together before securing her to the trunk of the weeping willow tree. He left her there shirtless, her bare back pressed against the boy's drying blood. He kneeled in front her, watching her breathe in and out. He touched the side of her face, gently, with care, stroking her tearstained cheek.

"I am going to save you," he whispered into her unconscious face, his sour breath washing over her skin. "I am the angel of God sent to prevent the sins of the world. I am your salvation."

His eyes dropped to the pale skin of her stomach and the pink bra she wore. He saw the band of her pink panties peeking up above the top of her shorts. He licked his lips as a shudder passed through his body. There was an ache inside him, but he knew he couldn't satisfy it. He couldn't be the source of sin in another's life.

"Won't do, won't do," he told himself, standing back up. He walked over to Max and freed him from the limb. "We'll come back later for her," he said before looking out over the water. He saw the body of the boy drifting slowly away downstream. It was face-down in the water. He knew eventually the body would be found, but he hoped it would be far away from here when it was. The body snagged on a pile of debris and hung up for a moment before continuing down the river. Michael watched until he couldn't see it any longer in the fading light. "He deserves nothing better," he thought to himself. "Maybe the water will wash away all his sins."

Michael returned to Martin Park well after midnight. He parked behind the pool, sitting there for several minutes making sure he was all alone. He picked his way back through the trees and found the girl where he had left her. She was awake now. Tears and dirt streaked her face. Tiny red bumps from chiggers and mosquitoes covered her chest and stomach. She no longer looked appealing with so many welts covering her skin and he wondered if she had an allergy to mosquitoes or chiggers.

"I should have covered you up," Michael said with just the right amount of concern in his voice. "I should have taken better care of God's prize." The girl tried to scream around the tape over her mouth, but the only sound Michael heard was a choked muffled cry. He smiled at her and freed her from the tree. "Do you understand that I saved you from that boy?" Michael said, tossing her over his shoulder. "I am an angel sent from God to preserve you from sinning." Ashley cried against his back as he carried her through the forest. She saw a dog walking beneath her. It was one of those small dogs that everyone liked. Branches lashed at her face, forcing her to close her eyes.

At the edge of the forest, Michael paused just behind the pool. His car was parked just a few feet away, but he wanted to make sure nothing had changed while he had been gone. Everything looked just as it had when he arrived in the park. He stepped from the protection of the trees and walked quickly to the rear of his car, opening the trunk with the remote dangling from his keys. He placed Ashley in the trunk quickly and closed the lid, placing the palm of his hand on the cold steel, stroking it tenderly. He had a hard-on but ignored it. "You be quiet in there," he whispered at the trunk before walking around to the driver's side door.

Chapter 29

The room where Ashley found herself was dark and cold. She guessed it was a basement somewhere inside a house. She was tied down to an exam table of some kind with her legs up in the air strapped inside a set of stirrups. The exam table was uncomfortable. The fake leather beneath her naked back was sticky and cold from her relieving herself during the night.

There were no lights on in the basement, but she was sure it was daytime outside because of the thin sliver of light showing at the top of the lone window she could see. The light wasn't much but it chased away a few of the shadows crawling around the room, and that was enough for now.

The basement stunk something awful. It smelled of piss and shit and things long decomposed. It reminded her of the convalescent home where her grandfather had died two years before. The hallways there had always smelled of pee and shit and other things she was sure were more disgusting than she could imagine. She had hated that place and had resented the fact that her mother had sent her grandfather there to die. She didn't understand why he couldn't have lived with them. She would have helped take care of him.

Goosebumps covered her naked body and her skin itched between her legs from pissing on herself. She had given up trying to escape because the ropes that were holding her down were secured tightly to the table. They cut into her skin whenever she pushed against them. She could flex her toes and her fingers but that was all the movement the stirrups would allow. The tape over her mouth had become this slimy strip of goo where her tongue had touched it all night long.

She could taste it in her mouth whenever she tried to swallow. It was disgusting and almost enough to cause her to vomit.

Above her head Ashley saw naked rafters weaving across the basement, disappearing into the shadows. She could see a spider's web clinging between two of the rafters. Every time someone walked on the floor above, the web vibrated and the spider stirred from the middle of the web where it was waiting for its next meal. She wondered if she would be its next meal while watching this fat hairy creature crawl along its silk strings.

Shortly after the sliver of light appeared at the top of the boarded-over basement window, she began to hear sounds from inside the house. A television played somewhere. She couldn't make out what was being said, but she knew the difference between the boxed sound of a television and real voices. From time to time she heard footsteps or the patter of an animal walking overhead. She wondered if it was the dog she remembered seeing in the woods after the man had come back. She had no memories of anything after the man had tossed her into the trunk of the car. After that, everything was a black hole.

While listening to the sound of the television, Ashley thought of her mom and dad. She wondered if they were as scared as she was. She thought that they might be. Her mother would be crying in the kitchen while her father paced back and forth like he did whenever he was worried about something. Her mother might even be smoking a cigarette, something she hadn't done in many years. Ashley wished she was with them right now. She would give anything for just one more moment with them.

An image of Steve crept into her mind, but she pushed it away before she could remember how he looked the last time she had seen him. *Poor Steve*, she thought, sobbing. The image of his smashed face swam through her thoughts despite her efforts to drive them away. She cried even harder, the tears mixing with everything else on the table beneath her back.

Michael sat in his recliner watching the evening news. His activities were everywhere now, but the police and the FBI were clueless. He wanted to hear more about the missing girl he had down in the basement. To see her mother and father standing in front of the cameras pleading for her life. It always thrilled him to see what failures their parents were. The cops had no idea who he was or where he lived. They were so far beneath him. God was his protection.

Grinning, Michael reached into a bowl and snagged two chocolate-covered almonds, popping them in his mouth while watching a commercial about cold medicine. The news came back on a few minutes later with a big breasted woman smiling into the camera. *She's a sinner for sure*, he thought, listening to her speak.

"We're going live now to the Manchester Police Department where Agent Jerrod Shelby of the FBI is answering questions."

"Do you have a description of the suspect?" a reporter in the front row asked.

"We believe he is a white male in his twenties or thirties. He looks normal, like any one of you. He may have a family. A wife, kids. He could be a neighbor of yours. He lives and works among us every day trying to fit in, but something about him stands out despite everything he does to blend. If you see something, anything, say something. Let law enforcement decide if it's important or not."

"Stupid man," Michael whispered at the screen, chewing on another almond.

"To the perpetrator of these crimes," Agent Shelby said, looking right into the cameras. "Turn yourself in. Don't wait for us to catch you because we will catch you."

"No, you won't, Mr. Fucking FBI man," Michael snarled at the television.

"We know you're hurting, crying out for help," Agent Shelby continued. "We know you're feeling like everything is out of control and your world is slipping away, but it doesn't have to be like that. We can help you get the help you need. You just have to turn yourself in."

"You're so stupid, stupid, stupid," Michael growled, standing up from his recliner. "I hate your fucking stupid face, and I hate you," he screamed at the television.

"Agent Shelby," a reporter shouted from the crowd of reporters. "Is the suspect sexually assaulting his victims?"

"No, he's not. We believe that he's incapable of engaging in anything sexual with them."

"You scumbag son of a bitch," Michael screamed, throwing the bowl of almonds at the screen. The television rocked back and tipped over in a shower of sparks. "Incapable! I'll show you how fucking incapable I am."

Ashley felt a cold wave of fear wash over her as the sounds from above echoed in the dark basement. The vibrations from the person upstairs moving around made the light jump above her only window. It made the shadows clinging to the walls and corners vibrate with each pounding footstep or crashing object overhead. She struggled against the ropes again, wishing she could free herself. It didn't matter; no amount of effort worked.

The commotion inside the house became more frantic and confused. Feet pounded on the floor overhead, and shouted curses rained down like a summer downpour. Ashley was terrified. "I'm going to die here," she thought, struggling even harder against the ropes, but to no avail.

The basement door flew open, slamming against the wall. Ashley jumped at the sound and froze, her eyes tiny little pinpricks searching her surroundings. A thick shaft of white light flooded into the basement, chasing away the shadows furthest from the exam table. Thundering footsteps pounded down a flight of wooden stairs. She heard every creak and rattle as the basement stairs struggled against the assault.

"I'm not some fucking impotent sissy boy!" the man shouted, walking with heavy footfalls across the dusty concrete floor. Ashley cut her eyes in the direction of his approach but couldn't see anything until the man stood over her. He looked like a giant straight out of her worst nightmares. His face was contorted and misshapen in his rage. He held his hands out toward her, the fingers bent like the claws of a dragon.

"I'm going to die, I'm going to die," Ashley thought over and over, feeling as if she were drowning in an ocean of fear.

Michael looked down at the frightened girl. She looked so perfect there on his exam table. So naked and exposed for all to see. She trembled with fear. Tears fell from her eyes, running down her cheeks. He reached down and wiped away a tear from her face while admiring how her tiny butt was lifted up just so from the table because of the stirrups. He could see the fear in her eyes as he wiped away another tear. "So sad," he thought.

"That man on the television said I can't," Michael whispered. Ashley didn't understand what he meant. "He thinks he's so fucking smart, but he's not. He's stupid, just like the rest of them. They can never stop me."

Ashley moaned from behind the tape covering her mouth. The man placed a shushing finger over the tape and looked at her thoughtfully.

She doesn't appreciate the fact that I saved her from that animal, Michael thought. *She doesn't deserve God's salvation.* A tight smile creased his face; his hands began to shake. He felt himself growing, becoming painfully hard. A red haze fell over his eyes.

"I'm going to die here," Ashley thought, looking up into the madness filling the man's face. "I'm so sorry, Mommy, I'm so sorry. I should have listened to you."

The man leaned down closer to her. His breath crawled over her skin. It smelled sweet, like chocolate. His mouth cracked open and Ashley saw something brown stuck between two of his teeth as his lips pulled back in a snarl. His nose wrinkled as if he smelled something disgusting and Ashley wondered if it was her. She hoped so. The man pulled his shirt up over his head revealing a chest covered in a thick patch of dark hair. The hairs looked like black curled wires, twisted into knots. His nipples stood out through all that hair looking like tiny round disks of stale bologna.

Oh my God, he's going to rape me, Ashley thought, suddenly more frightened now than she had been at the idea of dying. "Daddy, please help me," she cried silently behind the tape.

Michael undid his pants with trembling fingers. They dropped to the basement floor, puddling around his feet. He stepped out of the pants and his underwear followed. All he wore now was a pair of black dress socks which were pooled around the tops of his ankles. He climbed up on the exam table, placing his body between her legs. He looked into her frightened face, hearing the words of that FBI agent playing over and over inside his brain. The red haze grew darker until only the girl beneath him existed.

Ashley looked up in the red bloodshot eyes of the man kneeling between her legs, propped up on his hands. His face was only a few inches from her own. The sweet odor of chocolate was making her nauseous. She tried to look away, but that only allowed her to see his penis dangling down between his legs. It was soft and limp. The man grabbed it with one of his hands and began pulling on it.

"Come on, come on, you're not impotent. You can do this," Michael pleaded as he yanked harder on his dick, but nothing happened.

Ashley tried to shrink away from the man, but the ropes held her. She tried to force her legs together, but the stirrups kept them apart. She tried to look away from the man, but her eyes kept coming back to him yanking on himself, pleading for something to happen.

The man glared down at her. His face was just as red as his eyes. "It's your fucking fault, it's your fucking fault!" he screamed into her face, spittle flying. She watched as he climbed off the table, his dick just hanging there, limp between his legs. "It's your stupid fucking fault," he whispered, bending and disappearing below the exam table.

Michael bent down and reached into his black bag, which sat on the floor beside the exam table. He brought out his knife—the knife that he kept there for his special work. He dragged the tip of a finger across the blade. Blood dribbled down over his knuckle, dripping to the floor. His nostrils flared. He stuck the bleeding finger into his mouth and sucked on it, tasting the coppery flavor of his blood. The bleeding finger left a bright red streak across his tongue when he pulled it back out.

Michael straightened back up, smiling down at the girl. Her eyes fixed on the knife as he climbed back up on the exam table. His penis was no longer limp. It stood out straight and hard pointing at her face. He grinned as he grabbed it and lowered himself onto top of her. He forced himself inside her, pressing the tip of the knife against her breast as he did so. Blood flowered beneath the tip of the knife. He pulled it back, pulling himself out of her at the same time.

Michael watched the blood running down either side of her breast. It puddled in the valley between the breasts. He held his bleeding finger over the puddle of blood, allowing his own blood to drip down and mix with the girl's. He grunted low and deep and plunged the knife through her breast to the hilt just as he plunged himself back inside her. The feeling was amazing as he thrust in and out faster and faster, stabbing her with himself as he stabbed her over and over with his knife. He came inside her with an explosive rush of pleasure and horror.

Michael fell on top of the girl with a splat when he finished, his breathing coming in wild gusty gasps. Blood covered everything. Tissue clung to the wiry hairs of his chest. His face was bathed in the girl's blood. He tasted it on his lips, on his tongue, in his throat. Inside her, he felt himself softening but that did nothing to diminish how incredible he felt.

Michael ripped the tape away from the dead girl's mouth and leaned down and softly kissed her lips. He forced his tongue into her mouth, tasting the sliminess of the tape on her tongue. He pulled back and looked into the lifeless eyes. He was suddenly disgusted with himself. He leapt off the exam table and saw the gaping hole where her chest had been. It was full of blood and tissue and bits of floating bone. He cried. He fell across the body and cried and cried until his tears fell into the gore-filled cavity he created.

As the tears stopped, Michael stood back up. The basement floor felt cold through his socks. It felt like he was standing on an ice-covered pond. He reached for his clothing. The underwear, the shirt, and the pants were drenched in blood, but he put them on anyway. The basement floor around the exam table was covered in blood and gore. Looping tendrils of blood dripped down from the exam table. It looked like something out of his worst nightmares. He felt his gorge rising in his throat.

"I've done a really bad thing," he thought. "I've become the animal now. I made an innocent sin. Oh God, please forgive me, please," he cried into the half-lit basement, falling to his knees. The concrete bit through his pants. The cold chilled his skin. He remained like that in the blood and piss, praying over and over for forgiveness.

Max barked at the top of the stairs, snapping Michael out of his prayers. He looked over his shoulder and Max barked again. He sighed and stood, his clothes feeling tacky and stiff. He shed them, leaving them in a pile on the floor and walked toward the stairs wearing only his black dress socks again. He climbed the steps one step at a time. At the top, he opened the door and sat down on the tiled kitchen floor. It felt cool beneath his skin, but not cold like the concrete. Max placed his paws on his chest, whimpering, licking the blood and tears away from Michael's face.

"I failed, Max. I hurt that girl and made her sin. I'm no better than the animals. She'll never enter paradise now because of me." Max licked the dried blood from Michael's fingers. Michael continued sitting on the kitchen floor, leaning against the door jamb and Max continued licking until he tired of licking and simply curled up against Michael's leg and fell asleep.

Michael picked himself up from the kitchen floor as the last of the day slipped from the house. He made his way up the stairs to the master bathroom and turned on the shower.

Hot steaming water fell into the tub. He listened to the water falling, replaying over and over what had happened down in the basement. More tears fell from his eyes. He felt horrible as he got into the shower and sat down on the floor of the tub. The hot water fell on him, kneading his shoulders. He closed his eyes and willed the world away as pink-colored water ran down the drain.

After showering, Michael went into his bedroom and dressed. He kneeled in front of his bed beneath the shadow of a large wooden cross where Christ hung in painful agony. The cross had belonged to his mother once upon a time, but now it was his. He looked up into the dying eyes of the crucified Christ.

"Dear heavenly Father, in faith I pray to you with the knowledge that you forgive all sin. I ask that you not hold what I have done to this girl's account. Let her enter into your paradise as a child free from sin. Cover me in her guilt, hold me accountable, for it is I who has failed."

Michael remained on his knees for over an hour, praying for himself and for the girl. The sound of Max entering the room snapped him from his prayers. He opened his eyes and saw a shaft of moonlight falling across the bed. The shaft looked like the finger of God and he felt comforted by it. Tears fell from his eyes again, but these were tears of joy now. "I'm forgiven," he thought, standing up slowly. "Max, I'm still an angel." Max wagged his tail and rubbed his body against Michael's leg. *I'm forgiven*, he thought, leaving his bedroom to go back down into the basement to clean up. Max followed close behind, happy his master wasn't upset any longer.

Chapter 30

The shrill ring of Bruce's cellphone forced him to open his eyes and glare at the tiny bit of sunlight that had forced its way into his apartment through the blackout curtains. He tried rolling over to see who it was, but that proved to be more difficult than it should have been. A sharp stabbing pain ran through his injured shoulder, settling somewhere in the back of his head like a neutron bomb. He tried twisting his body around to his good shoulder but fell from the bed, landing on the floor with a head-jarring thump that sent fresh waves of pain radiating through his body.

On the other side of the bed the cellphone continued to blare. Bruce forced himself up onto his knees and crawled around the front of the bed. The cellphone stopped ringing just as he reached the other side. Bruce leaned his head back against the side of the bed and closed his eyes, wishing silently that he were dead. A moment later the cellphone started ringing again. He cursed at the instrument and wished evil thoughts against whomever was calling.

Bruce swiped at the cellphone from the floor and glared at the screen. He had four missed calls that morning from his brother. "Fuck, fuck, fuck," Bruce mumbled just as the cellphone stopped ringing again. "Fuck me," he cried, dropping the cellphone onto the floor. He ran his fingers through his hair and rubbed his eyes. This brought another sharp twist of pain through his shoulder. He tried to remember the night before, but all he got was a few broken memories.

He remembered going to Nick's and downing two slices of pizza along with three of the pain pills that Veronica had given him. He had a vague memory of a bar somewhere, but he couldn't remember where it had been. He had no memory of coming home or how he had managed to get into his apartment. He guessed it was better than waking up in some strange guy's bed and not knowing how he had gotten there or who the guy was lying beside him.

The cellphone remained silent for now, so Bruce pushed himself slowly away from the bed, standing up on wobbly legs. He looked down at the silent cellphone on the floor thinking about those missed calls and decided his need to use the bathroom was more pressing at the moment. He stumbled across the small apartment in near darkness and did what he had to do in the bathroom, not bothering to wash his hands when he finished. Slowly, he made his way back to his bed and sat down on his old worn mattress, ready to fall back to sleep.

The cellphone rang again just as he was about to place his head on his pillow. He snarled down at the cellphone and saw that it was his brother again. "Somebody better fucking be dead," he mumbled, reaching for the cellphone and regretting his choice of words. "What?" Bruce growled into the cellphone.

"Where the fuck have you been all morning?" Jeffrey shouted from the other end of the phone.

"Sleeping, asshole," Bruce answered, looking around his dark apartment once more.

"Well, we have another body, and it's not good," Jeffrey explained. "Best we can figure, she was taken the day before yesterday and murdered twenty-four hours later. It's bad, really bad. Our boy has totally lost it."

"Where?" Bruce asked, scratching the side of his head.

"Newington," Jeffrey answered. "The bastard dumped her body at Mill Pond Falls in Newington, beneath the foot bridge."

"Mill Pond, got it," Bruce said.

"No, you don't got it, brother. The feds are all over this scene. You can't get anywhere near it after that shit you pulled the other day at the station."

"So, what the fuck do you want me to do?" Bruce asked, looking around for his pills.

"Wait. I want you to wait until I call you back and say it's clear for you to sneak out there. Tonight, most likely, but wait for me to call."

"Great, wonderful. I'll sit here with my finger up my ass waiting for those assholes to finish screwing everything up."

"They're assholes for sure, but they know their shit. Give them some time and you'll have your chance," Jeffrey said. "Just answer your fucking phone when I call back."

"Yeah," Bruce replied, hanging up. *Asshat,* he thought, walking back across the apartment to take a shower. At the mirror above his sink, he glanced at his reflection. In the dim light he looked a thousand years old. The bruise around his shoulder was a sickly shade of yellow and gray. He tried lifting his arm above his head, but he couldn't. "Fuck my life," he thought, wondering what he did with the pills.

Chapter 31

Michael paced anxiously back and forth across the worn hardwood floors of his living room. A ceiling fan spun weakly overhead, the ball bearings squealing softly. Broken light spilled in through the curtains over the picture window chasing the shadows into the corners. Max sat on the recliner in the center of the living room watching his owner pace. He was nervous and excited at the same time, sensing all the pent-up energy in the room. It smelled like danger and adventure and all things wonderful and exciting to him.

"I did what I was supposed to do," Michael shouted at the ceiling fan. "I followed your plan. I disposed of the body in the water to wash away the filth of its life. I allowed the waterfalls to wash away its sins. To baptize it in the newness of life everlasting." The fan continued to revolve along its crooked squealing path, mocking him as he spoke. "Why don't I feel relief? Why didn't the itch go away?" Michael screamed, swatting at a gold ball hanging by a string dangling down from the fan. The ball swung up into the blades. The thwack of metal and pretend wood met so violently that it echoed loudly inside the house. Michael winced at the noise and went back to pacing.

Max barked at the sound of the ball striking the blades. Michael looked at his dog, his eyes wide and sad. "Why doesn't he let me feel any relief, Max? Why is God still punishing me?" he cried. "I said I was sorry. I asked for his forgiveness." Max barked at his owner, wagging his tail swiftly back and forth. Michael studied the dog for a moment. "A walk, of course. We always feel better after a walk, don't we?

What a wonderful idea, Max. Fresh air and sunshine, that's just what we need."

Max leapt from the chair and ran into the kitchen, his paws click clacking on the floor. Michael followed and found him sitting beneath his leash hanging down from the hook by the back door. "Good dog, Max," Michael said, putting on his ballcap and sunglasses before putting the harness and leash on Max. He opened the door and stepped outside. It was warm, but not uncomfortable. A squirrel raced across the driveway and Max tugged at the leash, huffing at the rodent. Michael held onto the leash tightly, leading Max to the car. He opened the door and Max jumped inside, the squirrel forgotten. Michael followed, shoving the dog across the seat. Max pressed his nose up against the passenger side window.

Michael drove randomly up and down several streets in East Hartford and Manchester until he finally entered a neighborhood close to Globe Hollow. He parked his car on a side street and got out, looking up and down the quiet suburban street while Max peed on a fire hydrant.

"Come on, Max," Michael said, starting down the sidewalk at a slow pace. The two of them walked along the edge of the sidewalk farthest from the street, enjoying the shade of the tall old oaks and wide maples that grew in the yards. The neighborhood where he walked was a mixture of homes old and new. Some were built in the early 1900s and others in the 2000s, with many of the homes covering all the years in between. Michael preferred the older houses with large front porches because they had what his mother called character. He also liked the trees in the yards of these older homes. Most were far older than the houses they grew around and were tall and hardy. He liked how their branches twisted every which way, full of life. Birds and squirrels settling on their limbs, living or dying as God saw fit. Max didn't seem to care about any of this; he simply enjoyed sniffing and peeing on the trees and the occasional signpost and fire hydrant.

Michael followed Dartmouth Road to Spring Street, turning so he was strolling in the direction of the town pool. He slowed at the edge of the parking lot and gazed at the pool in the distance. Max strained on his leash to keep going, but he held him back, wrapping the end of the leash around his fist. A few cars drove by on Spring Street but not much else was happening. Michael felt himself stiffening, the excitement of being so close to so many in need of salvation becoming a fire inside his body. He wanted to go to them now but knew that was foolishness. He couldn't allow himself to be caught by those who thought themselves above God's law. They would never understand what he was doing.

"Do you remember, Max? We set one of them free just over there," Michael whispered, tugging on the leash. Max glanced up as if he understood everything his owner said.

Taking slow deliberate steps, Michael forced himself to continue walking down the street. He listened to the sounds of the children at play, sounding so innocent, so sinless. He wanted to make up for his fall from grace so badly, but he knew he had to resist the urge to act. As bad as the itch was right now, he had to resist. *No time for mistakes,* he thought.

Michael led Max down the sidewalk until he no longer saw the parking lot and the pool beyond. He turned onto Arvine Place and then onto Comstock Road. He followed Comstock around until he was sure there was no one there to see him. He glanced quickly at the houses across the street before darting into the woods behind Globe Hollow. He walked to the edge of the reservoir, following it around until he could just see the pool through the trees. The reservoir was a special place.

So many children, he thought as he tied the end of Max's leash to a thin tree struggling to reach for sunlight through the thick growth overhead. Max sat down on a carpet of pine needles and began licking one of his paws, not interested at all in what his owner was about to do.

Michael crept to the edge of the trees that grew along the top of the hill above the pool until only a thin line of growth and shadow hid him. He slowly undid his pants, allowing them to fall to the ground. His underwear fell next, landing on top of the pants. The slight breeze blowing off the water and through the trees raised goosebumps on the exposed flesh of his legs. A wild jolt of electricity ran through his body. His skin felt like it was on fire. He focused on the teenagers gathered on the platform in the middle of the pool. His dick was hard, pointing straight out, waving slightly in the breeze.

"Lost, so lost," he rasped, wrapping his hand around himself, slowly stroking himself. His breathing was shallow little breaths that hitched after every few strokes. A soft moan of pleasure escaped from between his lips and he began stroking faster and faster. His eyes rolled up into his head and he came with a low, deep-throated groan as he dropped to his knees. Tears fell from his eyes and he forced himself to look away from the pool, the guilt of what he had just done so overwhelming.

"Why, Father? Why won't you forgive me?" he whispered. The only answer he received was the soft whisper of the wind through the trees and the shouts and laughter of the children down below at the pool. He gathered up his pants and released Max from the tree. At the edge of the water, he stopped and gazed at the spot where the path wound its way into the trees to the clearing. "We found her there," he whispered.

Michael and Max walked back out onto Spring Street ten minutes later. They returned to where they had parked the car and drove back home. Michael didn't feel any better even though the act of relieving himself did ease the itch beneath his skin. The guilt was still there like a dark stain that couldn't be scrubbed away, and even though he had eased the itch, it still gnawed at him, eating at him from the inside. The guilt of what he had done to that poor girl just refused to go away. This was a new feeling for him. Never before had he ever felt any guilt about what he was doing, but now it was threatening to drown him because he had disobeyed God's plan. He knew he had to do something soon to make up for what he had done so God could forgive him. He had to make God forgive him, so he could again be that angel his mother had always said he was.

Michael pulled into his driveway and parked his car just in front of the garage door. He picked up Max in his arms and carried him from the car to the house. The back door closed softly behind him. The kitchen was dark, full of shadows. He replaced the leash and harness on the hook by the door and set Max down on the floor. Max ran into the living room chasing ghosts. Michael sighed and went upstairs. He walked into his bedroom, dropping to his knees in front of his bed, and began to pray.

Chapter 32

"Carl, I don't think we should go out tonight," Matthew's mother said, standing in front of the kitchen sink, a dish towel in her hand, looking out the small kitchen window above the sink. Matthew looked up from where he sat in the living room, a *Spectacular Spiderman* comic book sitting in his lap. His eyes shifted away from the colorful pages to listen to his parents' conversation, an expression of worry drawing temporary lines across his forehead that resembled the permanent ones etched across his father's forehead. He wanted his mother and father to go out that night on what they called a date night. He wanted them to do whatever it was they did on date night, but most of all, he wanted to binge-watch scary movies on Netflix that his mother thought of as inappropriate for someone his age.

"It'll be fine, Mother," his father replied, sitting at the kitchen table with a cup of coffee in front of him. "Mary will keep an eye on Matthew and Matthew will keep an eye on Mary," he added before blowing into his cup and taking a sip of the dark liquid.

"I'll watch her like a hawk," Matthew chimed in, lending his support to his father. Mary flipped him the bird from behind her purple-sequined cellphone. She was sitting on the couch texting with someone.

"Nothing is going to happen to us, Mom," Mary said without looking away from her cellphone, sounding exasperated. "You two should just go out and have a good time," she added, eyeing her younger brother over the top of the phone. Matthew flipped his sister off and then mimed flicking a booger at her. "Fuck you, dickhead," Mary whispered just loud enough that he could hear, but not her parents.

"Mary used the f word, Mom," Matthew shouted, grinning at his sister.

"Mary!" her mother called from the kitchen.

"Just go, Mom," Mary moaned. "It's date night and you have hotel reservations. If anything happens, I'll call you," Mary said, trying to sound more grown up than she really was.

"No going out tonight while we're gone and I mean it, both of you," their father said, standing in the entrance of the kitchen now. "They haven't caught that sick bastard yet from the news who's been killing young girls."

"Carl, language," their mother said, stepping up beside her husband. "I'm still not sure about this. Those poor girls and their families."

"I don't want either one of you to answer the door for anyone, either," their father added, pointing a stern finger at each of them. "In fact, once we're gone, just keep them locked."

"Yes, Dad," Mary said in that voice that only a teenager can manage when speaking with her parents.

"I guess we can still go out tonight," their mother said, sounding unsure. "But we'll check in every couple of hours to make sure they're fine."

"Sure thing, sexy lady," their dad said, winking at his wife.

"Gross, get a room, you two," Mary said, sticking two fingers into her mouth and pretending to gag.

"Mom and Dad, sitting in a tree," Matthew sang, and Mary jumped up from the couch, covering her ears.

"I don't want to know what they're doing in a tree or anywhere else," Mary shouted, darting up the stairs before he could finish the rhyme.

Chapter 33

Bruce left his apartment around noon. He drove to the Dunkin' Donuts on Main Street and paid for two cups of coffee and six glazed donuts. Back in his car, he drove to Saint Christopher's Catholic Church, parking at the back of the lot behind the church annex beneath his favorite tree. He sipped at his coffee for a few minutes, studying the doors, remembering how his mother use to hold his hand every Saturday afternoon as they passed through those same doors to attend the five o'clock service. *Those were good memories after Dad died*, he thought, sighing over his coffee cup.

Bruce exited his car with the two cups of coffee and the donuts. He walked along the side of the church to the front of the building, opening the large wooden doors in front of the church. The doors felt thick and heavy, worn smooth with age and the many, many hands that had touched them over the years. The hinges groaned as the door swung open. They closed softly behind him, plunging him into a shadowed-filled vestibule. He stepped forward, dipping his fingers into a small bowl of holy water on the pedestal beside the next set of doors. He made the sign of the cross, whispering, "Father, Son, and the Holy Ghost."

Bruce opened the second set of doors and stepped into the sanctuary. Shadows stretched across the walls like long-deceased saints keeping watch over the faithful. The sanctuary was quiet. No one else was there; the pews sat empty. Bruce walked up to the front of the sanctuary and sat down in the front pew, setting the bag of donuts and cups of coffee beside his leg. He looked up past the altar at the large wooden cross that hung on the far wall. He looked into the face of the crucified Christ hanging on the cross, noting how the artist caught the totality of his agony and suffering. His gaze settled on the eyes and he looked away, feeling like he could never measure up to the image looking down at him.

"Forgive me," he whispered, standing up. The bag of donuts crinkled in his hand, the sound echoing inside the quiet church, causing him to feel guilty for disturbing the silence of the sanctuary. He could almost feel the disapproving eyes of the shadowed saints upon him as he stepped up onto the altar. He walked quickly to a door on the left side hidden behind a thick red curtain, knocking softly. The door opened.

"Bruce Westman," Father Murphy said, bathed in shadows. He wore jeans, a dark shirt, and white New Balance sneakers. His hair, what little there was, was not combed and stood out along the sides of his head. He looked a little like Albert Einstein in that picture where his hair is sticking out everywhere and he's sticking his tongue out at the person taking the photo. He looked nothing like a priest standing there in the open doorway.

"Father," Bruce said, smiling, holding out the donuts and coffee.

"A bribe," Father Murphy said, taking the bag of donuts from Bruce and stepping aside.

Bruce followed the old priest down a short hallway to an office at the end. Father Murphy walked in first and sat down behind a small desk. Bruce took a seat in front of the desk while Father Murphy took a donut from the bag and began to eat. Bruce set his coffee down on the desk and removed a donut from the bag.

"So, why the visit on a Friday afternoon?" Father Murphy asked after finishing his first donut and taking a second one from the bag. He tore this donut in half and shoved one half of it into his mouth. Glazed sugar fell in crumbles upon his desk.

"Things have gotten bad out there, Father. This guy I'm hunting is losing it and I'm no closer to stopping him," Bruce explained.

"I saw that agent on the television the other night. Are you still working with your brother?"

"Sort of," Bruce said. "I'm not allowed to be anywhere near the investigation right now, but you know how that goes. Jeffrey keeps me clued in as best he can, and I still get things."

"Those things as you call them are gifts, Bruce. Gifts from God," Father Murphy said. "I will not pretend to understand what it is that you can do, or how you can do it, but it is a gift just the same."

"I don't feel so gifted right now, Father. The things I see, they stain my soul. There's a darkness inside of me, Father, that's trying to take over. I'm scared."

"That's just not true, Bruce. You're just troubled by what you see because down deep you are a good person. I know this, and God knows this. I don't believe a God of love would allow you to suffer for no reason. Trust him, Bruce. Have faith and all will be revealed in His time." Bruce nodded, snatching another donut from the bag.

"Father, do you really believe in the Devil? In evil?" Bruce asked before biting into his donut.

"I have to believe. It's part of the job description."

"How can someone so evil exist if God is real, Father? It doesn't make any sense."

Father Murphy set what was left of his donut down on his desk. He looked at Bruce without blinking. "You can see into the minds of others. You've told me so, though I have no proof that you really can, but I believe you because I believe in who you are. I believe in God simply because I know He is real. I do not need physical proof of His existence, though I believe there is. Everything in nature testifies to the fact that He is real. We are such intricate creations that nothing, and I mean nothing, can explain it other than a Divine Creator. Everything about nature is balance and if there is something that creates nature, then there will be something that uncreates nature. The Devil, if you will. For surely if there is a God of love then there must be a Devil that hates."

"And something evil living here among us? Why does God permit that?" Bruce asked, wiping his fingers on his shirt. Crumbs dribbled down into his lap.

"Bruce, God is not corruptible, only man is. Everything bad, everything evil in the world, is just a result of that corruption." Bruce nodded, standing up. Father Murphy stood up as well and stepped around the desk, offering Bruce his hand. "Are you seeing someone at the VA, Bruce?" Father Murphy asked.

"No, Father. The things I need to share, I can never share with them. They'd just lock me up and toss away the key," Bruce answered, shaking Father Murphy's hand. "Thanks for the talk though. It helps. It always helps."

"Anytime, Bruce, and try coming to church every once in a while. You may find the act of worshipping within a congregation fulfilling."

"I will, Father," Bruce said, walking out of the office and into the short hallway. He left the church feeling better, a little less tainted than when he entered.

Bruce drove around East Hartford looking for a man walking a dog wearing a Red Sox ballcap. He found no one that matched that description, so he drove into Manchester and found his way back to Globe Hollow. He sat in his car at the back of the lot with the windows down to clear his head. He wanted a drink really bad but resisted the urge to open the glovebox and grab the bottle hidden there. He closed his eyes instead and allowed himself to drift away to wherever his mind wanted to take him. Sometimes, most times, this didn't work. Physical contact with an object was always best. He needed that connection to drift, but not this time.

The drift came quickly together, taking on shape and form. Bruce stood somewhere in a forest. There was water just beyond the trees where he stood. The water was dark and green and covered everything beyond the trees. It looked like a large pond or small lake. He was excited. There was a kind of nervous energy cruising through his body. This energy felt familiar and foreign. He was inside the killer's head.

A light breeze blew through the trees from over the water, tickling his skin. He looked down at himself and saw that he wore no pants, no underwear. He was naked from the waist down. Goosebumps covered his legs, though it wasn't really cold outside. He had an erection that pointed straight out, screaming for release. He saw and felt what the killer experienced. He was the killer, but he was Bruce Westman too, so he fought against these feelings of desire and lust and need. He forced himself to take in his surroundings and ignore this rush of electricity.

In the distance, he heard children playing. The sound of their laughter and shouts focused his mind and turned his attention away from himself. He saw now that he was above the pool at Globe Hollow. He could see the children below running and swimming. Joy of their laughter touched him, and he realized suddenly he was masturbating. He couldn't help himself. He couldn't stop himself. He was being forced to watch the children at play in a pool while stroking himself faster and faster until he came on the ground at his feet. He fell to his knees and began to cry deep sobbing tears of guilt.

He looked away and then back at the pool through a haze of tears. The water didn't look right. It was darker than it should be. "It looks like blood," he whispered. "The water in the pool has turned to blood," he moaned. "Oh my God, he's killed all the children."

Bruce's head snapped back up. He was in the parking lot again sitting behind the steering wheel of his car. There was an uncomfortable bulge in his pants, but he ignored it. He looked around the parking lot, half expecting to see the man and his dog looking back at him, but he only saw people milling around the entrance to the pool. A few of the mothers were pointing at his car. He felt like the star in a stranger danger video. One of the mothers was on her cellphone.

Bruce started his car and drove to the exit. Spring Street was quiet. He wasn't sure which way to go. "Fuck me," he whispered. *This guy was here, right here today and I missed him*, he thought, sitting back up again. "He might still be here somewhere," he said out loud, looking to the left and then to the right trying to visualize where the killer had to be standing above the pool. "The motherfucker might just be somewhere close by," he whispered. Closing his eyes, he took several deep breaths. In his mind he saw the woods again. He saw where the killer stood among the trees hidden by the shadows. Opening his eyes, he turned left onto Spring Street, allowing his inner mind to guide him. At Arvine Place he turned left again and followed it around to Comstock. He drove by intuition, creeping along the street, knowing he was close. Where Comstock curved, he stopped in front of an early, white 1900s colonial. The front yard was large, allowing the house to be set back from the street. A carport hung over the driveway attached to the house. An elderly woman was sitting beneath the carport smoking a cigarette.

Bruce turned the car off and got out. He looked at the trees across the street and then down the driveway where the woman sat. He pulled out a notebook from his back pocket and a pen from his shirt and started down the recently tarred driveway.

"Excuse me," Bruce said, halfway between the woman and the street. The woman eyed him suspiciously. For a second Bruce thought she was going to ignore him. "Can I ask you a question?" Bruce persisted, taking a step closer. The woman blew out a long stream of gray smoke that rose to the ceiling of the carport.

"If you stay there and come no closer, you can," the woman said, her voice raspy from years of smoking. Bruce noticed that the hand holding the cigarette trembled like a leaf on a branch caught in a breeze. He could even see the yellow nicotine stains discoloring her fingers. Beside her was an oxygen tank with a tube and mask draped over it.

"Did you see anyone out here today? Maybe a man with a dog?" Bruce asked, holding out the notebook so he looked like he was going to write down everything she had to say.

The woman took another long drag from her cigarette, her features disappearing for a moment in the cloud of smoke that spilled slowly from between her pursed lips. As the smoke was expelled, she coughed several times, fighting to catch her breath. Bruce watched as she reached for the mask and placed it over her face. She swallowed several mouthfuls of oxygen before hanging the mask back on the tank.

"I saw a fellow earlier today. Maybe a half-hour, forty minutes ago," the woman said, dropping her spent cigarette at her feet and stamping it out with the toe of one foot.

I bet you did see him, Bruce thought. *So. Fucking. Close.*

"He had a small dog with him, too. One of those Bostons, I think. Little thing but not too little."

"Did you see the car he drove?" Bruce asked.

"No car, young man. He walked up the road and into the woods there, just across the street from where you parked. He came back out later," she said, smiling a toothy grin. "He never saw me though, of that I'm sure."

Bruce took a few steps but paused when he saw the woman tense up. She fumbled another cigarette from her pack and lit it without taking her eyes away from him. She coughed once as she took a drag.

"I'm a private investigator, ma'am, hired by his wife. She thinks he's cheating on her and I'm just trying to get the evidence one way or another." The woman relaxed a bit and took another drag from her cigarette. Bruce noticed then how skeletal she looked each time she sucked on the cigarette.

"He was older than you; tall but not too tall, but taller than you," she said. "He had on a blue polo shirt, dark pants, dark sunglasses, and a ballcap."

"Was it a Red Sox cap?" Bruce asked, glancing over his shoulder at the trees across the street, trying to picture the killer as he stepped out of the trees.

"I don't know about that," the woman answered, flicking ash onto the driveway. "Always been a Yankee fan myself," she cackled. The cackle quickly turned into a fit of coughing. Bruce waited as she swallowed more oxygen, wondering how the hell she hadn't blown herself up yet lighting cigarettes so close to the oxygen tank.

"Is there anything else that you can think of that might be helpful?" Bruce asked, ready to slip the notebook back into his pocket. The woman eyed him and Bruce saw the deep wrinkles around her eyes, the valleys that cut across her forehead, and the spiderweb of wrinkles that formed at the corners of her mouth from years of smoking. Her skin looked like old worn leather. *New England tough*, he thought.

"I'm not so sure about all this cheating you're telling me about, young man, but I can tell you that he looked deeply troubled even from this far away. He was a nervous type, like he was afraid of being caught with his hand in the cookie jar, or maybe somewhere else."

Bruce nodded, thanking the woman before turning around and walking back down the driveway. He forced himself to stop at the end of the driveway and count to three, even though what he really wanted to do was race into the trees. Stepping into the street, he casually walked to the other side and stopped again on the sidewalk, standing just in front of the trees. He looked up and down the street noting how quiet it was. Not a single car had driven by since he stopped and spoke with the old woman. He glanced over his shoulder and saw that from where he stood, the old woman was hidden in the shadows beneath the carport. "He had no idea she was even there," he thought, stepping into the trees and disappearing.

The old woman watched the strange man walk into the forest and disappear. He left his car parked at the curb so she figured he would return. The woman took a drag on her cigarette before dropping it on the driveway at her feet. A fit of coughing proceeded that last drag so she had to reach for her mask and take a pull from the oxygen tank. The cool, medically-produced air rolled down her throat and she drank it in greedily, filling her slowly failing lungs. *Death is a real lonely bitch*, she thought, slowly standing up from her lawn chair, glancing once more across the street at where the investigator had disappeared. *He seemed like such a troubled young man,* she thought, grabbing the handle on the tank trolley and rolling it toward the side door.

Standing at her tiny kitchen table a few minutes later with a view out the front window, the old woman kept an uneasy eye on the trees where the second man that day had disappeared. She wore an oxygen mask over her face attached to a machine, listening to the pfft sound it made as it dispensed measured doses of oxygen into her diseased lungs. Soon she would need a breathing treatment because the effort of walking into the house had been too much. "I'll be dead soon enough," she whispered into the empty house. "Then the madness will begin," she crooked, laughing until she began coughing.

Bruce picked his way through the trees until he came upon the Globe Hollow reservoir. He could hear children at play in the distance off to his left. He made his way through the thick copse of trees until he could just see the pool below. From where he stood, hidden by the trees, the water took on a dark green color that looked so terribly cold. An involuntary shiver passed through his body. Twisted shadows played over the surface of the water like hidden demons waiting for a careless victim. Another chill wormed its way across his spine in spite of the warm afternoon.

"This is a perfect spot," he whispered, looking down at the pool. "He had a clear view of everything and everyone, and no one could have seen him from below. I bet he's been coming out here for some time now."

Bruce turned away from the pool and walked to the edge of the reservoir, looking out across its dark otherworldly expanse. Tiny ripples played across its surface as unseen fingers disturbed its stillness. Licking his lips, he looked across the water toward the trees where the path led to the small clearing. He couldn't see the path from so far away, but he knew it was there just the same, creeping its way through the trees.

I bet this is how he discovered where the older kids went to hang out, Bruce thought. "I bet he spied on them from here, not having the courage to cross to the other side," he whispered aloud. "I bet the sick fuck played out all his fantasies hidden here among the trees." Bruce studied the far side of the reservoir, nodding his head, liking the idea. *So, what changed, asshole? What drove you to act that day?* he wondered. *Was she your first? Was that why it was different? Were there others before her that we just haven't discovered yet?*

Bruce found a clear spot along the shore with just enough cover to hide himself if anyone should come along. He sat down, leaning against a thin tree that grew a few feet from the water's edge. He looked out over the water and waited. Bugs flew across the dark surface, darting this way and that. Sunlight sparkled in a dazzling dance that exhausted his eyes until they slowly fell shut. Ants mingled between his legs, carrying their bounty back to their nests. His breathing slowed.

"Why did you act?" Bruce whispered without opening his eyes. Dull light played just on the other side of his eyelids as the sounds of the children at play faded. Everything slowly disappeared until he wasn't there any longer.

The drift was gentle. He felt himself slowly floating up and then down, up and then down, until all at once he was standing at the edge of water. It was almost dusk, the sun setting slowly to west. Dark shadows filled the reservoir; a cool breeze blew out over the water, leaving ripples in its wake. Down below, the pool was emptying out for the evening. Children and their parents or older siblings were pouring out into the parking lot. The lights along the deck were off.

Bruce glanced down and saw that his pants were puddled around his ankles, and he was holding his limp dick in his right hand, semen dribbling from the tip. *You came here to jerk off*, Bruce thought.

Laughter drifted across the water as he bent to pull up his pants. Movement through the underbrush caught his eye as he grabbed at the waistband of his jeans. He saw a boy and a girl walking into the trees on the other side of the reservoir. Teenagers had come and gone before but this time he felt anger and rage at seeing the boy's hand on the girl's ass. He knew what was going to happen and the thought enraged him as the two teens quickly disappeared inside the trees, the sound of their laughter reaching back as they went forward.

He's forcing her into those trees, he thought. Looking down at himself, he saw that his dick was no longer limp. It was poking out from between his unzipped fly. He left it like that, pointing across the water like a dowsing rod in search of a hidden well. He thought about grabbing it and jerking it off again, but then another thought crossed his mind. He smiled, stuffing himself back inside his pants and yanking up the zipper.

"Stay here, Max," he whispered. Max looked up at him, looking so sad sitting there tied to a tree among the fallen pine needles. It was almost comical how its ears flattened out along its head and its eyes widened. He looked like a furry sealion begging for attention.

Before Bruce knew what was happening, his body was moving along the edge of the reservoir safely tucked away in the shelter of the tress, hugging the shadows in the space between the water and the forest. He crept along the bank like a burglar stalking his next target. It was disconcerting how he was himself and the killer at the same time. How the two of them were able to exist as one. At the path, they paused and looked back the way they had just come, contemplating turning around and fleeing, but that desire, that need, was just too much.

Bruce could feel the electricity flowing though his blood, rushing through his body like lightning across a night sky. His skin was on fire. The nerves at the tips of his fingers sizzled like licking the ends of a nine-volt battery. He was excited and terrified all at the same time, fully aware of everything going on around him and totally oblivious to the danger all around him. It was like nothing he had ever felt before. It was the world's ultimate narcotic, and he was riding its high for everything it was worth. *No wonder he kills*, Bruce thought. *If this was the thrill he felt each time, how could he ever hope to resist?*

At the end of the path where it emptied out into a clearing, he stopped and listened. Giggles from a female filled the air just beyond where he stood. He glanced around for the girl, but she was hidden by shadows settling over the forest. Silently, he stepped into the trees at the edge of the clearing and circled around until he was on the other side. He could just see the boy and the girl now through the trees. They were making out on an old mattress, stained and yellowed from many such encounters. He reached down and felt himself through his pants. He was so incredibly hard. The touch of his hand sent even more electricity through his body. His breaths came in short slow gasps. He could barely contain himself. He thought he might be ready to explode right there right inside his pants.

In the clearing, on the mattress, the boy lifted the girl's shirt up over her head. She raised her arms, so it was easy for him to remove the shirt. Smiling shyly, she dropped her bra into her lap. Her breasts, tiny and firm, looked so perfect, so young and so smooth. Even in the shadowed darkness he could detect the nipples standing out. The girl fell back onto the mattress, arching her back, and the boy fell on top of her. He was fumbling with her pants and she helped him until they were off followed quickly by her underwear. The girl removed the boy's pants without any trouble, the whole time kissing him while he placed one hand between her legs.

A red light swam through Bruce's vision as he watched the two of them. It was the rage exploding in front of his vision at witnessing the act of sin. He burst through the trees like a grizzly bear attacking its prey. The boy and the girl didn't see him or hear him at first because they were so focused on each other. Bruce grabbed a handful of the boy's hair, lifting him up off the girl. The boy cried out in surprise and pain, his face twisted into a mask of terror. He drove that face down into the ground beside the mattress. The cries became strangled gasps as the boy fought to breathe. He dropped the struggling body and lifted a booted foot, smashing it down onto the boy's head, once, twice, three times, until there was nothing left alive. The girl on the mattress sat there naked, screaming one long endless scream that seemed like it would never end. Bruce paid it little attention, noticing how her nipples were still erect.

When he could no longer ignore the screaming, he reached out and took hold of the girl, grabbing her by her throat, lifting her off the mattress, and choking off her screams. Her eyes were wide and terrified as she clawed at the hand that held her. Her struggles weakened, and her face began to take on a darker, purple color until her hands fell away. She hung there, naked and limp, at the end of his arm. She was still alive, her breaths coming in tiny, short, painful gasps.

"I am here to save you," Bruce said, the sound of his voice off. "I was sent by God to save you before you sinned and damned yourself to hell and a separation from the Father."

The girl's eyes were large red spotlights in the shadow-filled forest. Her tongue, fat and swollen, fell from her mouth. Bruce's hand squeezed tighter. Her eyes grew wider, dark red lines exploding inside the whites of her eyes. Bruce squeezed tighter until he felt something break beneath his hand. He watched the life slip away from the girl. It left her eyes in a slow fade and he felt himself explode inside his pants.

He released his hold on the girl. She fell to the ground like a lifeless ragdoll, her dead eyes looking up into a forest canopy. Bruce studied her motionless body. He kneeled down beside it and touched the skin beneath one breast. A tingle of electricity ran through him and he felt himself twitch. He was already becoming hard again. His nostrils flared.

"Motherfucker," Bruce whispered, snapping out of his drift. He vomited into his lap, noting that he had a hard-on. Looking across the water, he shuddered and threw up again, this time managing to turn his head so the vomit landed in the weeds. "Motherfucker," he mumbled, wiping his mouth with the back of his hand. He crawled to the edge of the water and used it to wash away most of the vomit from his pants and shirt. *It'll have to do,* he thought, standing up. He made his way back out to the street, needing to get as far away from that place as he could. He felt filthy and dirty, wishing he had a drink in his hand. He felt disgusted at what he witnessed and wished he could put it out of his mind, more determined to end the son of a bitch before he could hurt another child.

Bruce broke free of the trees and out onto the street a few minutes later. The woman was no longer sitting beneath the carport smoking her cigarettes. The street was empty. He looked down the driveway again. *Inside the house watching an afternoon soap or Doctor Oz,* he thought, walking over to his car.

Inside the house, the old woman watched the young man get into his car. He looked scared and angry, she thought as he slammed the door. She watched him do a U-turn in the street and drive away quickly. She noted the license plate as he drove off, jotting down the numbers on a pad of paper she kept by the window. Next to the plate numbers she wrote a description of a young man. She didn't know if he was a good guy or not, but she knew you couldn't be too careful nowadays. Above Bruce's license plate and description was a description of the man who had come by earlier and his dog. Beside that was a note that read: *walked into the woods. Came back out thirty minutes later.*

Chapter 34

Jeffrey Westman sat in his city-issued car in the parking lot of a gas station watching the entrance to Mill Pond Park as the last of the federal crime scene investigators drove away. Agent Shelby was the last to leave in his gray government-issued sedan. He did not notice Officer Westman watching him from across the street as he drove away. Jeffrey flipped him the bird as he waited until the car and Agent Shelby disappeared out of sight. Once he was sure the agent wasn't coming back, he picked up his cellphone, glancing down at the time. It was eight-thirty in the evening and about to get dark. He punched a number into the cellphone. The phone on the other end rang in his ear three times before it was answered.

"What?" Bruce answered, sounding irritated.

"Do you ever sound happy when you answer the phone?" Jeffrey asked.

"Yeah, just not when I see it's you who's calling," Bruce answered.

"The last of them assholes have just left. I'd give it an hour and then you can head out this way."

"Okay," Bruce said.

"I'm going to grab a bite, but I should be back across the street from the park by the time you get here," Jeffrey said.

"Got it," Bruce replied, ready to disconnect the call.

"Everything alright, brother?" Jeffrey asked, worried by how disconnected his brother sounded.

"I missed him today," Bruce said. "Thirty minutes, an hour, no more than that. I was that fucking close to getting this bastard," he explained. "An old woman saw him with his fucking dog walking into the woods behind the Hollow. He came out maybe thirty minutes later and walked away. I checked the area, but he was gone. I was so fucking close."

"Son of a bitch," Jeffrey exclaimed. "Motherfucker."

"Yeah, I know how you feel," Bruce said, feeling like he let his brother down.

Jeffrey heard the guilt in his brother's voice. He understood how he felt because he had felt that same way so many times on the job. You could have all the pieces to the puzzle and still the puzzle refused to fit together, and sometimes even when they did fit the bastards got off on a technicality.

"You want me to grab you anything to eat?" Jeffrey asked, hoping to distract his brother from falling down the rabbit hole.

"Sure, whatever you're having is fine," Bruce answered.

"Okay, I'll see you when you get here."

Bruce hit the end call button and tossed his cellphone on the bed before walking across the bedroom and looking out the window. His mouth was dry and his tongue felt like sandpaper. He needed a drink in the worst way. His hands were shaking as he opened the freezer door and took out a frosted bottle of vodka. Licking his lips, he unscrewed the cap and drank straight from the bottle, enjoying the sensation of fire and ice as the alcohol-fueled liquid ran down his throat. He closed his eyes and took another sip before shoving the bottle back into the freezer and closing the door. He leaned against the refrigerator and closed his eyes, trying to clear his head. What he wanted was to take another drink and another one after that until the bottle was empty, but he fought that urge. *Work first*, he thought. *You can go out later if it isn't too late and get shitfaced.*

Pushing himself away from the refrigerator door, he walked across the small apartment. His keys were on the nightstand and his cellphone was still on the bed. He snagged both from where they lay and walked to the door, grasping the knob with his right hand.

Righty tighty is always righty, Bruce thought, twisting the knob three times before opening the door and stepping out into the hallway. He closed the door and twisted the knob three more times to the right before locking it. "Where the fuck did that come from?" he asked himself, turning away from the door and heading down the stairs.

Bruce drove around East Hartford and Manchester looking for his killer but found nothing suggesting he was out prowling the streets. It was so disturbing how normal things looked even though children were being hunted by a serial killer. It was a typical summer evening and children were outside playing as if everything was normal. A few older kids walked the sidewalks engrossed in their cellphones while smaller kids played in yards or rode their bikes on the sidewalks. A few mothers and a couple of fathers were outside as well keeping an eye on their children, but he didn't think that was anywhere near enough.

If I had a kid, especially a girl, she wouldn't be out until this asshat was caught, he thought, glancing down at the time on his dashboard. He jumped on the highway a few minutes later, heading toward Mill Pond in Newington.

Bruce found Jeffrey parked at a gas station across the street from the park sipping from a straw. He parked alongside his brother's car and got out, walking around to the passenger side of the unmarked police vehicle. He picked up a bag from the seat and sat down. A burger and fries were in the bag and a coke sat in the cup holder sweating drops of moisture.

"Cheese and ketchup only?" Bruce asked, removing the burger from the bag as he spoke and peeling back the paper it was wrapped in.

"Yeah, what else would I get you?" Jeffrey answered. Bruce took a bite of the burger and smiled. He shoved a handful of fries into his mouth between bites of the burger. A loud burp escaped from between his lips as he shoved the last bit of the burger into his mouth, followed by the last fistful of the fries.

"Disgusting," Jeffrey said. Bruce smiled around a mouthful of food while sipping from his drink to chase it all down. Jeffrey pointed at the corner of his mouth. "You're wearing some of it," he said, shaking his head. Bruce tongued the ketchup from his face and finished off the coke, burping several more times before setting the empty cup back in the cup holder.

"Next time you can starve," Jeffrey said, tossing a handful of napkins at his brother. "Clean yourself off, ya pig."

"And I'll tell Mom how you let me starve," Bruce said, wiping his face with the back of his arm instead of using the napkins Jeffrey had given him. "You can deal with her Italian guilt trip for a change."

"Whatever, dickhead," Jeffrey said, rolling up the windows and turning the car off. "Let's get this over with."

"Will the cars be alright here?" Bruce asked.

"Yeah, I badged the cashier. We'll be fine."

"You sure they didn't leave anyone behind?" Bruce asked as they walked across the street.

"Don't think so. I counted nine going in and nine coming back out."

"And people said you weren't good at math," Bruce said, laughing. Jeffrey shot him the bird before slipping a notebook from his pocket.

"A couple found the body this morning floating in the water beneath the falls," Jeffrey read. "They had come to the park early to exercise and were walking along the path up toward the bridge." Bruce nodded and continued walking. "It was bad, Bruce, really bad. Paramedics had to sedate the woman. She was hysterical. The man wasn't much better. Stephen King has nothing on this shit."

"What the fuck did they find?" Bruce asked, remembering the boy he had seen in the clearing and the booted foot smashing down on the head.

"She looked like an animal had gotten to her. Where her chest should have been, there was just a big gaping hole," Jeffrey explained. "That asshole stabbed her so many times there was nothing left. And he raped her this time. There was vaginal tearing and bruising that was like nothing I've ever seen. It was as if he went at her with a sledgehammer. There was so much blood and damage down there. He must have been stabbing her the whole time he was raping her. I've never seen anything like it before, and I've seen some crazy shit, brother."

Bruce was silent. He didn't want to tell his brother that the craziest shit he thought he had seen didn't even come close to what he had seen in the sandbox. Other than Father Murphy, he had never told another soul what had happened over there.

They walked in silence for several minutes before Bruce looked up. "You're going to want to suggest that they send a diver to the reservoir behind the Hollow. I think he dumped a boy's body back there," Bruce explained, picturing the boy's pulped head again. It had sounded like a pumpkin being smashed against a wall. He couldn't get the image out of his head, or the sound.

Jeffrey made a note and continued walking. Bruce followed, enjoying the silence. He didn't want to tell his brother what he had seen earlier. He wasn't sure how to put it into words. *How can this be a gift?* he thought as they approached the bridge over the falls. At the center of the bridge, they stopped. Bruce looked down into the water below. It was dark and full of shadows that wobbled up and down as the water flowed over rocks. The falls were loud as they twisted over and down to the stream below. The meager lights beneath the bridge provided very little to see by.

To wash away her sins, or his own this time? Bruce thought, leaning out over the railing, listening to the water drown out everything else. The drowning out of nature didn't last very long before another power to swept over him. He closed his eyes and allowed the drift to take over.

He settled on the bridge. It was dark outside. The killer stood before him holding a girl's mangled body in his arms. He held her tightly against his chest as one might hold a sleeping child. There was a tenderness to how he was carrying the body. Bruce could feel his anguish and guilt pouring out.

Her head hung over his shoulder, her lifeless eyes looking across the bridge. The killer was a mess, his clothing covered in gore. He set the girl down gently on the railing, holding onto her hands as her body leaned out over the falls. Her flesh was horribly mangled and torn. Dried blood covered her stomach and legs. Her chest was an abyss of the terrible violence unleashed upon her. It was all jagged and tattered ribbons of skin, flayed and torn like the puckered remains of a mouth beaten and abused.

The killer was sobbing. Tears ran from his eyes. He gazed into her face pleading for forgiveness. Whatever had happened he hadn't wanted it to happen.

"Forgive me, Father, for I have sinned," the killer cried, his head shaking back and forth several times, spraying snot and shed tears everywhere, before shoving the body out into the falls. The killer fell to his knees, screaming and pulling his hair. "Please forgive me!" he cried over and over, yanking out tufts of hair with each plea offered up to the empty sky overhead.

Bruce snapped back, falling away from the railing and landing on his backside. He bit down on his tongue. "Motherfucker," he cried, holding a hand to his mouth, tasting the blood.

"Hey, you okay?" Jeffrey asked, reaching down for his brother.

"Yeah, I'm fine," Bruce answered, getting up without assistance. He looked over the railing again. "This wasn't supposed to happen like this," he said, looking down at the water. "He feels guilty for the rape. He was supposed to have saved her, not taken from her," he explained. "He's lost it. He's gone over the edge. He's going to act again soon because he can't handle the guilt of his failure. He has to save someone soon or he won't be able to live with himself."

"He's accelerating," Jeffrey said.

"He's out of control," Bruce explained. "Whatever it was that pushed him over the edge, there's no coming back from there now. We have to catch this asshole, fast, or it's going to keep getting messy."

Jeffrey swallowed hard and slipped his notebook back in his pocket. "Let's get the fuck out of here. This place is giving me the creeps."

"I could use a drink," Bruce said, walking off the bridge.

"I'd like to join you, but I can't. I have to get home or Annie will have my ass in a sling."

"Whipped," Bruce said, a weak smile creasing his face. Jeffrey shot him the bird.

Bruce started across the bridge and paused. He glanced at a fence post and walked over to it, bending down.

"What are you seeing over there?" Jeffrey asked. Bruce snagged a tuft of something stuck to the post and stood.

"Hair. The killer's hair," he explained, holding it out to his brother.

Chapter 35

"Where ya going?" Matthew asked his sister as she approached the back door. She paused, her hand resting lightly on the doorknob. He knew she was planning to go out because she was wearing too-short shorts, a black Misfits t-shirt knotted at the bottom, and more makeup than was necessary for spending the night at home with your younger brother watching movies.

"Out," Mary answered, grasping the doorknob and twisting it.

"I'm going with you," Matthew said, getting up from the couch.

"Fuck that, turd," Mary said. "You're staying here."

Matthew picked up his cellphone, holding his finger over the word Mom, and smiled. "Hello, Mom," he mimicked, speaking into the device.

"Fine, fine. If you stay here, I'll pay you five dollars and you can watch whatever you want on my Netflix account."

Matthew studied his sister with a serious expression on his face that made him look much older than he actually was. He set his cellphone down on the coffee table and rubbed at his chin, pursing his lips and narrowing his eyes. "Ten dollars, and you do the dishes for a week," he countered.

"You're an asshole," Mary said.

"You can always stay here with me eating popcorn and watching horror movies, or I can tag along with you," he said, smiling. "I'm fine either way."

"Fine," Mary said, opening the back door. "You're a little shit stain, you know that?"

"What time are you coming home?" Matthew asked before she managed to step all the way outside.

Mary looked over her shoulder at her brother. "No later than midnight," she answered, sounding perturbed, and then she was gone.

Matthew watched his sister walk out to the sidewalk in front of the house. A brown car pulled up to the curb, music blaring from inside. He watched as she opened the passenger side door, illuminating the interior. In the driver's seat sat Andy Andrews, an on-again-off-again boyfriend of hers that Matthew didn't care for because he was such an asshole.

You can do so much better than that red-headed showoff, Matthew thought, backing away from the window. He sat down on the couch and selected his sister's Netflix account on the remote. "What to watch, what to watch," he sang, scrolling through the list of horror movies available for his viewing pleasure.

Several hours later it was well after midnight. Matthew woke up on the couch, having fallen asleep while watching *The Shining*. The movie was over now, and Netflix suggested he try watching *The Amityville Horror* next. Matthew shook his head and rubbed his eyes. "Redrum," he whispered at the screen, grabbing his cellphone from the floor.

"It's after one in the morning," he groaned, glancing over at the back door, wondering if his sister had come home and just left him there sleeping. He looked upstairs and then at the back door again. The house felt empty. An uneasy feeling swept through him as he sat up, setting his feet on the living room floor. The hardwood floor was cold and sent a shiver through his body.

Matthew stood and walked over to the back door. It was still unlocked. He glanced through the glass, looking into the backyard and along the driveway. *If she had come home, she would have locked the door*, he thought. He looked into the backyard again beyond the glow of the porch light and saw that it was empty. Sighing, he turned and walked over to the living room window and looked out at the street, hoping to see his sister making out with Andy in the front seat of his shit mobile, but the car wasn't there. Somewhere in the neighborhood a lonely dog barked.

"Mary, are you home?" Matthew shouted up the stairs. Only silence came back. He climbed the stairs to the second floor and went to his sister's bedroom door. The door was closed, a black and white do not disturb sign was his only greeting. He knocked on the door, hard, several times before opening it. The bedroom was empty, and her bed was still made. The clothes she had been wearing earlier before their parents had left lay discarded on the floor where she had dumped them. He called his sister's cellphone and it went straight to voicemail. He called a second time and it rang over and over before going to voicemail again. Now he was beyond worried. As much as he fought with his sister, he loved her and he didn't want anything to happen to her.

Chapter 36

Mary's night had started out with a red plastic cup of Southern Comfort and coke sweating moisture into a cupholder. Andy had it ready for her when she got into the car. She knew it wasn't the best idea to start drinking with him, but she didn't want to disappoint him either.

"To lighten the mood," he said, holding the cup up to her as she sat down inside the car. Liquid droplets splashed down on the center dash. Mary watched them roll away somewhere off in the darkness as she allowed Andy to shove the cup into her hand. He smiled at her as she drank from the cup. The alcohol burned going down at first, but then quickly faded to a warm comfortable feeling that left her all tingly inside. She took another long sip and set the cup back down, leaning across the seat to kiss her boyfriend. Andy kissed her back and drove away from the curb. Mary finished her drink before they were a mile from the house. Andy refilled the cup with a double shot at a light, letting her top it off with coke.

By ten-thirty, Mary and Andy were parked deep in the trees along the Connecticut River on the East Hartford side of the river. The lights of downtown Hartford glistened off the water, dancing like tiny little fairies just above the surface of the river. The car radio was set to an oldies station, the music just loud enough to be heard but not so loud that it interrupted anything. Mary and Andy lay sprawled in each other's arms enjoying the feeling of naked skin against naked skin. A light sheen of sweat glistened off their bodies as they enjoyed the sensation of coming down from just having sex.

"You're so beautiful," Andy whispered into her ear as a soft breeze drifted in through the open windows. Mary smiled, nuzzling her face into the fine hairs covering his chest. She had wanted to tell Andy that she loved him, but the words wouldn't come, so she just lay there, content to enjoy the smell of his body and the feeling of the after-buzz from the alcohol.

Maybe it had been the music, or maybe the fact that she had drunk three cups' worth of Southern Comfort and coke, or maybe it had been the afterglow of the sex, but whatever it had been, Mary hadn't heard the sound of the car creeping down the ramp toward the river. She hadn't noticed that its lights were out, and she didn't see the man that had slipped out from inside the dark interior of the car.

The attack came like the flash of a strobe light in a dark room. A hand came from out of nowhere, shooting through the open driver's side window. Andy yelped as fingers wrapped themselves around his shoulder-length red hair, yanking him straight out of the window. Mary scrambled against the passenger side door, watching in horror as Andy's face was slammed over and over into the windshield. Cracks appeared in the glass. Blood smeared everywhere. Andy's face became a fractured broken thing that she hardly recognized. A tooth slid down the windshield through a stream of blood, leaving a twisted path in its wake.

Mary's screams reached another level when Andy's head finally smashed through the window, exploding into the front seat of the car just above the steering wheel. Blood sprayed everywhere through the shattered remains of the windshield. One of his eyeballs dangled on his cheek, hanging by thin bloody threads leading back into his eye socket. Grisly gore splattered onto the steering wheel. Blood ran from his torn and lacerated face. His scalp was peeled back over his forehead, revealing the red and white bone beneath. He looked so mangled and damaged. She wanted to reach out for him, but before she could, the head was dragged back out through the hole in the window.

Outside, in the dim light of the moon and the distant lights of the city, Mary saw a hulking man dragging what remained of Andy Andrews behind him through the trees. Andy's body didn't move or protest its treatment. His arms hung limply at his sides, bouncing up off the ground as the man walked down to the small dock. At the end of the dock, he lifted Andy up over his head and launched him into the river as if he were nothing but a bag of trash to be discarded.

Inside the car, Mary took a deep breath and screamed as loud as she could as she scrambled across to the driver's side. Glass from the busted windshield cut into her exposed skin but she hardly noticed as she set herself behind the wheel. She fumbled with the ignition, twisting the key, but the car wouldn't start even though the dashboard lit up. She jerked the key in the opposite direction and the car roared to life. Still screaming, she tried shoving the shifter into first gear like she had seen Andy do so many times before, but nothing happened. She tried again and this time felt it slip into place with the grinding sound of gears mashing together. The car lurched forward and stalled. She screamed in frustration at the steering wheel, slamming her fists into it, honking the horn. The sound jerked her head up and she saw that the man was close.

"Fuck, fuck, fuck," she cried, giving up trying to figure out how to drive a standard shift car. She looked through the windshield again and the man was even closer now. "Fuck!" she screamed at the glass, throwing open the driver's side door and spilling out onto the ground. Forest debris dug into her knees and the palms of her hands, but she ignored all of it and clawed her way to her bare feet, looking over her shoulder at the same time to see where the man was this time. He stood at the front of the car. He stood in the shadows with the lights of the city behind him making him seem like some dark figure from a horror movie. He was Freddy and Jason and Michael all mixed together. She couldn't see his face. He had no features. He was a monster hunting hapless teenagers. Mary turned blindly and ran. Behind her, the man ran after her. She could hear his feet pounding on the concrete, his breath whooshing in and out as he chased after her. Halfway up the hill the man was right behind her. She could feel the weight of his presence on her naked backside.

Mary felt a hand grab her from behind by the hair. The pain was immediate and all encompassing, and then she was completely off her feet. The man easily lifted her up off the ground and just like that the sky was rushing at her. Mary took a deep breath, believing that Andy's killer was about to launch her through the air as he had done to Andy down at the river, but then just as suddenly as she was lifted into the air, she was being driven toward the ground. Here chest hit the edge of the concrete driveway where the curb meets the dirt. The breath in her body exploded out in a wild rush of air that left her gasping. The man bent over as she fought to breathe, his grin exposing impossibly white teeth. From out of nowhere Mary felt the palm of his right hand slam against the side of her face with so much force that the world flamed white before simply fading to black.

Mary woke up slowly. Her head felt like it was ready to explode; it hurt so bad. The side of her face was swollen and tender. She tried to move but something held her down, preventing her from sitting up. She opened her eyes and looked around. She had no idea where she was. The room was dark and cold, and she was strapped down to a table of some kind. Her legs were tied to a set of stirrups like in a doctor's office so that they were held up in the air and wide apart.

There was a strip of tape over her mouth. She tasted blood in the back of her throat as she pressed her tongue against the tape. It didn't give and it left a sticky slime on her tongue. She looked down her body and saw that she was still naked. Dirt and blood clung to her skin. She hurt everywhere. There were stinging cuts and scrapes all over her body and each breath brought a flash of fire inside her chest.

Matthew, she thought. *He must be so worried.* Mary looked around again as best she could, looking for something that might help her figure out where she was, but found nothing. There were no lights and no windows that she could see. All she knew was that she wasn't in a hospital.

Where the fuck am I? she thought, remembering Andy for the first time since she had opened her eyes. Tears fell as she relived every detail of what had happened to him down at the river. *Oh God*, she thought. *Oh God, oh God, oh God, it's that guy that's been killing people. He has me.* More tears fell.

Chapter 37

Bruce's cellphone rang and the ringtone cut right into his brain like a knife. He reached out and seized the cellphone with his left hand, glaring at the screen ready to toss it against the wall. He didn't recognize the number and he didn't want to answer it.

"Shut the fuck up," he mumbled at the phone, and thankfully it went silent. The screen let him know that he had three missed calls from that same unknown number. He snorted at the phone, dropping it on the bed, and rolled over to the other side, letting his right hand hang over the edge. He swept that right hand blindly along the floor for the bottle that he knew was down there somewhere. He found it and rescued it from the dust bunnies patrolling beneath his bed. The bottle was half empty and warm, but he didn't care as he twisted off the cap and tipped it up to his mouth, but before he could take a swig, his cellphone rang again. Growling at the rude interruption, he set the bottle back down and reached across the bed, snatching the cellphone up from mattress and mashed the green answer button.

"Motherfucker, I don't know who you are or what you want," he shouted into the cellphone.

"Mr. Westman," a child's voice asked, sounding scared and unsure. Bruce squinted at the phone and took a breath to calm himself.

"Yeah, who is this?" Bruce asked, feeling silly now for shouting into the phone.

"It's Matthew Shovinski, and I think my sister is missing."

Bruce sat up straighter, rubbing his eyes. "What do mean missing?" he asked, setting his feet on the floor.

"She went out tonight and hasn't come home. She said she'd be home at midnight the latest but it's after two o'clock and I'm worried."

"What about your parents?" Bruce asked.

"It's date night," Matthew answered. "They won't be back until sometime tomorrow."

"Can't you call them?" Bruce asked, pulling on the pair of jeans he had worn earlier that day.

"I think he has her, Mr. Westman. That bad man killing kids, he has her, I know it," Matthew cried, panic creeping into his voice.

Bruce paused, standing in the middle of his apartment now. He knew the kid was smart. After all, he had helped him find that clearing behind the Hollow. He trusted that he wasn't overreacting. "Give me your address, Matthew," Bruce said, snatching a pen from the kitchen counter. He wrote the address on the countertop.

"I'm going to call my brother—he's a police officer— and then I'm coming over to your house," Bruce explained, stepping into his sneakers. Matthew thanked him and disconnected the call. Bruce shoved the phone into his pocket and grabbed his keys. He started for the door and paused. "Fuck," he whispered at the door, turning back around and walking over to his nightstand. He opened the drawer and removed a Glock 26 9mm semiautomatic pistol that he kept in there to go along with the revolver he carried most of the time. He picked up an extra clip as well and checked to make sure the one in the gun was loaded. He racked the slide, chambering a round and slipped the gun into the clip on holster that sat in the drawer beside it.

"Fuck, fuck," he whispered, hating how the gun felt as he clipped the holster to his belt in the small of his back. He hated how it reminded him of Iraq and all the bad shit that happened over there. For a moment he felt himself slipping into that dark hole standing there in the middle of his apartment. "Not now, asshole. Don't lose your shit," he shouted at himself, swallowing hard, willing himself to ignore the weight of the weapon. "One foot in front of the other," he mumbled, walking to the door and stepping into the hallway.

Outside, the street was dark and quiet. His car for a change was parked correctly along the curb. He gave the middle finger to the house across the street and got in, starting the engine and pulling away with a screech of rubber. At the corner, he stopped as a black cat crossed the street in front of him. He gave the cat the same middle finger he had given the house across the street before taking his cellphone from his pocket. He called his brother's number, waiting beneath the glow of a streetlight. The phone rang several times and then went to voicemail. At the beep, he spoke.

"Hey, dipshit," he said. "I'm going to this kid's house in Manchester. His sister is missing, and he's scared," he began. "He lives near the Hollow so I'm going to check it out. It's probably nothing, but give me a call when you get this just in case it turns out to be something." He ended the call and dropped his phone on the seat.

Fifteen minutes later, Bruce pulled up to a gray two-story rancher in a quiet, upper middleclass neighborhood. Several lights were on in the house, the soft yellow glow leaking out into the front yard and along the driveway. Bruce saw Matthew watching him from a window facing the street and his worry meter went up a notch. He put the car in park, turned off the engine, and got out at the curb. Matthew lifted a hand, pointing toward the side of the house and disappeared from the window. He reappeared a moment later at the top of the driveway. Bruce followed Matthew through a side door into the house.

"You hear from your sister, kid?" Bruce asked, stepping into the kitchen.

"No, and I've called her over and over. She wouldn't ignore me like that," Matthew said. "We have to find her, Mr. Westman."

"Bruce. Call me Bruce."

"We have to find her, Bruce," Matthew said, close to tears now.

"Tell me everything you know," Bruce said, slipping the notebook from his back pocket. He shuddered a bit as his hand brushed the firearm resting back there just to the right of the pocket. *Not tonight,* he thought. *You can go down that rabbit hole another time.* He ran his free hand through his hair to steady it before continuing.

Matthew took only a minute or so to describe what had happened that evening. Bruce took notes and asked a question or two and Matthew answered the questions as best he could. He was on verge of crying when he finished.

"You know it's probably nothing, right?" Bruce said, setting the notebook down on the kitchen table. Matthew shook his head.

"It's not nothing, I know it," Matthew said. "We fight and pick on each other all the time, but I know she would never do something like this to me. She just wouldn't."

"Is she having sex with this guy, Andy Andrews?" Bruce asked, wondering how his parents could have named their son Andrew Andrews.

"Gross. God, I hope not," Matthew said. "He's such a big loser.

"If you saw his car could you identify it?"

"Yeah. It's a Chevrolet something or other, but I'd know it if I saw it," Matthew answered. Bruce looked thoughtful for a moment. "You're not leaving me here," Matthew said, picking up on his thoughts.

"Fine," Bruce sighed. "Leave a note on the counter for your sister to call you in case she comes back. We're going to drive around and see if we can find them while I wait for my brother to call back." Matthew nodded and began to write his note. He left the small slip of paper on the kitchen table beneath a saltshaker. "You're to do everything I say, and at no point are you to get out of the car." Matthew nodded and followed Bruce to the car. He sat down in the passer side.

"Thanks, Bruce," Matthew said as they drove away from the house. The lights were still on, the soft yellow glow spilling out into the front yard chasing away the shadows.

"No problem, kid," Bruce said, leaving the neighborhood.

Bruce drove around Manchester for forty-five minutes checking out one make-out spot after the other. He even went down to the Hollow and jumped the fence with Matthew and checked out the clearing, even though there were no cars parked in the lot. They found the clearing empty, though it did look as if someone had been there earlier that night.

Bruce crossed into East Hartford after that and began searching the known make-out spots there. It was almost four-thirty in the morning when he pulled into the small riverside park on the East Hartford side of the Connecticut River.

"Come on, we'll walk down here and check things out, but stay close to me," Bruce said, parking the car in the lot instead of driving down toward the dock. Matthew exited the car with him and followed Bruce down the paved hillside. The lights of the city shone over the Connecticut River, but Bruce and Matthew hardly noticed them. At the bottom of the hill, they turned to the left and Matthew came to a stop. Bruce followed his gaze to a car parked beneath the trees hidden in deep shadows. Bruce knew right away the car was empty.

"That could be it," Matthew said, his voice sounding unsure.

"Stay close to me," Bruce said, creeping closer to the car. He didn't want to startle anyone trying to have sex, though his gut told him he wouldn't.

"That's the car, I know it," Matthew whispered, sounding positive now that they were closer. Bruce held up his hand.

"Stay here," Bruce said in a hushed voice. Matthew stopped and watched Bruce walk up along the driver's side door.

Bruce knew right away that something bad had happened here. He saw the busted out windshield and the streaks of blood left on the paint. He looked over his shoulder to make sure Matthew was where he had left him, and he was. "Don't come up here," Bruce said, looking into the car. The front seat and the steering wheel were covered in gore. Bits of flesh and bone and a few teeth clung to the vinyl seats. Blood had splashed everywhere inside the car. Whatever had happened here had been extremely violent.

Clothes lay crumpled up on the passenger side floorboard and a red condom wrapper sat in the center dash along with two red Dixie cups. The odor of alcohol drifted out from inside the car mixed with the coppery sweet odor of blood. Bruce wrinkled his nose as he slipped his phone from his pocket. His mouth felt dry as he dialed his brother's number. He wanted a drink so bad right now. The phone rang and rang several times before going to voicemail.

"Hey, I have something bad down at Riverside Park in East Hartford. When you get this, call me, and have the East Hartford Police send units this way to secure the scene. It's a green Chevy Cruz parked in the trees. Fucking call me, will you?" Bruce ended the call and pocketed the phone.

"Mr. Westman," Matthew said, suddenly standing beside him. Bruce looked down and shook his head.

"I told you to stay where you were," Bruce said.

"I know, but I had to see if she was here," Matthew explained, tears falling from his eyes. Bruce nodded, wishing he had left the kid at the house.

"Look, I have to do something and it's going to look strange, but it's what I do to find things and people," Bruce said. "I need you to go back to where you were and wait while I do this." Matthew took a deep breath and let it out slowly before walking away. Bruce watched him walk until he stopped well back from the car.

Bruce turned away from Matthew and faced the driver's side door. He knew he was going to contaminate the crime scene, but he had no choice; time felt so incredibly short. As lightly as he could, he set his hand on the sill of the door just inside the open window. The blood there was still tacky beneath the palm of his hand, and he knew that they weren't that far ahead. A shard of glass bit into his skin, but he didn't pull his hand away; instead, he gripped the door harder, feeling the glass slice deep as he closed his eyes and allowed his mind to drift.

The drift came upon him fast like the rush of an oncoming subway car. The events of the night swept over him like a tidal wave of violence. All at once he was there as the killer was viciously murdering the boy and taking the girl. He saw everything in such vivid detail that he felt nauseous and dizzy from the experience. It was like being on one of those tilt-a-whirls at the carnival. His inner mind whiplashed all around.

The killer was slipping even further away from reality. He was a monster acting on his worst instincts. What he had done here tonight was so brutal and violent and unnecessary. There was no sympathy, no pity, no remorse. He was no longer a human believing he was doing God's will. He had become an animal driven by an instinct to kill.

Bruce let go of the door and stumbled up the hillside, stopping where the killer had taken Mary as she ran from him. He dropped to his knees and placed his hand in the dirt, drifting away once more, the whiplash motion of it all setting his head spinning.

He saw the killer placing Mary's unconscious body over his shoulder. She was naked, but he didn't know if that was how the killer had found her or if he had taken off her clothes. He watched the killer walk up the hill, dumping her body into the trunk of a blue nondescript Impala. The dog was in the car looking out the passenger side window. His mouth was open so it appeared that he was smiling at his master. The killer closed the trunk, got into his car, and drove off. Bruce watched him turn left out of the parking lot and disappear into the night.

Bruce opened his eyes, looking back down the hill. "Matthew, get up here," he shouted, turning quickly and throwing up. Vomit splashed all over the asphalt but thankfully he missed his shoes. Getting into the car, Bruce paused, waiting for Matthew to catch up. Once the kid was seated, he started the engine and drove away, turning left out of the parking lot, focusing on the last image of Mary he had in his head. There was just enough of the drift still flowing through his mind to direct him. He wasn't sure if it would work or not, or for how long, but he had to try.

At the Main Street light, Bruce closed his eyes and waited. The light changed to green and he knew to turn right. He did this over and over again, feeling the drift leading him along the killer's path. For several miles it went on like that until he found himself driving through a Glastonbury neighborhood.

"We're close," Bruce said, looking over at Matthew. He felt exhausted from all the drifting. The gun in his back was digging into his spine. He wanted a drink in the worse way, but refused to give in to the urge.

"How do you know?" Matthew asked, looking out the passenger side window.

"Trust me, it's something I do," Bruce explained. "I call it drifting," he added. "I think because everything is so fresh right now, I can follow the killer's path, but it's beginning to grow faint, but I know he lives around here somewhere. We're close."

At the next stop sign, Bruce didn't know which way to go. It was after five in the morning now and the sky was beginning to lighten. A boy rode down the sidewalk on a bike delivering the *Hartford Courant*. An older man in a fedora hat was walking a poodle across the intersection. Bruce drove through the stop sign once the man with the poodle had crossed. He began driving around the neighborhood streets randomly hoping something would jump out. Matthew sat beside him yawning, exhausted from the long night.

"We're looking for a blue Chevy Impala with four doors. It's not a new car. but it isn't that old either," Bruce explained. "Keep your eyes open and check your side of the street while I check mine." Matthew nodded and began to scan all the cars parked in their driveways. At five fifty in the morning, Bruce stopped the car. "Motherfucker," he whispered. Matthew looked around him and through the driver's side window. At the back of a driveway parked beneath a large oak tree sat a blue Chevrolet Impala, not brand new but not too old, either. A porch light lit it up in the driveway.

"Motherfucker," Matthew whispered. Bruce nodded and continued down the street to the next corner. He turned and parked his car along the curb.

"Stay here," Bruce said, opening his door.

"I will not," Matthew said, grabbing the handle to his door. "I can help you; I can. And if I have to, I can run away really fast and get help. You need me." Bruce looked into Matthew's eyes and saw that the boy was dead serious. He knew that no matter what he said, Matthew wasn't going to stay in the car.

"Fine, but if I say run, you run and don't look back. Do you understand me?"

"Yes," Matthew said, getting out of the car. Bruce watched him as he walked around to the driver's side. He seemed so much older than he had the day they met.

"This is a horrible idea," Bruce mumbled, making sure to lock the door before they walked away.

Chapter 38

Michael sat in his living room watching the street outside his home as the morning dawned. His body and his mind were on fire. He wanted that girl in his basement. He wanted her in a sinful way, but so far had resisted that urge to do to her what the Devil was trying to get him to do—what he had done to the last girl. He hated this feeling that was working its way through his body, grinding on his nerves. It was the purest evil imaginable. It wasn't what an angel of God did. It wasn't what he was called do. He was to protect these girls just as he had protected his mother so long ago, but that release felt so good. Ever since that night it was all he could think about.

His knife rested in his lap with his hand wrapped tightly around the handle. Images of what he had done to that other girl played over and over in his mind like a filthy pornographic movie. He was so hard, so ready to do whatever he wanted to do to her, but he kept fighting against those urges, kept trying to stay on the righteous path. He just needed to resist, or he was no better than the animal that attacked his mother on that long ago night.

"I must save her from herself," he whispered into the shadows crawling along the walls. Max glanced up from the floor, looking at his owner, sensing a change in him. His tail slowly curled between his legs.

"No," he growled. You can't save her from herself because she's already a sinner and beyond salvation." Michael glanced over his shoulder as if someone else had spoken. His eyes searched the shadow-filled room expecting to see either an angel of light or a demon of darkness. He saw neither.

"No, no, no," he cried, pressing his hands against the side of his head. "Get out, get out!" he shouted into the empty living room. Max rose to his feet, sniffing at the air. His ears were up trying to discern the problem. Unable to figure it out, he spun in a tight circle, and dropped back down, hiding his nose in his paws.

Michael rose from his chair and walked slowly to the basement door. He held the knife down along the side of his leg as he opened the door and glared down into the darkness flooding the basement. "Take her, take her, take her, she's yours," he whispered through his teeth, starting down the stairs, one slow step at a time. He stopped halfway down.

"You are here to save her, not have your way with her. She belongs to God, not to you," he snarled, his head swinging back and forth as if he were having a conversation with another person.

"Shut up, shut up. She gave herself to that filth and now she is beyond salvation."

Michael reached the bottom step and paused again, waiting to see if there was anything else, but only silence reflected back at him. He stepped down to the concrete floor looking out into the shadowed darkness, again waiting to hear a voice, a message, anything that might turn him from his course. Nothing came—no voices, no messages, nothing. He sighed, his eyes adjusting to the darkness now. He could see the exam table in the center of the basement and the girl strapped down to it. He rubbed his chin, feeling the stubble there and sighed deeply. Dropping down and kneeling on the cold concrete floor, he clinched his hands into fists in front of his face until the knuckles turned white. Tears fell from his eyes.

"Help me," he pleaded into the shadowed darkness, looking up into the rafters, the blade of the knife just in front of his face. He felt nothing. The only sign he had was the stiff hardness pressing against his pants.

"She's already lost," he whispered. Sighing once more, he stood and slowly began to undress. One piece at a time he removed his clothing, leaving everything on the floor where he stood. He walked barefoot across the cold concrete floor once he was finished, feeling all the dirt and grim beneath his feet.

At the exam table, he stopped and turned on the overhead light. Licking his lips slowly, he stared down between the girl's legs. She was almost hairless there. Just a thin patch of hair above her vagina. His throat felt dry as he contemplated the split there between her legs and how wonderful it would feel when he slipped between those folds of skin hiding her sin.

The hand holding the knife trembled. He swallowed hard, forcing his eyes to look away. They fell on her small petite breasts, lingering for several minutes until he had to force them away. He found her wide frightened eyes. She looked so scared. She looked terrified. He smiled.

"It's going to be alright child," Michael whispered, touching the bottom of her foot with the tip of a finger. Mary groaned and tried to pull back from his touch, but her bonds held her. Michael grimaced at her reaction and brought the blade of his knife to the bottom of her foot. "You're the sinner here!" Michael shouted. "You did this to yourself. It was you who allowed that animal to touch you—to do those filthy dirty things to your body. You are beyond salvation now." A thin line of blood ran down from the bottom of her foot, dripping to the floor.

Bruce and Matthew crept on their hands and knees through the thick wall of bushes that grew around the house. A thin beam of light leaked out from the top of a boarded over basement window hidden behind the bushes. Bruce crawled over to the window and peered through the thin crack at the top. He could just make out a naked man standing beneath a circle of bright light. He stood over a naked girl tied down to a table. He was speaking to her, but Bruce couldn't hear what he was saying. He saw the knife in his hand reflecting the little bit of light inside the unfinished basement.

"Son of a bitch," Bruce whispered, looking at Matthew. "Take this, call 9-1-1, and tell them an officer needs assistance. Give them this address and tell them that a girl is about to be murdered in the basement of this house." Matthew nodded and took the phone. "Then call my brother Jeffrey. His number is the last number I called. Tell him to get his ass out here. And no matter what, do not come into that house." Matthew looked wide-eyed at Bruce for a moment and then began punching in the numbers.

Bruce didn't wait for Matthew to make the call. He stood and ran to the back of the house, kicking in the back door. Inside the kitchen, he drew his gun and looked around for a basement door. He found it and took a step that way, but had to stop when a dog attacked him by leaping up and grabbing a mouthful of crotch. Luckily it was all pants and no balls, but Bruce still had to pause, reaching down and forcing the dog's mouth open. He threw the dog out the back door and watched it run away before turning back to face the basement door.

Michael heard his door being kicked in. He heard the loud crash and Max barking and growling. He looked at the girl and then back up at the stairs. He heard Max yelp.

"Don't you hurt my dog!" Michael screamed, forgetting all about the girl and the fact that he was naked. He ran across the basement and flew up the stairs.

Bruce saw the naked man explode through the basement door before he reached it. The man's face was twisted in rage. He ran at Bruce with a knife clutched in his upraised hand. Bruce fired his weapon and a round hole that looked like the petals of a rose appeared on the man's chest, but the man kept coming. Bruce fired again, the shot going wide this time, and then the man was on him.

A white hot flair of pain exploded in Bruce's right shoulder and the gun fell from his hand, landing somewhere on the floor. The man stabbed Bruce again in the same shoulder, shoving the knife in with such force that Bruce felt it shatter bone. The pain he felt was incredible. It was like nothing he had ever felt before and he screamed as everything around him turned bright white.

Matthew heard the first gunshot and then the second. He got up from behind the bushes and ran to the back of the house, leaving the 9-1-1 operator shouting into an empty line. The back door of the house hung open by one hinge. The doorjamb was a shattered mess. Inside the house, Matthew saw Bruce on the kitchen floor struggling with a naked man. The naked man had a knife and he was stabbing Bruce. Matthew ran through the open doorway and saw the gun on the kitchen floor beneath the kitchen table. He scrambled under the table and picked up the gun, pointing it at the naked man. His hands shook as he pulled back on the trigger. The gun exploded in a roar of flame and sound. Matthew cried out and dropped the gun.

Bruce heard the gunshot and stopped screaming. His eyes focused and he saw the killer was on top him. His eyes were wide. His mouth hung open. There was a surprised look on his face. He gagged once and expelled a long rancid breath before settling on top of him like dead weight.

Bruce felt the killer die. He tried to roll him off, but he didn't possess the strength. "Help me get him off," Bruce groaned, the knife still sticking out of his shoulder. Matthew helped Bruce shove the naked man off of him. The body offered no resistance. Bruce used the kitchen table to get to his feet. He glanced at the knife in his shoulder. It looked so ugly and so lethal sticking out. He wanted to yank it out with his left hand, but he was afraid to try. His right arm was useless.

"Basement," Bruce groaned, taking a step toward the door the killer had exploded out of only minutes ago. "You follow. Stay behind me." Matthew nodded. At the basement door, Bruce stopped and looked around the kitchen and into the living room. He swallowed hard, clearing his throat. "Yank those curtains down from that window," he said. Matthew did as he was told, quickly joining Bruce back at the door. Bruce started down the stairs. Matthew followed.

Bruce and Matthew walked across the basement floor together, stopping at the exam table. Matthew draped the curtain over his sister and undid the straps holding her to the table. She sat up slowly and removed the tape from over her mouth.

"Are you alright?" Bruce groaned, leaning against the table for support. Mary looked at Bruce standing there with a knife sticking out of his right shoulder and then at Matthew. She wanted to answer, but only tears fell from her eyes. She slid off the table and threw her arms around her brother. They collapsed to the floor holding onto each other, crying hard tears. Bruce watched, tears falling from his own eyes before passing out.

Chapter 39

Three patrol vehicles from the Glastonbury Police Department arrived a few minutes later with sirens blaring and lights flashing. Behind them came an ambulance and fire engine. The paramedics wanted to transport Bruce immediately after packing gauze around the knife and sticking an IV into his other arm, but he wouldn't let them take him. He had one of the officers call the Manchester Police Department and tell them to get hold of his brother. Jeffrey arrived thirty minutes later looking like he had just woken up. Bruce gave him the quick version of what happened and then allowed the ambulance to transport him to Hartford Hospital.

Matthew stayed with his sister the entire time. He refused to leave her side for any reason. He rode in the ambulance with her to the hospital and stayed with her while the doctors checked her out. She had a mild concussion and a few other minor injuries but otherwise she was physically fine. Jeffrey arrived at the hospital an hour later and spoke with Matthew and his sister for a few minutes. Matthew's parents called shortly after Jeffrey arrived and he assured them that both of their children were fine. They informed him that they were on their way to the hospital. Jeffrey kept hopping between Mary's room and Bruce's room while they waited for the mom and dad to arrive. Bruce slept through it all.

Jeffrey finally took a seat in Bruce's room after the parents arrived. He smiled at his brother lying there in a bed with an IV attached to his arm, feeding him pain medicine. A heart monitor beeped away while a jagged line ran across a green screen. Everything said he was alive and that was a good thing.

"What the fuck are you looking at, grinning like that?" Bruce slurred around noon, not feeling much pain. The knife was gone from his shoulder, but the world felt so wobbly.

"You son of a bitch. You saved that girl without me," Jeffrey said.

"Your phone?" Bruce asked, closing his eyes for a moment before opening them again. It took him a moment to focus on his brother. "You never answered."

"Yeah, it was dead. Somehow the charging cord slipped out and it died while I was sleeping. I missed all the calls. The department sent a cop over to wake me after you had that officer call, and they couldn't reach me."

"Stupid," Bruce said, closing his eyes again and drifting back off to sleep.

"I'll see you later, brother," Jeffrey said, getting up and leaving the room once he was sure Bruce was asleep.

***

Bruce woke the next day. His shoulder hurt like a son of a bitch and there was a large bandage wrapped around it. He wasn't all that sure why the bandage was there. He couldn't remember anyone putting it there. Foggy images of a struggle kept floating through his brain, but he was having trouble focusing on anything too concrete. A nurse came into the room. She smiled down at him and took his vitals. He watched her go about her business and then fell back to sleep.

Bruce woke again, several hours later. He didn't feel so drugged out and his eyes no longer felt like there were weights tied to them. He looked around his room and saw a get-well card on a food tray beside his bed. Matthew walked into the room and Bruce smiled.

"Hey, kid," Bruce said. His voice sounded raspy, and his throat felt like he hadn't had anything to drink in weeks. "Can you get me some water?" Bruce asked.

"Sure," Matthew said, filling a cup from a pink plastic pitcher. Bruce drank slowly, enjoying the cold liquid as it slid down his throat.

"How's your sister doing?" Bruce asked, pushing a button so he could sit up in bed more.

"She's okay physically, but not in the head, you know what I mean? She's scared and jumpy, and she cries whenever one of us leaves the room. She's afraid to be alone."

"It takes time, Matthew. I'm sure with you and your parents and a good therapist she'll come out this just fine." Matthew nodded. "How about you? How are you doing?"

Matthew looked at Bruce for several seconds before answering. "I tell everyone I'm fine, but every time I close my eyes, I see him on top of you trying to kill you, and then I see myself pulling that trigger and shooting him," Matthew explained. "Will it ever go away?"

"I wish I could tell you yes for sure, but I can't, I'm sorry. I understand how you feel though, and if you need to talk to someone you can call me anytime you want, day or night. When I get out of this place we'll go out for a burger or something and I'll tell you how I know how you feel."

"Thanks. Please don't tell my parents about any of this. They have enough to worry about." Bruce smiled and nodded his head.

"It will be our secret as long as you promise to call me. We'll work through our demons together, understand?" Matthew nodded.

**

Bruce was released from the hospital two days later. Jeffrey drove him to his house. His car was parked in the driveway in front of the garage door. At the front door, Anne and his mother stood. His mom looked worried. Anne had a smile on her face. Bruce looked at his brother and shook his head. "Asshole," Bruce said. "I could have gone to my apartment."

"Payback for playing hero," Jeffrey said. "Now get out and smile; they were worried about you." Bruce exited the car and held up his left hand, waving at his sister-in-law and mother. William stood on the other side of the door. He looked scared. Bruce waved at him and winked.

"Come on out here and give me a hug," Bruce said. William stepped out the door and approached his uncle. He carefully wrapped his arms around him and squeezed.

Chapter 40

Bruce walked into the Manchester Police Department three days after being released from the hospital. He sat in front of Jeffrey's desk. Agent Shelby sat on the other side of the desk sifting through a stack of papers. Several officers sitting in the bullpen gave him encouraging looks. Many congratulated him for taking out the Hollow Killer. In truth, he enjoyed none of it, nor sought any of it out. He would have rather gone unnoticed at the station.

Agent Shelby stopped what he was doing and looked up at Bruce. His expression was blank. He took a deep breath and swallowed. "I want to apologize for being such an asshole," Agent Shelby said. Bruce nodded, studying an old coffee stain on the desk. "The agency really appreciates everything you did to rescue that girl. I won't pretend to understand how you did it, but just know you have my respect."

Bruce looked up and eyed Agent Shelby. He didn't like the man very much, and he was right—he was an asshole. Bruce smiled a smile that never touched his eyes. "I appreciate that, agent," he said.

"Jerrod. You can call me Jerrod," Agent Shelby said.

"Thanks, Jerrod."

"Hey, it looks like you two have buried the hatchet, and thankfully not into each other," Jeffrey said, walking up with three cups of coffee. He set the cups down on the desk and dragged a chair over.

"I was just telling your brother how much we appreciate everything he did," Agent Shelby explained.

"He's special like that," Jeffrey said. "A little touched-in-the-head special, but he gets the job the done."

"Well, gentlemen, I have to be going. If there is ever anything you need, please call me," Agent Shelby said, gathering up his paperwork and standing.

"Another case?" Bruce asked, standing up from his own chair.

"Missing call girls in the Big Apple. Probably some nut job whose mother didn't love him enough or whose father smacked him around too much or touched him in his no-no parts."

"Well, you can have that shit," Jeffrey said. "I've had my fill of psychos. I'm ready to get back to solving the boring cases again."

"Amen to that," Bruce said. Agent Shelby looked over at Bruce for a moment.

"Here's my card. I've got your number too, so if I need a consultant, I'll be sure to call you first," Agent Shelby explained. "I can promise you this: the federal government pays a lot better than your brother," Agent Shelby said, holding out the business card. Bruce took the card and looked at it.

"Well, let's get you moving along," Jeffrey said, setting a hand on Agent Shelby's shoulder. Agent Shelby glanced at the hand but allowed Jeffrey to guide him out the door. Bruce stayed behind.

"Just so you know, I told him to leave you alone," Jeffrey said, returning a few minutes later. "They got their own profilers in the Bureau. They don't need you, and definitely don't need them."

"I don't know, it felt good catching the bad guy," Bruce said. "Going back to cheating spouses and lost items seems boring now. I made a real difference."

"I'll feed a case here and there to keep you from getting too bored. I'm sure Manchester has enough knuckleheads to keep you busy."

"I guess," Bruce said, standing up. "So how about you pay me for my services and take me out to lunch?"

"Pay you? You're lucky the city doesn't charge you for that ambulance ride and the hospital stay," Jeffrey said. "That shit isn't free, you know."

"Motherfuckers, what cheap bastards," Bruce said.

"Hey, no one told you to let that nutcase stab you in the shoulder twice. You should have just shot him in the head and been done with it."

"Son of a bitch," Bruce said. "I risk my ass and you treat me like this. Well, you better take me out to lunch then while I figure out how I'm going to make rent this month." Jeffrey laughed and grabbed his keys from the desktop. Bruce followed him out of the station and into the bright Southern New England sunshine.

Chapter 41

The next morning, Bruce walked into Saint Christopher's Catholic Church with a half-dozen donuts and two cups of coffee. Father Murphy was waiting inside the sanctuary sitting in the front pew. Bruce walked up the center aisle and paused when he saw that the priest was praying. He waited until Father Murphy was finished.

"Good morning, Father," Bruce said as the priest sat back.

"Good morning, Bruce. I hear you caught your bad guy."

"Something like that, Father," Bruce said.

Father Murphy stood, noticing the coffee and donuts. He smiled and waved for Bruce to follow him to his office behind the altar. They walked in silence down the dark hallway and into the office. Father Murphy sat behind his desk, turning the lamp on so there was some light to see by. Bruce sat in front of the desk, setting the donuts and coffees down in front of him.

Father Murphy took a donut from the small box and one of the cups of coffee. He ate the donut in three bites and drank half the cup before setting it back down on his desk. He licked glaze from his lips as he snagged a second donut from the box. Bruce took his time with his donut and only sipped at his coffee.

"So, what can I do for you today, Bruce?" Father Murphy asked, taking a bite of his donut.

"I want to bring someone by here so they can talk to you," Bruce explained, filling him in on Matthew and Mary.

"Are they Catholics?" Father Murphy asked. "Not that it matters, but it would help."

"I don't know if they even believe in God, to be honest with you," Bruce said.

"It doesn't matter," Father Murphy explained. "Bring them by Monday morning around ten. We'll start out on the basketball court and see how things go from there." Bruce nodded, finishing his donut. "So how are you doing now that it's over?"

Bruce took a sip of coffee from his cup and set it down. He looked across the desk and forced a thin a smile. "I'm better. Not perfect, but the feelings I was getting from that guy are gone now, so that helps."

"Good," Father Murphy said.

Thirty minutes later, Father Murphy and Bruce stepped out into the sanctuary. Defused sunlight shone through the stain glass windows, casting warped shadows across the room. At the doors, Father Murphy stopped as Bruce stepped through into the vestibule.

"Take care, Bruce, and I'll see you Monday."

"Just so you know, Father, I won't be taking it easy on you Monday," Bruce said, pointing a finger at the priest. Father Murphy smiled.

"I've never needed a handout in my entire life, Bruce," Father Murphy said, stepping back inside the sanctuary.

"I bet not," Bruce said to the closing door.

Bruce drove away from the church with no particular destination in mind. He thought he was driving aimlessly, but quickly found himself rolling down Spring Street. He turned into the parking lot for Globe Hollow and parked in his usual spot beneath the oaks, pulling alongside Peter Briley's Volkswagen. There were only a few other cars in the parking lot besides his own. The day was cloudy and promised rain. Through the fence he saw a handful of kids running around.

Bruce rolled down his window and rested his head back against the seat. He closed his eyes and reached out for the rhythm of the world around him. It was silent. There was nothing for him to latch onto, so he couldn't drift away. *It's really over now*, he thought, smiling. A few minutes later he fell asleep. No nightmares disturbed him.

Epilogue

New York. Hunts Point in the Bronx

He saw her standing on the curb just beneath the glow of a streetlamp on Hunts Point Avenue. She stood just south of Spofford Avenue working the edge of the curb. She had pink hair, down to her shoulders. "A wig," he thought as he drove slowly down a street. She wore fishnet stockings and a short brown skirt that allowed the bottoms of her ass cheeks to show in the pale yellow light of the streetlamp. Her top was a plaid shirt, unbuttoned three quarters of the way down so it showed off plenty of cleavage. She wore a black bra beneath. She was big breasted, and he liked what he saw. She was young, early twenties, and the street hadn't taken much of her youth away yet, but it was working on her. She had a hardness around the eyes that told a long story of abuse at the hands of others and she appeared hungry, as if her last meal might have been a day or two ago. He pulled to the curb and rolled his passenger side window down, looking across the seat.

"What ya looking for?" she asked, sounding like she was from Jersey. Her voice made him hard as the East Coast accent played across his ears.

"Blowjob," he answered in a husky voice, his nostrils flaring. He wanted her in a bad way now.

"You a cop?" she asked, looking up and down the street for other vehicles.

"Do I look like a fucking cop?" he replied, ready to leave if she looked like she was spooked.

"You're white, your hair is short, you work out, and you're sort of good-looking. So yes, you look like a fucking cop to me." He frowned, unzipped his pants and whipped out his dick, holding it with his right hand.

"Would a cop do that?" he asked, giving it a rough jerk before stuffing it back into his pants. The girl looked down the street again and smiled. Her teeth were crooked and there was a slight gap between the front two. She opened the passenger side door and got in the pickup truck. It was a blue Ford Ranger that had seen better days, but still ran.

"Thirty dollars to suck you off, another ten if I have to swallow," she said, still holding the door open, one foot outside the truck.

"Forty it is," he said, tossing two twenties on the seat. She licked her lips and shut the door. He drove away from the curb and she snatched the money up from the vinyl seat.

"Go behind that warehouse over there through the open gate," she said, sticking the money inside her bra. He did as she said, parking all the way in the back of the deserted parking lot. It was almost pitch black back there and he had a clear view of everything in case someone should approach. Leaning back in his seat, he undid his pants. She pulled them down to his knees along with his underwear and began to do what she had been paid to do. He finished quickly with a loud groan, his hand on the back of her head, shoving her face into his lap making sure she got all of it.

"You can take me back now," the girl said, wiping her mouth with the back of her hand as she sat back up.

"You are a good little slut," he said, laughing as he pulled his pants back up.

"Look, asshole, I did what you wanted, now take me back," she said, sounding angry.

The attack came fast. Faster than she could react. The man was on her before she knew what was going on. He pinned her against the passenger side door with one arm across her throat. Something pricked her in the side of her neck, and she felt a quick flash of pain, and then the man was off of her. Fumbling with the passenger side door, she fell out of the truck. Outside, on her feet, she tried to speak, but the words wouldn't come. Her thoughts were jumbled, and the world was tumbling and spinning all around her. The dark asphalt came up at her like a slap across the face. A moment later, a booted foot appeared beside her. She wanted to stand, but her body wouldn't respond. She tried to focus on the boot, but it seemed to swim in an ocean of grays and whites even though it was dark outside. She felt a hand grabbing her roughly and lifting her into the air. A face appeared in front of her; it was the man from the pickup. He smiled at her. His teeth were so perfect, so white, while everything else was a dirty shade of gray. She tried to touch that face full of teeth floating in front of her, but the world slipped from gray to black and then she was simply gone.

Acknowledgments

I want to thank John Fitts who had to read the first draft of this story and plow through my many errors. It was because of your hard work and dedication that I am a better writer today. I also want to thank family and friends who have had to listen to me endlessly as I ran ideas by them all throughout the process of creating this novel and the stories that follow. Finally, I want to thank God for giving me this desire and ability to write and create and to entertain others.

Acknowledgments

About the Author

C.L. Thomas grew up in Southern New England in the 70's playing outside every chance he could, and one of his favorite games was playing cops and robbers. Little did he know that as an adult, in the United Sates Army, and later for the City of Houston, he would get to play cops and robbers for real. On several occasions he would come home from work and tell his wife, "I would have done this for free." For eight years, C.L. Thomas was a member of a tactical unit in one of the worst parts of the city. Working alongside five highly trained and dedicated officers, C.L. Thomas put his life on the line every day for the citizens of Houston.

C.L. Thomas has been writing stories since he was a sophomore in high school growing up in East Hartford, Connecticut. He brings his gritty work world reality to the pages of *The Hollow*, painting a picture of the world that very few people ever get to see.